A Novel

MacCullough's Women

For Kathleen,
I hope you like it.

Kathleen

KATHLEEN FERRARI

ROSKERRY.

ISBN 13: 978-0-9836354-0-6
LCCN: 2011936476

Credits:
Lisa J. Jackson, Editor
Delaney-Designs.com, Layout

Dedication

To my parents:
John L. Ferrari and Gertrude M. Ferrari,
who gave me everything.

Acknowledgements

My thanks to my early readers who provided feedback to draft versions of this book: Karen Eber Farley, Daragh O'Brien Taylor, Linda Booth, Stephanie Whiting, Marie Hislop, Maureen Costello, Nancy Bradbury, Karen Ferrari, Mary Kay Spahl, Elizabeth Tallon, Susan Logan and Amanda Heeney.

Special thanks to:

Mary Kelly, Daragh O'Brien Taylor and M.G.C. aka "The Dog Nanny" for their invaluable insights on specific content in this book.

Karen Eber Farley who read the first chapters and convinced me that I did have a story to tell.

Nancy Bradbury whose encouragement at a critical stage in the writing of this book gave me the courage to continue writing.

Desmond Beirne, Dalkey, Ireland, who loaned me the use of his wonderful name.

My editor, Lisa J. Jackson and my cover designer, Kristina J. Hickman.

MacCullough's Women was born and shaped under the careful eyes of the Souhegan Writers Group, my fellow writers for the last nine years: Beth Blodgett, Cherie Konyha Greene, Sue Spingler, Luci Osborn, Mike Robertson and Michael Sills. Thank you for listening to me all those Saturday mornings and providing me with your insights and support. I am truly grateful.

I can never adequately thank J. Michael Robertson, author of *Warrior of the Three Moons,* for mentoring me during the process of writing this novel. His thoughtful edits and choice of the title made MacCullough's Women a better book.

My thanks to Teal, Halsey and Patrick who live on in this book as Lucy, Oliver and Thomas for the love and joy they gave us while they were part of our lives.

My love and thanks to my daughter, Amanda Heeney. Without her support and blessing, *MacCullough's Women* would never have been written.

Last but never least; I want to thank my husband, Mike O'Connor, for walking this long, twisting path with me, and never losing faith in me or in the book. He was always there with whatever help I needed and a cheerful willingness to read the book one more time. He will always be "a chuisle mo chroí. "

PROLOGUE

D rew MacCullough sat in his office at Chayne Communications, smoking. Savoring each illicit puff, he realized the old cliché was true; the forbidden is sweet. He leaned back in his chair. The nicotine worked its evil magic and the tension began to melt from his jaw and shoulders.

"Are you crazy?"

He looked up and smiled at the sound of Kara Steuben's voice. "Not yet. I'm just having a cigarette." He pointed to the chair in front of his desk. "Have a seat."

"No. I don't think so." She cast a nervous glance over her shoulder. "You know that you can't smoke in here. What if someone catches you?" Kara looked anxiously around her.

Drew liked Kara. She was the administrative assistant to his boss, Johanna Caras, not an easy job. He sympathized with her. Johanna could be a witch and everyone who worked for her knew it.

"And who would that be?" Drew asked, his eyes crinkling at the corners, his raised eyebrows punctuating his question. His smile was defiant. He looked like a little boy caught doing something he shouldn't. "Look around you, there's nobody here. Don't you need to go Christmas shopping like everyone else?" The week before Christmas, people began slipping out early. It was close to five and the place was deserted.

"When Johanna's here, I'm here. I have pretty much finished my shopping. My guys get so much stuff. They are the only grandchildren on both sides. What about you?"

"I haven't even started. I do it all on Christmas Eve. I'm one of those clueless men you see wandering around the malls looking for the perfect gift." He laughed.

Far from clueless, Drew MacCullough had an air of confidence that bordered on, but only rarely became, true arrogance. Almost fifty, he was a handsome man. He was not quite six feet tall, but people always assumed that he was taller because he acted like he was. He carried no extra weight and had little patience with those who did. His thick black hair was beginning to go gray in a way most women envied. When he smiled it was with his entire face; the corners of his eyes disappearing into deeply etched laugh lines.

He nodded toward the clock on the wall. "You should get out of here. I'm leaving soon myself." He studied the cigarette in his hand. "When I started here, we could smoke in our offices. We all did it and thought nothing of it. You can't imagine how helpful a cigarette can be in a meeting. Someone asks you a tough question you smile, pick up your cigarette, and take a puff while you're figuring out your answer."

"I have to go. Johanna may have something that she wants me to do for her before she leaves. You don't want her looking for me in here." She glanced pointedly at the cigarette.

Suddenly, Drew looked tired; the weariness no longer deflected by his smile. "Don't worry. My office is the last place you'll see Johanna."

He wondered how much Kara knew about the blowup he had with her boss. Kara could have heard Johanna shrieking at him through the closed office door.

He swung his feet off the desk and stood up. "There. Are you happy now? No more breaking the rules." He ground the cigarette out in the ashtray he had found buried in the bottom of his desk drawer. "Go home. I am."

Nodding, Kara turned and started to walk toward the opposite side of the building where her own desk sat outside Johanna's office.

He called to her.

"I'm only in for half a day tomorrow. I may need about fifteen minutes with Johanna in the morning. Can you put me on her calendar if I decide that I need to see her?"

"Sure. Her schedule is light this week because so many people are on vacation." Kara said, turning back to smile at him once more.

He watched her walk rapidly away, admiring the way her shapely legs disappeared into her short black skirt. He weighed the idea of lighting another cigarette.

His glance fell upon the picture of his wife, sitting on the corner of his desk. It was not a recent picture, but he loved looking at the happy girl captured in the frame. They were antiquing the day he took that picture, determined to find something that Franny called a nursing rocker. She was almost seven months pregnant in the photo. The picture portrayed a radiant young woman with luminous brown eyes looking back at him like she had been handed an unexpected present. She was one of those women pregnancy agreed with. The picture was more than four years old now. It was still his favorite picture of her.

He sat down again and flipped open his phone to call home and let Franny know that he had returned a day early from his trip. Hesitating, he debated telling her about his meeting with Johanna. Changing his mind, he snapped the phone shut. He was going to have to talk to Franny, but not yet. The conversation about his meeting with Johanna could wait until he figured out what he was going to do.

An idea began to form in his mind and his grim expression

slowly dissolved into a smile. He selected Cunningham's Florist from the contact list on his phone. He pictured Franny's delight when she opened the long white box, her face lit with the spontaneous joy he found so enchanting. The woman who answered was slightly out of breath. Recognizing his voice, she explained he had caught her heading out the door. He ordered a dozen red roses to be delivered to his wife. "Sign the card, from the last man in your life," he said.

"Pretty cocky, aren't you, Drew?" The florist replied, laughing, before she assured him the flowers would go out in the morning. Pocketing the phone, he found himself thinking not of red roses, but of tulips – the dozens of tulips of every color he had sent to Brid, who disdained roses. Ah, Brid. Sighing, he reluctantly turned his thoughts from his ex-wife's love of tulips back to his meeting earlier in the day with Johanna.

Drew leaned his chin on his fingertips; closing his eyes, he made his decision. Turning to the laptop in front of him, he addressed a letter to Johanna, typing the day's date, a single sentence and his name. The printer on the desk next to him sprang to life, delivering the printed letter to his waiting hand. Signing it with the scribble that passed for his signature, he folded it neatly in three, pressed his fingers over the creases, placed the letter in an envelope, and slipped it into his briefcase. He reached for the ashtray, the lone cigarette butt now harmless in the center, and then changed his mind. Let them find it.

Shrugging into his coat, he shut down the laptop, slid it into his desk drawer, locked the drawer, and left his office without a backward glance. Walking through the lobby past the tall Christmas tree decorated with red balls and silver garlands, he stopped to say good night to the company security guard sitting at the front desk.

"Hi, Bill. All set for Christmas?"

"The wife does all that. Runs around like a chicken with her head cut off for Lisa's two kids. I only pay the bills." His grin told Drew that he didn't really mind. "What about you, Drew?"

"Not me. It's too early. I'm a Christmas Eve kind of guy. How's David? Is he back from school yet?" He groped his pocket for his gloves.

"He came home Friday with three months of dirty laundry. His mother had a fit. But, deep down I think she was glad." Bill chuckled. "Still needs his mom."

"I'm only going to be in for a little while tomorrow morning. I won't see you again before the holidays. Merry Christmas!" Drew said, extending his hand.

"You, too, Drew. See you in the new year."

Stepping through the glass doors into the December night, Drew shivered as the cold air slapped him. Turning up the collar of his topcoat he strode rapidly across the deserted parking lot toward the silver Lexus thinking, God, I need a drink.

CHAPTER 1

"**Y**ou're a klutz, Thomas, like me," Franny Mac-Cullough told the orange tabby cat as she watched him fighting to keep his balance on the edge of the high sleigh bed. Reaching out to steady him, she smiled ruefully, remembering the doubles game she and Drew played at the country club last week.

"All you have to do is stay out of my way and I'll return the balls," Drew told her.

She was ready to catch him if he fell, but Thomas gained his footing and purring, marched up the slope created by her hip and across the valley of her waist to sit in front of her face. He paused for a moment before increasing the volume.

"Hello, Thomas, my sweet boy, is it morning already?" Still thinking about her own clumsiness, she told him, "My serve is pretty good." What she couldn't seem to do was return the ball. She had taken a series of private lessons at Drew's insistence, but they hadn't helped much.

"You have this hand-eye coordination thing going on," the frustrated pro patiently explained to her. "You can't figure out where the ball is. It's not your fault. It's the way your eyes work."

Franny stretched, letting her legs splay out in a wide arc, her toes, painted with a pink polish called "Wanna Dance?" pointed to the opposite corners of the bed. She slid her left foot out from under the duvet and admired the tattoo of entwined rosebuds she had applied above her ankle the day Drew left on his trip.

I better remember to wash this off before he sees it, she thought. She laughed at herself. The tattoo was a small act of rebellion. It was not that she wanted one – not really. It was simply that Drew had forbidden her to get one. He hated tattoos, especially on women. She smiled, remembering his reaction when they were standing in the ornate lobby of the Wang Center during the intermission of a performance of the Boston Ballet. A tall blonde glided by them, talking on her cell phone. Franny could tell by the way Drew followed the girl's progress across the lobby that he liked what he saw. He abandoned the pretense that he was listening to her as his appreciative glance found the thick black snake curled around the girl's left arm, beginning at her shoulder. His eyes widened in growing horror as he followed the snake's body all the way down to where the head, fangs extended, splayed across the girl's hand.

"What the hell—" he sputtered as Franny dragged him out of earshot.

Franny yawned and considered rolling over and going back to sleep. Working for herself, her schedule was her own. She had no place that she needed to be this morning. She didn't sleep well when Drew traveled, thrashing fretfully until the early morning hours, when she fell into an exhausted sleep. She missed the warmth of his body and his knowing hands touching her with a familiar certainty sure of their destination and their welcome.

Thinking of those hands, she told the cat, "Drew says the

only sport I'm any good at is sex." She tapped lightly on Thomas's nose to emphasize her point. "He's right. I am good at sex. He's the one who taught me how to play that game, so I guess he should know."

Although she missed Drew, when she was trying to go to sleep, it was nice some mornings to wake up without him. Drew saw his role as being that of an interpreter of her time and he attempted to fill her day with his own expectations. He was a great believer in what he called a structured day. One of the drawbacks to marrying an older man was his firm conviction that he was entitled to lecture.

Franny didn't mind. Drew's certain grip on life made her feel safe. She loved him and knew that her life would be empty without him in it. She had literally fallen at his feet. The summer before her last year of college, she interned in the training department at Chayne. Racing down the stairs and unable to see clearly over the stack of binders in her arms, she tripped on the last step as Drew rounded the corner. He helped her up, made sure she was not hurt, gathered up the binders, and asked her to dinner. They were married six months later.

When she woke alone, Franny moved slowly to soak in the day's possibilities. When Drew was home, he catapulted from sleep to being wide awake as soon as the alarm clicked on, tearing a hole in the silence of the early morning. He swung his legs to the floor, decisively slapping the off button.

"Wake up, Franny. Let's go." He would order from the depths of the closet where he wrestled with his robe. She would pull the covers over her head, groaning in protest. He would go downstairs, feed the animals, and start the coffee. After finishing their breakfast, the dogs would race upstairs and leap onto the bed. They bathed her in doggy kisses to prove they had not forgotten her during the night. On his way to the shower, Drew would leave a mug of coffee next to her on the nightstand to tempt her awake.

This morning, without Drew to set off their morning march, the day waited to begin with the shimmering expectancy that hovers over the week before Christmas. Franny shut off the alarm before it shattered the silence; the hissing of the steam in the big cast iron radiators the only sound in the slumbering house. She picked up Thomas rubbing his face with her own. The cat purred contentedly and butted her back. She read once that when cats rubbed against you like that it was to put their scent on you. It was their way of saying, "Mine, mine, you're all mine."

"I love you, too, Thomas. Shall we go eat?" She let the cat go and got out of bed. Thomas jumped off the bed and followed her.

She was downstairs before she realized she had forgotten to put her slippers on. Her feet were cold on the tile floor of the kitchen. They lived in an old house built two years before the battles at Lexington and Concord. It was believed to be the oldest house in Hiram's Forge, New Hampshire; Drew was very proud of this and bragged about it to all their friends. Franny was more enthralled with the idea of all the other lives that had unfolded within the same walls that now sheltered her and Drew.

She opened the kitchen door and crossed the narrow porch that ran the length of the house to the garage. She walked on tiptoes to avoid having her bare feet touch the icy floor. The dogs, Oliver and Lucy, slept in the attached garage where Drew had built them a kennel. He painted their names over each snug box, telling Franny when Lucy was a puppy, "Dogs do not sleep in the house." A doggy door allowed them access to the fenced-in yard. This simplified life by removing the need to take them out on a leash to relieve themselves. She was tempted to sneak them in when he traveled, but decided it would be selfish of her to confuse them by bringing them into the house.

"Hey, puppies." She opened the door the tiniest of cracks. Oliver's white nose poked through, to be followed by his wriggling brown and white body as he pushed the door open. He "woof-woofed" his joy at seeing her, his handsome head thrown back in happy song. Lucy, their thirteen year-old black Lab, followed him through the door, her thick tail thrashing back and forth, indicating her pleasure at seeing Franny and the promise of breakfast ahead.

Franny bent down and caught Oliver's snowshoe paws in her hands and began to dance with him, singing softly. "It's beginning to look a lot like Christmas everywhere we go." Lucy leaned her head against Franny's thigh as she and Oliver swayed to the song. Gazing into the intelligent brown eyes of the spaniel, Franny felt an overwhelming rush of love, remembering with painful clarity the day he came into her life.

She had wrapped herself in the quilt her mother had given them as a wedding gift trying to get warm. She was always cold, no matter how high she set the heat. Drew would be happy that she was not in bed. He would see this as a good sign, a sign that she was getting better. He told people that. She had heard him. The kitchen door opened and she sat up. She reached down for her book abandoned on the floor and pretended she was reading, pushing the tangled hair out of her face.

"Hi, Hon. How was your day?" Drew didn't say anything about the empty bag of cookies and silver wrappings from the Hershey's kisses that littered the floor in front of the sofa. She tried to smile as he bent down to kiss her. "I brought you a present. I think you're going to really like it." Another purse or cashmere sweater to add to the gifts he had already given to

her, piled unused in the corner of their bedroom, she thought.
"I'll go get it. You wait here." Her heart twisted at the idea
that he believed her capable of moving from where she sat, that
there was somewhere other than her baby's grave she might
want to go. Drew came back into the room, grinning. Without
ceremony, he dropped a brown and white puppy into her lap.
Sure of his welcome, the way all puppies are, the dog launched
himself toward her face, feverishly licking her with his insistent
pink tongue.

Hungry, Oliver whimpered and scratched at the kitchen door, bringing Franny back from her memories. "Okay, you guys, enough singing. It's not Christmas yet. Let's go in and eat." Franny opened the door and Oliver rushed into the house. Franny and Lucy followed more sedately behind him. Franny filled the dogs' dishes with kibble. Out of the corner of her eye, she watched as Thomas, crouched on the granite counter, swatted a box of chamomile tea at Oliver who pranced impatiently behind her.

Smiling to show that she really didn't mean it, she reprimanded the cat. "Your behavior is appalling, Thomas." Once again, she thanked God for her animals. She thought indignantly about her mother-in-law's comment at Thanksgiving that her dogs and cat were her children. No, she had wanted to scream, my child is lying in Lynton Lawn Cemetery. I know the difference. She had chosen to ignore Elaine's remark. It was important that she not appear to be some kind of a psycho. Not now, when Drew was rejoicing about how well she was doing. "And I am doing well," she told the animals fiercely, as she placed the two dishes of kibble on the floor.

It had been four years since they lost the baby. The first year, she wanted to die, although she was too much a product of her

Catholic upbringing to do anything about it. The second year, she had not cared if she lived. Her therapist, Dr. Wohlander, had assured her that there was a difference. Slowly, over the last two years, the darkness had lifted. Each month, she felt more alive, no longer frozen by the icy grief that covered her after the baby's death. After all, she told herself, I still have Drew.

She was never sure of Drew's schedule when he traveled. His plans changed so frequently it was pointless to keep an itinerary. If a plane ever went down, her first thought would be that he probably wasn't on it. He always drove himself to the airport, preferring to have his own car waiting for him. Franny thought it was romantic to wait for him at the airport like the heroine in one of the old movies she loved, but Drew thought it was ridiculous in light of the delays and security checks resulting from 9/11. "Be romantic by waiting for me here in bed," he said, lingering to kiss her once more, reluctant to say good-bye.

He had called last night shortly before seven, telling her that he was going to take the red-eye into Boston. Over her protests, he had insisted that he needed to go directly into the office from the airport. He had done it before when there was something urgent he needed to do. He would be exhausted by the time he got home, but he would be on vacation for the holidays. She was looking forward to spending the time together. Smiling she remembered his last words to her. "Don't put the lights on the Christmas tree. You'll just screw them up. I'll do it tomorrow night." She tried his cell phone to see if his plane had landed, but the call went directly to voicemail. He had probably forgotten to turn the phone back on. She decided to call the office. Maybe Lorie was there. Drew was the Director of Marketing at Chayne and Lorie worked for Drew. She had started out as his administrative assistant. Impressed by her talent and ambition, Drew had encouraged her to move into graphic design, making arrangements for the company to pay for her classes at one of the local technical colleges. She had advanced to the position of lead designer and now she managed the graphics department. She always knew where to find Drew and when to expect him back.

"Lorie," Drew had said once, shaking his head in good natured exasperation, "is a flake, but she gets things done." Maybe she is a little flaky, Franny thought, but she's nice. Franny admired Lorie's ability to dress and act exactly as she pleased. She thought the modern hippie look suited Lorie with her flowing strawberry blonde hair, wide-spaced green eyes, dusting of freckles, and lean body. Lorie favored long skirts or leggings, tunics or draped tops in deep colors like teal or purple with dramatic scarves, chunky necklaces, and chandelier earrings.

Drew often grumbled to her about Lorie's clothes. He thought that they were inappropriate for the office. Franny told him he was being "old-school."

"Everything today is about a signature look and that's Lorie's look. She's a designer and they like to look edgy, you can't expect her to dress like an account manager or a corporate attorney," she tried to explain to him when he complained about what he called Lorie's latest "drapery."

His response was to tell her that he had in fact gone to an old school and he didn't like the way Lorie dressed. Franny wasn't sure if Drew ever said anything to Lorie. If he had, Lorie apparently had chosen to pay no attention to him because he was still not happy with what she wore to the office.

Drew's annoyance had increased with the discovery of Lorie's tattoo, a reflection of her growing obsession with angels. Franny had been there when Drew saw the angel, or to be more accurate, the angel's wings, at Chayne's annual company picnic. Drew arranged for them to meet up with Lorie, her husband, Steve, and their baby for lunch in the picnic area set back from the beach at Miller State Park. Franny was seated on the ground next to the stroller; she was entertaining the baby, Alex. Lorie, dressed in jeans and a tank top, bent over the diaper bag to get the baby his bottle.

"What is that?' Drew exploded; staring down at Lorie's exposed back. Franny craned her neck to see what he was glaring at. Rising majestically above the waistband of Lorie's jeans were the wings of an angel.

Before Lorie could answer, Steve stepped in front of her and said to Drew, "What's the problem? That tattoo is art. She designed it herself. It cost over eight hundred bucks."

Ignoring him, Drew asked Lorie, "Why would you ever let someone do that to your body?"

Lorie hesitated before she answered him, a wary look in her eyes as she glanced nervously at her husband and Franny. "I love this image," she said, tossing her hair back from her face. "I wanted to feel like I have an angel standing behind me. It's not a big deal."

Drew shook his head in disgust. Abruptly, he turned his back on them all and walked off toward the beach. They watched as he paused to light a cigarette. Embarrassed, Franny started to apologize for him, when Lorie cut her off.

"Don't worry about it, I know he hates tattoos. It doesn't matter. It's not like he ever has to look at it." Breaking the tension, she grinned at Franny. "But don't you ever get one!" Franny was pretty sure she heard Steve mutter the word, "asshole" under his breath.

On the way home, Franny asked Drew why he cared so much that Lorie had gotten the tattoo. "It's so ridiculous and ugly. But you're right. It's none of my business. She can get Noah and his ark on her ass next for all I care."

Giggling, Franny asked, "How would you know?"

Before calling Drew's office, Franny lit the fire in the antique wood stove to take the chill off the room. The old stove gave off enough heat to warm the entire kitchen. A battered armless oak rocking chair sat invitingly in front of the Victorian wood stove. The rocking chair was the one thing they had kept after the baby died because it was really only an old chair with no connection to the child she would have nursed while sitting there. Thomas, sated from his breakfast, sprawled lazily across the cane seat. Drawn by the warmth, Franny swooped up the cat and sat with him purring in her lap, her icy feet tucked under the stove. She spread her hands in front of the flames, resting her chin on Thomas's head, and stared into the fire.

Franny was pretty in the softly blurred way of women who are slightly overweight. Of average height, she had an open face and a pleasant smile, but would never have been called beautiful. She had always been old for her years. Her father had called her an old soul from the time she was a little girl. It had surprised no one when she had fallen in love with a man fifteen years older than herself. She had lost the weight she had gained with the baby, but she was always battling those last ten pounds. Drew never felt she was thin enough. He liked women to be lean. Her finest feature was her almond-shaped brown eyes. Eyes that often seemed to be looking at something only she could see.

Shifting her gaze from the fire, she looked out the wide bay window, drawn by the noise of the birds at the feeder outside, her hands stroking the cat's soft coat. The day was gray and forbidding. A light rain was falling. It was cold, but not quite cold enough to turn the rain to snow. It had not yet snowed even though it was the nineteenth of December. The backyard was a frozen palette of muted browns.

She watched the pushy rose-breasted grosbeaks fight for space at the birdfeeder, oblivious to the rain. Franny rooted for the smaller birds, but there wasn't much you could do to get rid of the grosbeaks or the blue jays. Oliver shoved his nose around the indignant cat on her lap and stared expectantly up into her eyes. She idly scratched his long curly ears and bent down to kiss his nose. I'll be glad to have my car back, she thought. Drew had taken her Lexus to the airport and left her his own car, a Land Rover, in case it snowed. He didn't trust her driving the Lexus in the ice and snow. She hated driving the SUV. Drew had initially bought the car for her. He was convinced the dark green Land Rover was exactly what she should be driving, once they had kids, completely ignoring the fact that she couldn't drive a stick shift. She still struggled with the clutch five years later.

"Okay, Thomas," she said, dislodging the cat as she stood up. "If his flight got in on time, he should be in the office by now." She crossed the kitchen, reaching again for her cell phone, still wishing for the warmth of her slippers, and watched the tabby cat effortlessly settle back once again into a striped ball on the seat of the rocking chair.

Mentally, she went over the list of things that she had to do, starting with finishing her Christmas cards, as she called Drew's office.

"Drew MacCullough's office." The voice was unfamiliar.

"This is Franny MacCullough. Did Drew make it in from the airport?"

"Lorie called this morning and said that she and Drew would be in late. They're meeting offsite."

Franny was surprised. Why had Lorie called? Had she been on this trip with him? Drew hadn't mentioned she was going. Franny was sure he had gone to Seattle alone. He had told her

Lorie was swamped with design work. "And when she isn't working, she seems to be tied up with one of those damned angel parties." Franny smiled thinking about the home parties that Lorie hosted offering products dealing with angels. Drew called it "Cherubim Tupperware." Lorie gave "angel readings" using a deck of cards similar to Tarot cards.

If Drew had let the battery run down on his phone, that would explain why her call went right to voicemail and if he was meeting Lorie offsite, he would have asked her to call the office for him. It made sense but she wondered why they were meeting away from the office. It was probably about something he didn't want his boss, Johanna Caras, to know about. She must remember to ask him when he got home.

"Okay. Thanks for your help." She stood for a moment with the phone in her hand. The only sounds in the kitchen were the snapping of the logs in the wood stove and the rumbling sounds of contentment coming from the sleeping cat.

Pouring a fresh cup of coffee into one of the reindeer mugs she only used during these two weeks of the year, Franny began to sort the pile of Christmas cards stacked on the granite island in front of her. She loved cards, obtaining a sensual pleasure from the words, images, and various paper stocks used to make them. She had been a collector of words from the time she first learned to read. She savored them. Drew called her "Little Miss Wordy." She was able slip into the pages as seamlessly as a pebble skipped across a pond. Sometimes the lives of the people in the stories she read seemed more real to her than her own.

She carefully selected every card she sent, spending hours searching for each one. She never looked at the prices.

"They see you coming, Franny," Drew had once said, laughing at her. "I should have a line item in our budget for cards."

She placed the cards in orderly rows of four. Studying them

carefully, she realized one was missing. Puzzled, she reached for the folded paper bags from which earlier she had dumped the cards onto the island. Each was empty. Stepping back, she said aloud, "I can't have forgotten to buy Drew's card," annoyed that she would now have to go back into the stores. How could I forget to buy his card? I remember looking for one, she wondered.

Franny loved Christmas, but unlike Drew, she also liked to finish her preparations well before the madness and the rush of the last week. She had been so sure that everything was done, and only the baking, with the details carefully itemized on a list hanging behind her on the refrigerator, remained. All her gifts were already wrapped, labeled, and stacked in neat piles on the bed in the guest room.

Behind her, the phone on the wall rang. It startled her because she almost never used the land line. She was weighing whether Billet Deux or Papyrus would be the better place to find the missing card. Distracted, she picked up the phone without checking to see who the caller was. "Hello."

"Mrs. Andrew MacCullough?" A disembodied voice came business-like over the line.

"Yes," Franny answered her mind on the missing Christmas card.

"This is the Sheraton in Lynton. Your husband, Andrew MacCullough, was a guest here." There was the slightest pause. "He's had a heart attack. The ambulance just left here. They've taken him to St. Luke's Hospital."

CHAPTER 2

The words didn't make any sense to Franny. Of course, Andrew MacCullough was her husband. It was the other words that kept skittering up and down the sides of her mind: guest, Sheraton, heart attack, St. Luke's, ambulance. These were the words she couldn't seem to understand.

"Thank you," she answered, asking no questions, shocked into her best Catholic school girl's voice. Numbness crept over her as she hung up the telephone. She was aware that she needed to hurry, that she needed to go. Now! It was this sense of urgency that made her break into a run as she headed upstairs toward her bedroom.

The two dogs looked up from where they sprawled beside the wood stove and followed her. Oliver raced past her on the stairs. He acted like this was some new game. On the way through her bedroom, Franny gathered up the clothes she had taken off the night before. In her bathroom, she stripped off her flannel nightgown and took one step into the shower. Reaching to turn on the water, she stopped, her mind transported back to a time during the first year after she had lost the baby.

She needed a shower, but the idea of taking a shower exhausted her. She counted moving from her bed down to the sofa in the family room as her big success for the day. The only time she bathed was when Drew succeeded in cajoling her into the shower with him. She leaned against his naked body under the gentle flow of warm water, feeling no desire, seeking only oblivion with her face buried in the wet mat of dark hair on his chest. He shampooed her hair and washed her body, stopping at times to try and press the cake of soap into her hand.

"Come on, Franny, Sweetheart," he crooned softly as he closed her hand around the soap. "You do it, Honey."

She opened her fingers and let the soap fall to the floor where it skittered aimlessly to the far end of the shower stall.

Drew picked the soap up and began again.

The clock in the living room began to chime. I have no time for a shower. I have to get to Drew, Franny thought, turning around to retrieve the clothes scattered on the floor. Dressing quickly, she brushed her teeth and pulled a comb through hair. Back downstairs, she grabbed her jacket and Drew's keys from where they hung on the hook next to the kitchen door. The dogs followed her anxiously from room to room.

It had begun to rain harder; Franny felt the icy drops falling on her face as she left the house. Climbing up into the Land Rover, she remembered to push in the clutch as she turned the key, something she often forgot to do when she started Drew's car. The engine roared to life. Jerking the gears, she began to reverse the car. Suddenly, she slid her foot off the clutch. The car shuddered to a halt. Something was missing. She realized she didn't have her purse or her cell phone. Shifting into park, she pulled up the emergency brake, opened the door, and returned to the kitchen. The forgotten items retrieved, door firmly shut behind her, she climbed shakily back into the Land Rover and headed south toward Lynton.

Hiram's Forge was fifty-five miles north of Boston and eleven miles north of Lynton. It was a bedroom community known for its landscaped neighborhoods, excellent schools, and carefully hoarded Yankee charm. One of those nouveau riche communities with enough remnants of the small New England town it once had been to make it an ideal place for raising children. This was reason that Drew and Franny bought their old colonial there ten years earlier.

They had each grown up in Lynton, although a world and fifteen years apart. The Chiesas owned a modest ranch near the Massachusetts border. Franny's mother sold it after her father's death. Drew grew up in an old brick house with white pillars and manicured lawns in the prestigious north end of the city where the early mill owners and other men of means had built their large homes a century before. Drew's father, a retired banker, and his socialite mother still lived there.

Franny drove, instinctively heading south. The windshield wipers seemed to whisper "hurry, hurry, hurry" as the car ate up the wet road. Her thoughts were on the condition in which she would find Drew, not the road or anyone else on it. *Don't let him be dead don't let him be dead don't let him be dead* played over and over in her head. She was not a good driver, everyone said so, and as a result, she hated to drive. Drew said she was a menace behind the wheel. "I drive better drunk, than you do sober," he told her when once she offered to drive because he had been drinking. She was flying now. The windshield wipers worked overtime to keep up with the freezing rain and the spray from the cars and trucks she was passing. She blew by an eighteen-wheeler. He honked at her, his full-throated air horn piercing her thoughts like a claxon. It was then she looked down to see the speedometer hovering near ninety-five. Slowing down, she felt the Land Rover slip on the wet pavement as she carefully made her way over into the right lane. Behind her, the trucker flashed his lights in what she took as approval. Good girl. Slow down.

What if he's already dead? The thought slipped into her mind without warning. She shook her head in an attempt to remove it from the place where it lodged itself. Turning off the highway, she followed the back road into the downtown, drawing a shaky breath as the granite façade of St. Luke's Hospital came into view. The large marble statue of the saint, Patron of Healers, stared at her from the courtyard in front of the hospital. She turned right into the parking garage. She usually avoided garages, sometimes resorting to parking blocks away from her destination. Today, she had no time to indulge such weakness. Parking the car in the first spot she found, she ran down the stairs and outside onto the sidewalk.

She was vaguely aware of horns blowing as she raced blindly across the street and through the revolving door into the hospital's lobby. She forced herself to slow down as she approached the semi-circular information desk, reluctant to meet what news waited for her there. A woman in a pink volunteer's smock sat behind the desk. Her nametag, pinned over the pocket with St. Luke's Hospital neatly stitched in blue on it, read: Hello. My name is Charlotte. There was a small Santa Claus sticker in the corner.

"Can I help you?" the woman asked, smiling at Franny.

"I'm trying to find my husband," Franny said, taking in the decorated Christmas tree surrounded with brightly wrapped packages destined for some local charity.

"What's your husband's name, dear?"

Franny hesitated before answering, not ready to finalize the fact that Drew was even in the hospital. "Andrew MacCullough. I received a call that he was taken here."

"Can you spell the last name for me, please?" Charlotte asked her hands poised over the keyboard. Franny slowly spelled MacCullough. She thought she saw something flashing on the computer screen when the women finished typing in the name. Her heart began to race as she watched the smile on Charlotte's face freeze and then crack the way ice on a sidewalk does when you put your weight on it.

"He's in emergency. You follow that hall and turn to the right. There are red footprints painted on the floor marking the way," she said, biting her lip, looking everywhere but at Franny's face.

Franny felt the way she had when she had played tag at the lake as a child and tried to run through waist-deep water. She wanted to move fast, but some unseen force seemed to be holding her back. Following the bright red footprints, she drifted down the corridor toward the Emergency Room. A woman stood in the hall. A tall, slender woman dressed in skin-tight jeans and an embroidered poet's shirt, her long red hair gathered in a messy knot on top of her head. I know her, Franny thought as she walked towards her.

"Here's his wife." This woman said to someone Franny couldn't see. It was only then, after she heard her speak, that she realized the woman was Lorie.

They stood facing one another, surrounded by the antiseptic bustle of the emergency room. She surprised herself by asking, "He's dead, isn't he?"

Lorie hesitated before she answered, "I think so. He was blue when they took him out of the hotel room."

"Mrs. MacCullough? I'm Doctor Cantillio," a tall man said, stepping past Lorie. "Will you please come with me?" Gently, he turned her around and guided her into a small room. She was conscious of his closeness. He wore Polo cologne. She recognized it because Drew wore it, too. With the slightest pressure of his hands he eased her down onto a small sofa upholstered in a bright orange and green plaid.

"He's dead." Franny said. She was certain now as she stared up into the doctor's concerned face.

"Yes, he is. I'm so very sorry, Mrs. MacCullough."

It was the finality of what he said that took her by surprise. Dead. Drew was dead. Despite knowing it to be true, hearing it confirmed by the doctor made something inside her want to fight back. "No. He can't be. I can't live without him." She repeated herself to make sure that the doctor understood. "I can't."

"Your husband had a massive heart attack and we couldn't save him. I'm sorry." Franny said nothing. She had already stated her case. She couldn't live without him.

She found herself feeling sorry for the doctor. He was about fifty, the same age as Drew. A trim man who wore his hair in a no-nonsense brush cut. She thought his blue eyes behind his glasses looked tired. He wore green scrubs. His nametag read: Peter Cantillio, M.D. She noticed a small pattern of bloodstains, none larger than pinpoints on his sleeve. She supposed the blood was Drew's. She nodded slowly, confirming that, yes, she understood. "They took my mother into a room like this. I suppose it's a rule: Don't tell the wife that her husband is dead in the hall."

"Something like that." The ghost of a smile slipped briefly across his face. "Your father died of a heart attack?"

She nodded. "My father was sixty. 'First and fatal' they

called it." She fiddled for a moment with her wedding ring, twisting the wide gold band, left then right. "This is the same thing, I guess. What time did Drew die?"

"The death certificate will read that he died at nine o'clock, but, in reality, he was probably dead before the paramedics reached the hotel." The doctor's eyes never left her face.

"My father died at nine thirty-five in the morning." She said, steadily looking back at him.

She remembered Drew holding her in his arms that hot summer morning as she wept inconsolably. "I'll never die in bed like your father. I know I'll go in a car crash or on a plane," he had told her.

"Do you think that God has a sense of humor?" Franny asked.

"Mrs. MacCullough, who can we call for you? You shouldn't be alone now."

She could tell she was making him nervous. He was feeling bad about not being able to save Drew. And now here she was, inquiring about the personality of God. She was suddenly tired and closed her eyes to focus her thoughts. Who to call? Sofia, she thought.

"My sister. She works here in Lynton. I can call her."

Behind the doctor, in the doorway, a woman cleared her throat. "Dr. Cantillio…" she said, tentatively. He turned quickly, but not before Franny saw his expression of relief. He stepped aside so the speaker, a small woman with a gold cross pinned to the collar of her shirt could enter the room. She sat down next to Franny on the sofa.

"Mrs. MacCullough, this is Sister Moira Callahan. She will stay with you while you wait for your family." The doctor reached for Franny's hand. "I am very sorry for your loss. Take all the time you need here. You've had a terrible shock.

Would you like me to give you a sedative? It would probably help you."

"No." Franny answered sharply, thinking of the pills she had taken in the months after the baby died, all prescribed to make her not feel the pain of her loss. "Thank you. I really don't need anything. I'll be okay." She stood up. "I want to see him."

A look passed between the doctor and the nun who said, "Do you think that you should wait until—"

Franny spoke to the doctor. "I want to say good-bye to him by myself. I don't want anyone else there."

He nodded. "Okay. I need to have them clean him up a little bit. Things got pretty frantic in there. Give me a few minutes." Franny glanced at the blood on the doctor's scrubs. "Sister Moira will wait with you," he added as he turned to leave.

"May I call you by your first name, Mrs. MacCullough?" Sister Moira asked her.

"Of course, Sister."

The nun waited patiently. "What is your name, Mrs. Mac-Cullough?"

"Franny. My name is actually Francesca, but people call me Franny."

"Francesca. What a lovely name, not one you hear often."

Franny smiled, surprising herself. It was her first smile since the phone rang. It felt like a sacrilege. Quickly, she rearranged her face. "It's not a very common name. I was named for my father's grandmother, his Nona. I never knew her, but I know he loved her, that's why I was named after her."

The two women sat next to each other on the sofa waiting for the doctor to return. Franny felt numb. She had no idea how long they sat there, but it felt like forever. Finally, the doctor was back. "You can go in now, but first I want you to be prepared for what you'll see." He looked at her closely, and continued. "His skin will be bluish gray because the blood is no longer oxygen-ated. His body will be cool to the touch. We have covered him with a sheet. If you look under the sheet, you will see that several cut downs were made while we were working on him. Do you think you can handle that?"

Franny nodded. The nun started to get up from where she sat on the sofa.

"No," Franny said, "I want to go alone."

She followed the doctor down the hall, ignoring Lorie who was waiting where Franny had left her. The doctor stopped in front of the closed door to one of the small trauma rooms. Opening the door, he stood aside for her to enter. The curtain was pulled around the bed. The doctor placed his hand on her shoulder. "Remember, we'll be right outside."

She entered the room, closing the heavy door behind her. She shivered. The room was cold and very quiet despite the bustle outside. She walked very slowly to the end of the curtain and stopped. She didn't exactly turn the corner as much as she peered around it, her feet reluctantly following her eyes. She felt light-headed. She reached out for the foot of the bed to steady herself.

The harsh overhead light was off; the only light in the room came from the softer light at the head of the bed, muting slightly the stark reality of death in the room. Drew's eyes were open. Her own heart began to race as she looked down at him. She thought wildly, he's not dead. Then she saw that there was no light in his eyes, their blue-green sparkle dulled by death. The sheet was pulled tightly up under his chin. The only part of his body that was visible was his face. She was thankful he didn't look scared, only surprised. He appeared small, lying there in the bed. Drew was average height, but he had always seemed larger than life to her. She reached over and gently closed his eyes, unable to bear their emptiness.

"I told you that job was going kill you. But you wouldn't listen."

As if in answer, his left eye slowly opened. She started to close it again and stopped. She let her hand fall to her side. It was too late. Everything was too late. Turning away from Drew, she walked out the door into the hall, closing the door behind her.

She could see Sister Moira and Dr. Cantillio standing outside the door of the room with the plaid sofa, waiting for her. Someone stepped forward, reaching for her hands.

"I loved him too." It was Lorie, the freckles standing out on her strained white face.

"I know you did. He couldn't have done his job without you. He counted on you to keep things running smoothly." Franny said, not sure what else there was to say to her in the way of comfort.

"Can I go in and see him?" Lorie asked. "I just want to say good-bye."

Franny stared at her, weighing the woman's presence in the ER for the first time. Why were you and Drew meeting outside the office this morning? She wondered. I can't think about that now. Her answer was uncharacteristically terse. "No, I would prefer you didn't. There's nothing to see, he's not there anymore. Please go home. I'll call you when I know what's happening."

Lorie started to say something, but instead, pulled Franny into a hug. "Rely on your angels," she whispered in Franny's ear. "They're here. And Drew's, too, I can feel them." Looking at the closed door of the room where Drew lay, she added, "They'll guide Drew on his journey home."

"We should call your sister now," Sister Moira said to Franny. Extracting herself from Lorie's hug, she followed the nun into the room without a backward glance.

Franny reached into her purse and pulled out her cell phone. She searched through her list of contacts until she found the entry: **Sofia**.

"You can't use your cell phone here. Would you like me to place the call for you?" Sister Moira asked, indicating the beige phone on the table next to the sofa. Franny shook her head, reached for the phone, and punched in the number of her sister's cell. After three rings, Sofia answered, "Sofia Chiesa."

CHAPTER 3

Sofia Chiesa slumped disconsolately in her office chair and gazed at the print hanging on the wall opposite her desk. "The Scream" by Edvard Munch, was the portrait of a person, sex unidentifiable, standing at the end of a bridge, with mouth gaping open in the silent scream of the title. The eyes stared wide either from panic or surprise. She was sure it was a woman. It was her favorite painting. When she hung it here in her office, one of the founding partners, Neil Malone, commented dryly, "Are you sure that will engender confidence in the clients?" She didn't care. It was her office and if it scared the clients, that was too bad. She liked it. She had to admit that it rarely went unnoticed.

Examining the face in the picture more carefully than she usually did, she felt that she understood the emotions lurking behind those wild eyes only too well. God, my life is a mess. There were twelve days until the end of the year and she had two mergers expected to close by the thirty-first.

What was really bothering her was that her training times these last three days had been terrible. Shaking her head in disgust, she reached for her BlackBerry and recorded this morning's run. She had qualified to run the Boston Marathon this spring. She wanted not only to run, but to turn in a credible performance. If she couldn't do that, then she wouldn't run the race. She was not an I-only-want-to-finish kind of competitor. She banished the idea of not competing before it could take root in her mind, believing strongly in the power of positive thought, straightening her narrow shoulders as she did so. *Damn it, I will run Boston and run it well.*

Opening her desk drawer, she reached for the pack of Trident sugar free gum that she kept within easy reach. She didn't like to think about how much gum she chewed. It drove her brother-in-law crazy. "It keeps me thin, unlike your wife," she said aloud to the picture in front of her. Franny had taken that picture the summer their father died. The shot was of her and Drew sitting on his motorcycle. Picking up the picture, she examined it more closely. *I look fat,* she thought. Drew looked young and carefree, his eyes staring suggestively into those of his wife behind the camera. A sensuous half smile played around his mouth. *How could we have gotten through that terrible summer without Drew?* Staring at the photo, she found herself thinking of the conversation they had last week when he dropped into her office.

"You look exhausted," she said. "Can't you take a break from all this traveling?" Drew lounged in her client chair in front of her desk. He was completely at ease in any space he occupied. He laughed, and for a moment the animation in his face banished the weariness.

"You should talk. You look like a vampire in that getup. Do you ever wear anything that isn't black?" This was an old

battle between them. Drew liked soft colors on women. He was forever bringing home pale pink or lilac sweaters to Franny.

"This is a Max Mara and I'll have you know that I paid a fortune for it. It makes me look thin. I happen to like it."

Drew eyed her speculatively for a minute. "Hard not to look thin when you weigh what? Ninety pounds soaking wet? I like my women thin, but there's a limit. You run too damn much." He smiled at her, taking the sting out of his words. "Suit yourself. But you're not going to hook a guy looking like you should be on view at McKenna's," he said, referring to the local funeral parlor. As usual, she noted sourly, he completely dismissed her relationship with Brendan.

"I'm taking some time off after I come back from Seattle," he said. "I'm on vacation starting the nineteenth. I don't go back to work until January second." His smile flashed. "I'm going to sleep late, go to the club, play tennis until I drop, and soak in the hot tub. I'm going to try and blast your boss out of here to do some skiing." This caught her attention. She would love to go skiing, too. Silently, she cursed her caseload. If she worked late all this week and the weekend, she might be able to steal a day and tag along.

"I doubt you'll have much trouble getting him to take a day off. The only thing he loves better than practicing law is skiing," she said, smiling back at Drew.

"Yeah, but you forget he's such a faithful soul. The counselor is not a man for coloring outside the lines."

Unlike you, she thought, who has spent your entire life doing that with the equivalent of a big yellow marker.

His mood shifted and his face fell once again into the somber lines that had disturbed her earlier. He looked old and she didn't like it.

"I need you to promise me something," he said.

"What are you talking about? What's wrong?" She was surprised by the seriousness of his tone.

"Nothing's wrong. I'm calling in a favor. Remember all those times I took you out on the bike?" Drew nodded toward the

picture on her desk. "I want you to promise me you'll be nicer to Franny."

"You're unbelievable." She snapped, suddenly angry.

Not quite five feet tall, she insisted she was not "short," only reluctantly conceding to being "not tall." She added three inches to her height with the black Italian leather pumps she wore as part of a uniform with whatever black outfit she had chosen for the day. Seething with rage, she stood up and marched across her small office. She stopped when she could go no further in front of the bookcase to straighten a picture of her parents that didn't need to be straightened. Turning, she confronted Drew, feeling her face flushing with her anger.

"You and my mother. 'Be nice to Franny.' 'Don't upset Franny.' 'Don't say anything to Franny.' Doesn't it occur to anybody but me that what Franny needs is a kick in the butt?" It was the same old song. Franny was special. The rules didn't apply to Franny. Sofia had been hearing it her entire life.

"Look, I know that the two of you don't agree on much, but she's had a rough time." Drew was no longer smiling.

Here we go, Sofia silently fumed. Franny and her rough time.

"A lot of people have rough times, Drew, and they go on with their lives. They don't completely fall apart and not get out of bed." Her tone softened. "You had a rough a time, too."

"Yeah, well it's different for a guy. I had my job. Franny only had her dreams. Losing a baby is a terrible thing for any woman to come back from."

"Please don't suggest that every woman would have reacted the way my sister did. Most women have to get out of bed, they have no choice. It's an insult to all of us. As you and my mother keep reminding me, Franny is hardly typical."

Drew sighed. "I agree. There's nothing typical about Franny." He smiled. "Maybe that's why I love her so much. I don't want to fight with you about it. Let me put it differently. I am asking you to cut Franny some slack as a favor to me. Okay?"

Mollified slightly, Sofia nodded.

"Thanks, I knew I could count on you. Anyway, she has been doing a lot better. She is actually doing something with that little doll business of hers. She's going to be fine."

"Oh, yeah, that's right, the dolls." She snorted contemptuously, thinking, wonderful. My sister gets out of bed every day like the rest of us and plays with dolls.

Drew didn't react to the last comment. "If anything were to happen, I have to know you would be there for her. She would need someone to lean on and your mother can't do it."

Sofia wasn't about to argue with him there. She was worried about her mother, struggling with failing eyesight and the loneliness of widowhood.

"I want your word that you would look out for Franny if anything were to happen."

She shivered, suddenly cold. His intensity disturbed her. "What are you talking about? What are you trying to tell me?"

Drew smiled. "Only what you've already pointed out yourself. I've been traveling constantly. Soon, it will be winter. I need to know that if something goes wrong when I am in East Podunk, Franny has someone she can call. That's all. No big deal."

"Fine," she replied, disarmed by that smile. "You've got it. I'll look out for Franny if anything goes wrong."

"And..." He waited.

"And I'll be nice." She conceded, grudgingly

"Good girl."

Taking her eyes from Drew, she was suddenly aware that Neil Malone's large frame filled the narrow door of her office. He smiled at her over the top of Drew's head.

"What are you doing here, MacCullough? Slumming?"

Drew twisted around in the chair to grin at his closest friend. "Visiting with my wife's sister. I hope you don't mind."

"I hope she's billing you for it," Neil said, his smile making a lie of his words.

Her cell phone began to ring, bringing her back to the present. She smiled when she saw that it was Brendan.

"Hi, Brendan."

"Hey, Babe, how's your morning going?"

Her immediate reaction, when Brendan called her "Babe" was one of annoyance. Why he persisted in doing it, when she told him repeatedly that she hated it, she didn't know. She wondered if it wasn't time to end things with Brendan. There was no future in it, as Drew pointed out to her whenever the subject of Brendan came up. What could a lawyer who was a Phi Beta Kappa from Dartmouth possibly have in common with a firefighter who moonlighted as a carpenter? Brendan was fun to be with and he made her laugh. And lately, not much else in her life did. That, and the fact that he was great in bed had kept things going since she met him at the Y's running club.

"It's insane here this time of the year, Bren. I told you I have two deals that expect to close this month." She nervously chewed her thumb as she spoke.

"You sound stressed out. Did you run today?" His question automatically triggered a picture of him running in her mind. It irritated her. Where she planned and calculated, Brendan just ran. At five-foot-ten and weighing one hundred and fifty pounds, he had the slender build that made the sport effortless for him, or so it seemed to her. He was, as much as it pained her to admit it, a much better runner than she was.

"I did a very slow five. I just can't seem to improve my time."

"You try too hard and you don't eat right. You're supposed to fuel the body remember? Not starve it."

"What's up?" She asked, deliberately changing the subject, choosing not to have the food discussion this morning. Her eating habits were a constant source of friction between them.

"I'm off tonight and if you want, I could make a pot of Feeney's Finest Spaghetti. We could get some Chianti and a video. How does that sound?"

She was tempted. She would love to curl up on Brendan's cushiony sofa, watch some mindless video, and have someone take care of her. Brendan, when she let him, was very good at taking care of her. He would fuss over her, make her eat the admittedly delicious dinner he had cooked, and after the video they would make love. She stared at the neatly labeled manila folders in front of her and sighed. "Brendan, I can't. I'm way behind and I have to get this work done. You're sweet and I do appreciate it, but I'm stuck here tonight."

"I know that tone, Attorney Chiesa. But, hey, how about I bring you over a doggie bag about seven? No strings attached."

Her friends, Drew being first among them, didn't understand what she saw in Brendan Feeney. A very good finish carpenter, he had a waiting list of customers eager to have him do work for them. If he left the fire department and worked as a carpenter full time, he would make a lot more money. She was certain he could start his own construction business. But when she had pointed this out to him, he had shrugged and said, "Yeah, but I like being a firefighter. It's what I do. I have everything that I need." Thinking about it, she realized, to her chagrin, he did.

Brendan owned a small duplex. He rented out one side and lived in the other. He drove a ten-year old Ford truck that, he told her complacently, "Gets me where I need to go." His only extravagance was his running shoes. It didn't bother Brendan that she made more money than he did. There were times she wondered why she was attracted to Brendan rather than to some of the "more suitable" men in her own office and the other law firms with whom she worked. But tonight wasn't one of them.

"That would be awesome." She answered, flooded with gratitude that someone cared if she worked herself to death.

"Okay, then look for me around seven. Listen, Babe, please try to take it slow."

That was a good one, she thought closing her phone, take it slow! She reached for the top folder on the pile in front of her. She was reading the latest revisions to the Addison Chemicals merger when her cell phone rang again, breaking her concentration.

"Oh, shit!" She sighed as she reached for the annoying instrument. "Sofia Chiesa." She snapped into the phone, still concentrating on the document in front of her, not bothering to see who was calling.

"Sofia? It's Franny."

Damn, Sofia thought, I don't have time for whatever this is. "Fran, I'm kind of in the middle of something here. Is it important?"

"I'm at St. Luke's. Something's happened to Drew." Franny's voice broke.

Sofia shivered, as she gripped the phone. "What is it? Did he have an accident? Tell me what happened?"

"He's dead! Drew's dead!" Standing in the small waiting room at St. Luke's Franny listened as Sofia began to scream. Sighing, she shrugged her shoulders, looking over at Sister Moira and waited for the screaming to stop.

In her office across the city, Sofia continued to keen; her small body bent almost double in a paroxysm of grief. Erica, her administrative assistant, and Neil Malone almost collided at the door to her office. Malone held a carved blackthorn shillelagh in his hand.

"In the name of God, what's the matter?" He roared as he thundered into her office.

Still holding her phone, Sofia slid to her knees next to her desk, rocking back and forth as she wept.

Neil bent over her, checking her for any visible signs of having been physically attacked. Having assured himself that she was unharmed, he reached for the phone in her hand. She gave it up without protest. Clearing his throat, he said, "This is Neil Malone."

"Neil?" Franny sobbed, "Oh, God, it's Drew."

"Franny, calm down," he said, clearly articulating each word. An icy dread filled his heart, but his voice was steady as he continued, "Tell me where you are and what's happened."

"I...I'm at St. Luke's and...Oh my God, Neil...he's dead! Drew's dead."

Pain slammed into him, slicing his gut with the precision of a surgeon's scalpel. His eyes filled with tears that began to slide down his face, leaving dark splashes on the front of his imported silk tie. "Was he in an accident?"

"No. It was his heart. He had a heart attack. Oh, God, I don't know what to do." Franny sobbed.

"You don't have to do anything. Just wait there. Sofia and I will be there as soon as we can." He glanced uncertainly at the girl huddled at his feet. "You stay where you are. I'll take care of everything." He closed the phone.

He dropped to his knees in front of Sofia. He took her chin and cupped it in the sturdy hands he had inherited from his paternal grandfather who had dug ditches for city of Boston. "Sofia, you've got to pull yourself together. Do you hear me? We have to go tell your mother and get over to the hospital." Dazed, Sofia looked up at him with unfocused eyes and said nothing.

"Erica, in the bottom right-hand drawer of my desk there is a decanter of Jameson's. Bring it to me, please, along with one of the glasses you'll find there." He scanned the concerned faces of his co-workers crowded into the small hall outside the door to Sofia's office. "Everything is under control in here. Sofia has had some tragic news." People began moving away and returning to what they had been doing before hearing Sofia scream. Only his partner, Mike O'Shea, lingered in the door.

"Is there anything I can do, Neil?"

Neil answered tersely. "It's Drew. Heart attack." He looked away from Mike and swallowed deeply. "He's gone."

Mike took a step toward him. He stopped at the sight of the fortress Malone's face had become.

"I think we have the situation under control. Don't we, Sofia?" Sofia shuddered. She nodded slowly. Neil handed her his pressed white handkerchief. Taking it, she blew her nose.

Mike turned to leave. "Okay. I'll take care of things here. You two go and do what you have to do." He looked down at Sofia. "I'm very sorry for your loss." His eyes met those of the man who had been his friend since law school. "I'm sorry, Neil, I know how close you and Drew were. He was a great guy, he'll be missed."

Unable to speak, Neil bit his lower lip and nodded his thanks. He turned his attention back to Sofia. "We have to think of Franny now. Drew would expect us to take care of her."

Shock flooded Sofia. "Just last week when he was here, that's what he made me promise, that I would look out for Franny." Her eyes widened. "You don't think he had a premonition do you? That he knew—"

"No, I don't," Neil answered. "He was probably worried about Franny coping if she had to deal with a crisis with the car or the house and he wasn't here. I think he always saw her as impractical, but ever since she lost the baby, he worried about her even more." Looking at Sofia, he added, "You, on the other hand, he saw as being strong. Someone he could count on. Now is your chance to prove him right."

He reached for the Waterford decanter of Jameson's Irish whiskey and the matching tumbler Erica held out to him. He poured three fingers of the amber liquid into the glass and held it out to Sofia.

She shook her head. "I don't want it."

"Drink it. You've had a shock. You're going to need it."

She gave him a sarcastic smile. "You and Drew. You think this is the answer to everything. 'The cure for all that ails you.' That's what he said." Reluctantly, Sofia took the glass from his hand. Grimacing, she drank the whiskey like a child forced to swallow medicine.

Neil got to his feet and extended his hand to Sofia. "We have to go and get your mother."

His face was a stoic mask betraying nothing as she left to use the ladies' room, Erica hovering at her side. It was only after he shut the door behind them that he surrendered to his own grief. He stuffed his meaty fist into his mouth, biting down hard to keep from crying out. It would be two days before he would notice that he had broken the skin just below the thumb on his right hand.

CHAPTER 4

Brid Sheerin balanced on a purple gymnastics ball in the center of her living room. Taking a deep breath, she began bouncing up and down with the abandon of a six-year old. She matched her breathing to the motion of her body, inhaling on the way up and exhaling loudly as she came down. Her anger at Declan Molloy lessened with each bounce.

She used the gym ball to reduce stress and, despite how ridiculous she knew she looked, her approach was working. Stress, Dr. Kelly insisted, could kill her. "It's reckless to be walking around with your blood pressure reading," he said. She had a deep fear of all medication rooted in watching her mother die a painful death twenty years before surrounded by rows of brown plastic bottles lined up along the old marble-topped dresser like soldiers on parade. She believed that none of them had provided her mother any relief, and had contributed to the misery that marked Rosemary's last month on earth.

"I'm not swallowing a bunch of pills without trying something else, like meditation and exercise first!" Brid insisted. Knowing the futility of arguing with her, Tom Kelly reluctantly agreed to go along with her plan. To her delight, and the doctor's surprise, her blood pressure was normal when she came in to have it checked again.

"I don't know what you're doing," he said, looking at her over the top of his glasses, "but keep doing it."

Declan had called her as she was leaving her gallery. One of her main suppliers in Ireland, she had been after him for months to find the blown glass Christmas ornaments that she had hoped to showcase in the gallery this holiday season. The noise in the background, coupled with the hour in Dublin, made it clear that he was calling from Paedar Kearney's, his favorite pub. He informed her jovially that the shipment had finally been located, damaged, on the Aer Lingus freight dock. She wanted to kill him, would have killed him, if she had him in front of her. What she actually told him was, "I would like to squish your little ferret mug until your eyes pop." Declan seemed to take no offense. He had run afoul of her temper before. In an excellent mood, no doubt, she was sure, fueled by the pint of Guinness in his hand, he responded, "And a very Happy Christmas to you, too, Brid."

She felt the knot between her shoulder blades slowly begin to come undone as she continued to breathe deeply. Behind her, on the oak sideboard, her cell phone rang. Still bouncing, she reached for the phone checking to see who was calling.

"Oh, damn." She cursed. It was her father. Now what? "Da, I'm here. What's wrong?" Thirty-eight years in the States, and still, the lilt of Doolin, the Irish seaside town where she was born, could be heard in her voice.

She slid off the ball, resigned to hearing the latest crisis at Ceol agus Craic, her father's restaurant and bar. She watched the ball drift aimlessly toward the long cream-colored sofa covered in an array of bright quilts, standing in the semi-circle of the wide bay window. She stretched out to her full five-feet-nine on the polished oak floor and waited.

On the other end of the phone, her father was silent, a highly unusual state for gregarious Desmond Sheerin. She felt her heart begin to race in the old familiar panic, drumming relentlessly within her chest. Sharply, her voice rising, she asked, "For God's sake, Da, what is it? Did the place burn down?"

"It's Drew."

She snorted, rage beginning to burn under her breastbone. Of course it's Drew. Who else it would it be? "What's happened now? Is he passed out there on the floor?" The phone in her hand was silent. Behind her, the mantle clock chimed six o'clock. Her father cleared his throat.

"He's dead."

Her eyes were drawn to the corner of the room. Mounted there, nostrils flaring, legs prancing, stood an antique carousel horse. She was transported back to the day that she and Drew found him.

"Hey, Mick! Over here! Come look at this!" Glancing up from the box of old cameos she was picking through, Brid searched the antique stall for the source of Drew's voice. She found him, crouched in the baked dirt that turned to cracked clay in the late August heat. He beckoned her over to where he squatted, not taking his eyes from something lying on the ground in front of him. "It's a carousel horse." He lowered his voice "I think it could be authentic. Look at the wood," he said.

She looked down at the poor broken thing, lying forlornly in the dust, and answered, "Surely, it's dead, though."

"Brid, are you there?" Her father's voice pleaded, bringing her back to the present. Hearing the old man softly slurring his

words, she thought, he's broken his sacred rule about never taking a drop before the stroke of midnight.

"Brid!" Desmond's voice bellowed from the phone.

"I'm here, Da." She pushed herself into a seated position,
hugging her bent legs to her chest, the telephone held to her
right ear. "I'll be there in twenty minutes. I have to change first.
You've caught me exercising."

"You're coming here to Craic?" Desmond sounded confused. She almost never went to the bar anymore, not unless she
needed to deal with some urgent business matter. She preferred
to see her father here at her condo or the gallery. Places where
unpleasant memories did not haunt their conversations.

"Yes, I'll come down to Craic. Are you alone?" Realizing,
even as she asked him, how unlikely it would be for the bar to
be empty at this time of night.

"Harry's here with me." He sounded slightly less anxious.

"Good. I'll be there as soon as I can." Disconnecting the
phone, she sat motionless for a moment longer, before reaching
once again for the gym ball. She had a working artist's hands;
the nails cut short and left unpolished. She rolled the large rub-
ber ball aimlessly back and forth as her mind struggled to grasp
what her father had told her.

She rose from the floor. She began stripping her tee shirt over
her head as she crossed the long room and continued down the
hall into her bedroom. She had been delighted to find this condo, a second floor flat, in an old Victorian in the north end of
Lynton. She combined the two small bedrooms into one large
room overlooking the walled garden at the rear of the house.
It was painted the palest of green, a color called "tendril." The
room was dominated by a king-size bed with a white iron head-
board covered with a handmade quilt in the pattern known as
"Grandmother's Flower Garden." A fiery watercolor of a sun-

set at the harbor at Doolin hung over the bed. She had painted it herself.

Brid had the kind of looks often called striking, although she had been called beautiful, and not only by men who had too much to drink. Her features were strong and warred slightly within the confines of her highly expressive face. Her eyes were more green than brown, they were large and heavily fringed with thick sooty black lashes. She had a long nose with a bump almost at the end, marring its perfection, and the prominent jaw and high cheekbones so often seen in the Irish. Her mouth was large. Her smile, thanks to Des's religiously saving his tips for years for that very purpose, was perfect. It was a dazzling smile offset all too frequently by a scowl that was equally forbidding.

She caught a glimpse of her reflection as she crossed the room in the mirror standing in the corner. Still slender at forty-three, she had long legs and narrow hips. Her figure had changed little since she was eighteen. A lifetime of ballet classes and now yoga, coupled with the fact that she was almost constantly in motion, helped; but in the end, she had been lucky enough to inherit her mother's genes. It was her mother that stared back at her from the mirror. The old glass distorted the image, making it easy for her to believe for a moment that it was Rosemary, looking back at her. Thank God, Brid offered a silent prayer; she's not here to see this sad day.

Turning away from the mirror, she dressed quickly in faded jeans that molded her body like a second skin and a black cashmere turtleneck sweater that fell softly below her hips. Grunting, she pulled on her boots, actual riding boots, bought at a tack shop, and made of the softest of leathers. She swirled a scarlet cape around her shoulders, grabbed her purse, and started out of the room. At the door, she stopped. Turning back, she walked over to an old steamer trunk and lifted its gracefully curved lid. Dropping to her knees, she reached down inside. Pushing aside the old journals, stacks of cards and letters banded in faded ribbons, and high school and college yearbooks, she found what she was searching for near the bottom. Gently, she pulled a picture framed in silver, tarnished almost black, from the depths of the trunk.

Brid held the picture with both hands and stared at it. Her eyes flooded with tears she blinked angrily away. The camera captured the man in the picture in a moment when he was unusually relaxed, the cavalier mask he wore so naturally, gone. It was Drew as he might have been, and that was why she had kept it. It reminded her of a time long ago when she believed in happy endings. She brought the picture to her lips and held it there for a moment. Without glancing at it again, she reburied it at the bottom of the trunk.

She drove her ancient Jeep through the traffic, winding her way down toward the river past the brick mill buildings converted to pricey office space and condominiums. She drove with the sureness of a cat slinking watchfully through the hedges in search of prey. A block from Our Lady Queen of the Angels Church, she slid the car into the familiar alley behind the bar.

Turning off the ignition, she shivered and pulled the cape around herself. It was cold outside, the temperature a raw and wet 30 degrees. The red cape lined with beaver, discovered in a small boutique on Grafton Street in Dublin, was warm enough. The cold she felt did not come from the December night, but from within herself. Distastefully, she stared at the back of the ramshackle wooden building, at the staircase that rose to the second floor apartment where she had lived with her parents when they had come here from Ireland. A battered plastic candy cane hung forlornly on the door leading into the flat. Her mother had died in that apartment. Her father, surrounded by an ever-changing assortment of kin, both actual and honorary, still lived there.

I'll not go in the back, she thought, it will only make me feel worse. She ducked around the side of the building, passed the blue Dumpster and the stack of empty kegs waiting to be picked up, made her way carefully around the assorted trash, and came out on to Dock Street. The change from blue-collar near slum, to what had recently been called one of the best places to live north of Boston still caught her by surprise. The sidewalks were brick now. Gone were the wide concrete squares, separated by the chipped cracks she had fretfully avoided, according to the old wives' tale, lest she break her mother's back. The streets were illuminated by restored gas streetlights. The old mill buildings, diagonally across the street, once the manufacturing facility for the Storrs Shoe Company, had been divided into two and three bedroom condos, now called The Mill at 17 Dock. They were home to young professionals who either worked in Lynton or commuted into Boston or to one of the high tech companies dotted along routes 128 and 495. The block now boasted an upscale florist, McGonagles, whose windows sparkled with tiny white lights nestled in a sea of red poinsettia and a French bakery, La Boulangerie, famous for its brioche. Her father's bar and restaurant, Ceol agus Craic, had stood on the corner of Main and Dock Streets for thirty-six years.

The soft yellow light from the ornate Tiffany lamps glowed softly through the long row of multi-paned windows fronting each street. Over each set of windows was a sign, black letters outlined in gold: Ceol agus Craic. Pausing to gather her courage, Brid could hear her mother's voice from that long ago night when Des had painted the original sign that had hung over the door.

"Mother of our Precious Lord, Desmond, you can not call the place that!" Rosemary protested, aghast. Her apron bunched in her hands, she argued with her husband. "These people can't even pronounce it much less understand what it means. Call the place 'Sheerin's Pub' or even 'Pot O'Gold'."

"Well, that's the name it's having, woman," her father answered without bothering to look up from where he knelt carefully painting the sign. He wore a paper hat fashioned out of folded newsprint, a skill he learned from the pressman at the Lynton Ledger where he worked when they first came to America. "Let them learn the name if they want to buy a pint here. I'll do my part in keeping the language alive. Even the bastard Brits couldn't completely destroy it. Pot O'Gold," he snorted, stepping back to admire his work. Seated on one of the high bar stools, wearing her own paper hat, Brid wondered what it was that made Da so mad. She liked the name Pot O'Gold, maybe the leprechauns would come if he named the bar that.

The sound of a siren on a fire engine racing down Main Street brought her back to the present. In the end, she thought, they were both right. Craic's first customers did call the bar, "Sheerin's" or "Des's Place," but "Craic" was what the bar came to be known in Lynton down through the years and remained even now when the word "crack" meant something else. Des was satisfied. It was a rare night that he was not asked what the name meant. This allowed him to give his lesson on the lyrical beauty of the Irish language he loved and rail against the terrible tyranny of the "bastard Brits."

"Ceol Agus Craic" – music and fun. There will be little fun to be had here tonight, she thought. Her hand hesitated on the brass door handle, taking a deep breath, she opened the door and stepped across the oak threshold into the light of bar. It was a typical crowd for an early Thursday evening. The dining room tucked into the front room that ran along Main Street was empty. Craic served two dinners, by reservation only, the first at seven and the second at nine o'clock. It was six thirty. People would be starting to gather for the seven o'clock seating. She could see the two waiters, immaculately dressed in black tie, shoes shined to a high gloss, carefully checking table settings. She watched as Ronan, one of her father's newest waifs, carefully repositioned a Waterford bud vase.

As she stepped into the large open room, her eyes automatically swept the long oak bar. At the far end, slouched on their usual stools, nursing respectively a Harp and a Bushmills, she could see Tommy Mahoney and Barry Shanahan. Retired now, they had started coming to Craic when it first opened its door on their way home from the second shift at the shoe factory. Two stools away, Harry, his back to her, was in deep conversation with her father. In the glow of the long lamp over the bar, she saw that Harry's hair was more silver than blond. Now when did that happen? She wondered.

On the working side of the L-shaped bar, stood her father and from the color of his face he had definitely suspended his sacred rule. There were two men at the other end of the bar in their early thirties, dressed in pinstripes and red ties, sipping what looked like martinis. They were likely early arrivals for the seven o'clock dinner seating. A couple sat snuggled together on one of the two emerald green velvet love seats placed at right angles to the long windows overlooking the river. Giggling and touching each other, they hardly seemed old enough to buy the

Guinness on the table in front of them. Tommy Mahoney, taking his eyes from his Harp, looked up and saw Brid. He said something to Desmond and the old man turned. At eighty, despite a pronounced stoop, her father remained a tall man. He had a long cadaverous face dominated by deep set eyes and a hawk-like nose blotched with spidery red veins born of years of consuming his own products.

Watching her father walk unsteadily toward her, Brid's heart went out to him. She was dangerously close to tears herself. She knew what Drew meant to him, but not that his loss would shatter him to the degree that it clearly had. Looking at his red-rimmed blue eyes, she wanted to roll back time. She wanted to find him blustering away behind the bar, concocting a Black and Tan, or charming some wide-eyed customer with one of his fabulous tales about life in the old country. How his father had stood that day at the GPO on O'Connell Street with Connolly and Pearse and the rest. Reaching for him, she pulled him close, her senses filling with the stale musty smell of clothes not properly aired, sweat, and Irish whiskey.

"Oh, Da," she murmured into his ear. "I'm so sorry."

"He was a son to me." Her father's voice broke. "No man could have asked for better."

And that's the truth of it, Brid thought. "I know Da, I know he was." Letting go of her father, she turned to Harry – Elliot Harrison Winslow IV– who was patiently waiting his turn. Harry Winslow, Neil Malone, and Drew MacCullough – what a gang of little hooligans those three must have been, Brid thought, looking into the eyes of Drew's childhood friend.

"He's the one with the really old money," Drew told her the day he introduced them. Harry smirked sheepishly and said nothing. Brid knew the family fortune founded on the China Trade was long gone. Still, there was something about Harry that evoked old money, debutante dances, a certain courtliness no longer much seen. Brid's mother once said that of all Drew's friends, it was Harry who was clearly minted a gentleman. He held out his arms to her.

"I can't believe he's actually dead," he said in her ear.

She extracted herself from Harry's embrace. "I am not sure I have quite taken it in, myself. Someone needs to tell me what happened." She shrugged off her cape and draped it over a barstool.

Behind the bar, Desmond said, "I made you some fresh coffee, darlin'." His hands shook as he passed Brid a white cup and saucer, the aroma of freshly brewed coffee assaulted her.

Brid was grateful for the warmth as she held the heavy china cup in her cold hands. She eyed her father critically. He was in no condition to be working the bar. "Where's Pat?" She asked. Pat was a cousin of some degree of which she was never certain, her Aunt Cloddagh's grandson, over to make some big money working in construction. She vaguely remembered Desmond telling her that Pat had every other Thursday off.

"He's upstairs, watching the television and taking a load off."

"I'll be right back," she said. She walked over to the entrance to the dining room and called Ronan. When he came over, she said. "Go upstairs and get Pat. He needs to take the bar tonight. Da's into the Bushmills early."

"Ah, sure, I'll go up. Des's broken up for certain about the fella that died."

Ronan, newly arrived, had yet to meet Drew, and now, Brid thought with a pang, he never would.

"Thanks." She went back over to the bar and slipped onto the stool next to Harry. She took a sip of the coffee, wincing slightly at her father's bitter brew. A tea drinker himself, he had a heavy hand with the coffee. The kitchen made the coffee served in the dining room. Des's coffee was usually offset by liquor of one kind or another or used to sober up drunks who were beyond caring what it tasted like.

"Okay, Harry. Tell me. What did Drew do, drive his fancy car into a tree?" Even to herself she sounded callous, but Harry, long used to her acid tongue concerning Drew, didn't appear to notice.

"You won't believe it. It was a heart attack." Harry shook his head, indicating that he certainly didn't. "Drew MacCullough – the last person you would have thought would go that way. God, he would have been so ticked off."

She snorted. "Or the first person. He smoked two packs of cigarettes a day, drank buckets of coffee, and in case you've put it from your mind, he drank like a fish."

"Not recently. He was on the wagon."

"Ah, sure he was, probably getting ready to sign the pledge, too."

"Yeah, but, he was thin," Harry said. He groped in his breast pocket for his pack of Camel Lights. "What do you suppose that his blood pressure was?" Harry frowned. "You think that it was high? I take a pill for that, you know."

"His blood pressure was low. Although it's been a few years since I've monitored it, myself. He had that mad job on top of everything else."

"We all have a job, including you. How's the gallery doing?"

"Very well, thanks. Even without the holidays, I've had a good year."

Harry smiled and reached over to pat her hand. "He would have been glad. He really wanted your gallery to make it. He used to send people there. Did you know that?"

"No, but it doesn't surprise me. It's something he would

do." The ever-generous Drew MacCullough, she thought. "Was he at home when it happened?"

Harry shook his head. "No, he was on the road; coming back from Seattle, I think. He was driving home from the airport. He pulled off and stopped at the Sheraton. He collapsed there, I guess. I don't really know the details. They called an ambulance. He died at the hospital." Harry seemed about to say something more, but didn't, carefully examining the cigarette in his hand.

She frowned. There was something he wasn't telling her. "How did you find out, anyway?"

"Neil called me. I came right down to tell Des. I thought he should know." Both of them looked over at Desmond who, having turned the tending of the bar over to Pat, was slumped on the stool next to Mahoney, a glass of Irish whiskey in front of him, a glazed look in his eyes. Why he's an old man, a sad old man, Brid thought, stunned.

"I didn't want to tell him over the phone," Harry said.

"It was good of you to come, Harry. It must have been an awful shock to him." And to you, too, she thought.

Harry paused to shake a cigarette out of the pack lying on the bar. "How many cigarettes do you suppose Drew really did smoke a day, huh?" He pushed the pack toward Brid. She shook her head with regret; she could have used a cigarette. Shrugging, Harry stood up on his way outside for a smoke. He stopped and looked closely at Brid before he spoke.

"Sofia Chiesa works for Neil," he said. "Now there's a woman I wouldn't mind knowing better," obviously going over the attributes of the lovely Sofia in his mind. He had never married, but usually had a pretty girl on his arm, each one younger than the one she replaced.

"You old lecher! Sofia Chiesa is too young for you. She could be your daughter."

Harry laughed his deep belly laugh. "I'm not that old yet and she's not my daughter. According to Neil, Sofia Chiesa can take care of herself. He thinks she's a damn good lawyer, too. In this case, your motherly concern is misplaced. Maybe you made a mistake not having babies."

She was not surprised. She pictured Sofia, so different from her older sister, Franny. Not that Brid really knew either of the Chiesa sisters. Lynton was not that big. She had crossed paths with them once or twice at functions in the city. Franny... She thought briefly about Franny. Aloud she said, "Whatever will that poor girl do now?" Harry shook his head, his eyes meeting hers, indicating he had heard everything she hadn't said. He knew she wasn't referring to Sofia Chiesa.

"Here's Himself." Desmond rose unsteadily from where he sat and walked, rolling slightly from left to right, over to greet Neil Malone as he came through the door.

CHAPTER 5

Irish men, as they age, either shrink into themselves or run to fat. Always a big man, Neil Malone had played tackle at Boston College. Although he was lighter than when he played football, he found himself engaged in a pitched battle against the second fate. Tonight, he was distraught. His eyes were shadowed with exhaustion and a mixture of shock and sorrow. After hanging his coat on one of the hooks by the door, he reached both hands out to Desmond, assessing the old man with an experienced eye.

"Jesus, Des. Can you believe what's happened today? God, I need a drink."

"And so you shall have one. Bring the man a vodka gimlet, Pat," Desmond called out to the bartender.

"Coming right along, Des," Pat answered, reaching for the house vodka.

"Use the Grey Goose, lad," the old man admonished, "our friend, Lawyer Malone, is a man of discerning tastes."

Harry, still holding the unlit cigarette in his hand, asked quietly, "You coming from Drew's now?"

"Thanks, Pat." Neil took a long, slow, sip.

Watching him, Brid wondered idly if there was a woman in

Neil's life. There should be, she thought, he is such a good man. Moments later, with a start, she remembered that it was Drew who pointed that out to her one night in this very room.

"I still can't believe it. I was sitting there with Franny, Sofia, and Mrs. Chiesa and I tell you, I kept expecting him to walk in the door." Malone shook his head. "Forty-nine years old and he's gone."

For the first time since entering the room, his gaze fell on Brid, perched on the edge of the barstool, staring into her cup. Sliding his drink down the bar toward her, he stood up and opened his arms. "Brid, come here."

She couldn't remember a time when she didn't know Neil Malone's big open freckled face, set between two jugged ears; not a handsome face, but a sound one. She had watched him, resplendent in his hand-made lace surplice, worn so confidently over his black cassock, pace down the aisle in front of the priest, when she was a little girl. Clutching the dime Des had given her for the collection, but secretly saved instead for the candy store, she had stood on the steps of Our Lady Queen of the Angels, and listened as her mother and her friends speculated about whether young Neil Malone would become a priest. How proud he would make his mother if that were the case, the ladies said.

Every devout Catholic boy flirted with the idea, and he was no exception. In the end, he chose the law over the church and never looked back. Although there was not a person in the bar that night who knew it, something of that altar boy remained. His last act every day was to get down on his knees and say his prayers.

Brid allowed herself the comfort of being held tightly against Neil's broad chest. He whispered in her ear. "I'm so sorry, Brid. I know what he meant to you." She wondered how he could be so sure of something she didn't know herself.

Stepping back and reclaiming her stool, she asked, "What happened?"

Neil gestured toward the bartender with his empty glass and said reluctantly, "I am not sure." He sighed. "Remember how Drew used to say, 'This time I'm really in deep shit'? Well, this time he is."

Brid reached the limit of her patience. "For the love of God, Neil, what happened? You're not in the damn courtroom, so get to the point. He was with a woman, wasn't he?"

Malone sighed. "Let's say he died in a place where he shouldn't have been with someone he shouldn't have been with."

"You think he died in the saddle?" Harry asked, titillated, splashing his drink as he put the glass down on the bar.

"That son of a bitch," said Brid. Normally, she did not have a discernible accent, only a hint of something that suggested that at one time she had. But, when she was tired, or drunk or very angry, her brogue became as thick as her father's. "Ah, to be sure, he did. You could've made book on it."

She grabbed Harry's cigarettes and angrily knocked one from the pack. Reaching for her cape and the lighter on the bar, she made her way to the street. Drawing on long practice, she expertly flicked the lighter and lit her cigarette. Tilting her head back, she took a deep drag, allowing the rush from the nicotine to wash over her.

"I thought you quit," Harry said, materializing beside her and watching her through the haze of blue-gray smoke with an amused grin.

"I did, but as you don't see Drew MacCullough here for me to throttle as he's already gone and died, this will have to do." The cigarette calmed her. She took another puff, ruefully thinking of the hard fought four years since her last one. Dropping the cigarette in the can of sand near the door, she went back inside to rejoin Neil at the bar. "You might as well tell me. Does Franny know?"

"It's hard to say. Franny's main concern tonight seemed to be the Christmas tree lights." Neil answered. "I suppose she's in shock. She kept saying, 'Oh, God, who'll put the lights on the Christmas tree, now?'"

"Christmas tree lights?" Harry asked as he took his seat next to Brid.

"What the hell do you two know about it? You never had to live with him. He was a madman about the Christmas tree lights. There had to be a thousand lights on the damn tree, not nine hundred, not nine hundred and fifty, no, one thousand and they all had to be white." She laughed bitterly. "One year, he came home with some drunken fool in tow who refused to believe him. Of course, Drew made a bet with him. Do you know what he did?" The two men shook their heads, eyeing her warily. "He took every ornament off that tree and removed the ten strings of one hundred lights, lining them up in rows, still lit mind you, in front of that man. After collecting his hundred dollars, he put every last thing back on the tree exactly as it was before. I know why she is obsessing about those damn lights. The bastard's probably giving her orders from the morgue."

"Brid, darlin' girl, would you be wanting more coffee, or some tea, now?" Desmond joined them. He remained in command of his feet, but it was clear that the Bushmills was having an impact on his balance. He made one attempt to hoist himself onto the barstool next to Neil and failed. He managed to remain standing by gripping the edge of the bar, which he chose to lean against instead.

"I'm fine, Da. More coffee or tea and I won't sleep."

Satisfied, Desmond locked eyes with Neil Malone. "So tell us what happened? How could a man in his very prime drop dead like that?"

"And," Brid added, "start at the beginning, not with the damn tree lights."

Neil drained the last of the gimlet, waving away Des's offer of a third.

"This morning around ten o'clock, I was in my office when I heard Sofia start screaming. I grabbed that shillelagh I brought back from Ireland and ran to her office. I don't keep my gun there in case I'm tempted to shoot a client," he added, the briefest of smiles acknowledging his attempt at black humor. "I thought some nut was attacking her." He reached for his empty glass and regretfully put it down. "Today, you never know. Remember the guy in San Francisco who brought a gun into that law firm and murdered all those people? Anyway, I get into her office and found Sofia alone. She was doubled over, clutching the phone, crying hysterically.

He reached for his empty glass again, stared into it, and put it back down. Desmond nodded at Pat who mixed another gimlet. He placed it in front of Malone who picked it up without comment. He took a long sip.

"I took the phone from Sofia and I realized that it was Franny who was on the phone." He bit his lip and looked away, focusing on the young couple on the love seat. He took another sip of the gimlet and continued. "Franny told me that Drew was dead. I told her to wait there, that Sofia and I would be there as soon as we could. We stopped on the way to pick up Mrs. Chiesa. We found Franny in a room outside the emergency room. There was a nun with her. Franny was sitting there, like a little girl waiting outside the principal's office. When we came in, she looked up and said, 'He was supposed to come home today.'

That's all. She wasn't crying like she was when I spoke to her on the phone. The nun suggested that we take her home. There was nothing more to be done at the hospital, so I drove them back to Hiram's Forge. The only thing that Franny said to me during the ride was, 'I can't live without him, Neil. I can't.' She said it like it was up to me to get him back."

"Ah, the poor girl, her so young and after losing her baby that way," Des said sorrowfully.

"I made them each a stiff drink and I took a cab to the Sheraton and picked up Drew's car and the rest of his things." Malone ran his hand distractedly through his hair. "I had to sign a release to get them. The manager let me into the room. He told me the woman with Drew called the front desk around eight this morning and said she needed an ambulance."

"What woman?" Brid and Harry asked together.

"That I don't know. The manager was surprised she was there at all. Drew checked in last night around six thirty as a single guest. He had dinner in the restaurant and spent the rest of the night holding court in the bar."

Brid toyed with her coffee cup, using the handle to spin it back and forth in the saucer. She watched the cold coffee splash over the sides of the cup. *The manager was surprised she was there at all. He registered as a single guest.* She remembered another winter night when Drew, having picked her up at school and taken her to dinner, decided they should make a night of it.

Laughing, Drew looked down at her, the light from the entrance to the Holiday Inn shining on him, casting his sensual features in a way that reminded her of a painting she had seen once of Lucifer, the most beautiful angel. He pulled the collar of her coat up so that it covered her ears the way a doting

parent would bundle up a cherished child. He kissed the tip of her nose and as her cold hands cupped his face, his mouth slid down over hers, taking all the time in the world to linger there. "You stay here, Mick, and I'll register. I'll come back and get you once I have the key to the room."

"A bad way to go," Harry said, shaking his head sadly. He reached for the lighter in front of Brid, bringing her back to the small group gathered at the bar.

"Yes. And to make matters worse, he called Franny last night and told her that he was in Seattle and would be taking the red-eye home and going directly into the office." said Neil, staring morosely into his now empty glass. "It's every man's worst nightmare. Can you even begin to imagine what was going through his head at the end?"

"You are both despicable!" Brid exploded. "Is it the simple fact that you're men that makes you band together thick as sorry thieves? Can it possibly be that I am hearin' ya right? It's Drew you're feeling sorry for?" A patch of hectic color smudged each cheekbone. "What about his wife? You don't see that selfish bastard here do you, reaping the fruit of his latest mess? Damn him!"

"Enough, Brid," Des roared, the slurring gone. Conversation in the room died as people looked with interest at the four mourners at the end of the bar. "A good man is dead." Lowering his voice, Des went on, "And need I remind you, girl, he loved you. If you'd followed the beliefs of Holy Mother the Church and given him the children he wanted, he might be with us here tonight."

"Des is right," Neil said his voice filled with sadness. "Drew was still in love with you."

Harry, sobered by Des's tirade was quick to agree with Neil. "Drew told me once, right here at the bar, that, sure, he loved Franny, but you were the love of his life." Harry repeated himself. "The love of his life. That's what he told me."

Brid stood momentarily frozen by her father's harsh attack. And then her anger melted the ice and she was on the other side of the bar. "You want to see the love of his life?" She hissed through clenched teeth. She slammed the amber-colored bottle of Glenlivet down on the bar with a bang. "This was the love of his life, not me!" Harry and Neil sat stunned, but her father's Irish temper exploded.

"Go dté tú go hIfreann!" Des roared at her, his face scarlet.

Go to hell yourself, Da! She answered him silently. Without another word to her, Des turned to Pat. "A round for the house, on Craic." The dining room had been empty for almost an hour. There were about twenty people in the bar quietly watching the scene that had just taken place.

Brid was reminded, watching him now that her father had acted in minor roles at the Abbey Theater as a young man. He can still play to the house, she thought. She understood that his need to make a speech, at least for the moment, outstripped the hold the Bushmills had on him. He moved to the center of the room and raised his glass. "I'll ask you all now to lift your glass to the memory of Drew MacCullough, a good and decent man who died today. He was a son to me." He stared coldly at Brid who, unrepentant, glared defiantly back at him. Gathering his composure, he continued. "All of us who knew him and loved him will sorely miss him." Around the room, the words, "To Drew MacCullough," were murmured and the glasses were drained.

Harry turned to Desmond. "Des, why don't you sing one of those sad Irish songs? I think Drew would like that."

Nodding, Desmond placed his empty glass on the bar and made his way to the piano standing against the wall. Watching him, the other three could each remember Drew accompanying him in the traditional Irish ballads, like "The Boys from County Wexford" and "The Rising of the Moon." Tonight, it was Des who played the piano. Despite his age, his tenor was still clear and true. Brid knew what he would sing before he sat down.

The crowd joined him as he began to play, but it was only Neil Malone who remembered the words to all the verses of "Danny Boy." The two men had just begun the third when Brid fled.

> *But when ye come and all the flow'rs are dying,*
> *If I am dead, as dead I well may be,*
> *Ye'll come and find the place where I am lying*
> *And kneel and say an 'Ave' there for me.*

CHAPTER 6

Franny lay motionless in the center of the queen-sized bed, avoiding both her own side and Drew's. The neutral space in the middle felt less empty. Thomas slept curled tightly in a ball on the pillow beside her. She lay dry-eyed, watching the muted splashes of pink in the winter sky. She had spent a sleepless night trying to make sense of the last twenty-four hours, carefully laying out the individual pieces of the day.

All through the night, she painstakingly rearranged the jagged pieces of what she knew; trying to make them form a picture she could understand. No matter how many times she examined the facts, nothing made sense, and no clear image emerged. Now, watching the dawn of a new day in the winter sky, the only thing that remained true was that Drew wasn't here with her.

She was glad she hadn't slept, glad that she fought the need for sleep and won. At least she spared herself the pain she remembered waking the morning after her father died; that slow dawning of incalculable loss followed by an immediate plummeting into bottomless grief. The difference was that Drew had been there to console her then; reassuring her that he would always take care of her. He had even made her laugh, when she was sure she would never laugh again. Now, she had lost them both.

Last night, as she lay in bed listening to the clock in the living room marking the hours, she kept asking herself the following questions: Why had Drew spent the night at the Sheraton when he told her he was still in Seattle? What was he meeting with Lorie about? And why had he not called her? She refused to examine the larger question: What was she going to do without him?

Yesterday, her mother had asked her how much insurance Drew had. It was one more thing on an ever-growing list of the things that she didn't know about her husband. She knew that Drew was insured through Chayne, but not the amount of insurance that he had. The only thing she was certain of was that Drew was dead. She knew there were things to be done, important things, but she seemed unable to move beyond the trauma room at St. Luke's.

She looked at the clock next to the bed. The numbers glowed red in the dim light: 5:46. Twenty-four hours ago, Drew was alive. It was the first of many time markers she would observe in the new reality she would come to know as "since Drew died." Lorie called last night to see how she was doing and to ask if there was anything she could do to help. Closing her eyes, Franny went over again what Lorie told her.

"He called me the night before and told me that he had something urgent he needed to talk to me about. He didn't tell me what it was. He asked me to meet him at the Sheraton for coffee at seven thirty. When I got to the hotel and called him, he told me he was not feeling well." Lorie explained, when Franny asked her why she was with Drew at the hotel. "He told me that he had been sick all night. He asked me to come up to the room. He looked awful. I knew something terrible was happening because I felt the angels hovering all around him. He said he was having chest pains. I told him he was having a heart attack and asked him to let me call an ambulance. 'It's an anxiety attack,' he said. 'It's happened before. If you're going to get hysterical, then you better go.' Before I could even argue with him, he fell across the bed and I called down to the front desk for an ambulance."

At least that part made sense, Franny thought, smiling. Drew could be so bossy. He might possibly be the only man alive, and, she paused, stopped by the realization that he was dead, who didn't make the most of being sick or in pain. Her father was able to make a plague out of a cold. Not Drew. Once, when he was alone hanging sheetrock, the knife slipped, nicking the vein in his left wrist. Despite the blood that spattered all over the drywall, he used his belt to make a tourniquet, neatly noting the time in black pen on his forearm. Instead of calling for help, he drove himself to the nearest emergency room to be stitched up.

Turning on her side, Franny stared at the telephone on the table next to the bed. Twenty-four hours ago, her husband lay next to a similar telephone and he hadn't called her. Why? And why had he told her that he was in Seattle when he was he was already back in Lynton? These were the questions that she asked them yesterday: Sofia, Neil, her mother, and her father-in-law. Rod MacCullough drove over to the house when he learned that Drew was dead. They all glanced nervously at one another, each offering her a different empty answer:

"He came home early and he wanted to surprise you and he pulled in there on his way home because he felt sick."

"He was trying to protect you."

"He needed to be alone to think."

Underneath their hasty reassurances, Franny sensed something left unsaid, but nevertheless present in the room. It reminded her of the time she and Drew were in Rome and they had taken the subway back to their hotel from the Vatican. It was rush hour and they were surrounded by people on the train talking urgently in Italian. She hadn't understood a word that was said.

She knew there was something she had to figure out. Hastily pulling on the jeans and sweater she had dropped on the floor next to the bed, she opened the door and stepped into the hall. She paused outside the closed door of the guest room where her mother and sister were sleeping. She listened intently to make sure they were not awake. Downstairs, in the dim light of the kitchen, her fingers found the flashlight hanging on the hook next to the back door.

She let herself out of the house, wincing as the hinges on the door squeaked, and hurried across the porch to the garage. Her entrance woke the dogs. Lucy's tail beat a tattoo of welcome, but Oliver rolled his eyes up at her, as if to ask, "Are you crazy?"

"Go back to sleep," she told them. "It's not time to get up yet." The dogs settled back again in their beds.

Neil had taken a cab back to the Sheraton and picked up the Lexus along with Drew's bag and briefcase. They were still sitting inside the kitchen door where he left them. No one had touched the Lexus since he pulled it into the garage. She walked around the car, inspecting it carefully with the flashlight, coming back to look again at the front bumper, playing the beam of light from the left to right and back again. There was nothing to see. The silver metallic paint was as flawless as the day they picked the car up from the dealership. Not a nick or a scratch. She wasn't sure if she was relieved or sorry. If Drew had an accident and gone to ground at the Sheraton like some injured animal licking his wounds, it would explain a lot, answer a lot of her questions. She sighed. Who am I kidding? It would make sense only if he had been drinking.

Leaning wearily against the side of the car, she thought about Drew's drinking. She wondered when she realized that he had a problem. Had it been as early as their first year together? No, she thought, not that year. Then it had been, "Well, I know he likes to drink, but he can control it." Liked to drink? Drew loved to drink. Glenlivet, if he could get it, but anything in a pinch would do.

He promised to quit drinking. "I'll get a handle on it. I promise," he told her when his drinking had reached a point where even he admitted it was a problem. This, after years of incidents, tears, scenes, near misses, and embarrassment, finally ending in the inevitable loss of his license duly reported on page four of the *Lynton Ledger* seven years ago. He had given her no reason to doubt him, casually drinking tonic water and lime socially; making self-depreciating throw-away comments, like "I've already drunk my own and several other people's quota, thanks." She could not explain what brought her out to the garage this morning. Although she didn't know why, she wondered fleetingly, if Drew had started drinking again.

He had come home unexpectedly from a trip to a trade show in Las Vegas in late August. She was reading on the wicker chaise hidden in the corner of the porch when he drove into the driveway. Her first thought was: Wonderful, he's home a day early. She watched him, climb slowly out of the car, and she was transported back to the early years of their marriage. My God, he looks like he's coming off a three-day bender. She banished the thought, telling herself that she was crazy, that Drew no longer drank. Smiling broadly, she went to greet him, all her worries dispelled by the passion with which he pulled her into his arms.

Without warning, light flooded the garage, sending Oliver into a frenzied barking. Sofia stood shivering in the doorway, in her short, hot pink, satin nightgown. With its plunging neckline and spaghetti straps, she looked as out of place as an exotic bird against the backdrop of shovels, coiled hose, and neatly stacked bags of rock salt.

"Franny, what are you doing out here?" she asked. "It's not even seven o'clock and it's freezing!" Looking down at the dog as he continued his nervous whooping, she said, "Shut up, Oliver." Satisfied by this acknowledgement, Oliver returned to his bed. He circled twice before he found the perfect spot and settled down.

Franny looked at her sister. At first glance, devoid of make-up, her small feet in her running shoes, planted defiantly, she looked like a child playing dress-up. A second glance took in the swell of her generous breasts, a surprise in someone as tiny as Sofia, clearly visible beneath the skimpy nightgown. "I was looking for something and I thought..." She left the rest of her sentence unsaid, sensing her sister's growing impatience.

"Come inside before we both freeze to death." Sofia stood aside like a sentry or a prison guard waiting for Franny to pass her. "If there was anything in the car, don't you think that Neil would have given it to us?"

Not bothering to answer, Franny walked past Sofia into the house, the dogs crowding by her in search of breakfast.

Her mother stood at the stove and watched as they filed through the kitchen door. Franny knew that her mother wanted to comfort her but didn't know how. She had loved Drew, too.

"I promised your father that I would take care of his three girls," Drew told Franny the day her father was buried.

Biting her lip, she thought, and you did. Looking at her mother now, she remembered how good Drew had been to her that horrible summer. It was Drew who accompanied her to the Social Security Office and the pension board, reassuring her that she would be fine. Ever since her father died, Drew had stepped in whenever either her mother or her sister needed him.

"Franny, where do you keep the coffee?" Her mother gestured toward the open door of the cabinet where Franny kept her baking supplies. "All I can find is this herbal tea." She held the offending box of Quietly Chamomile in her hand.

"It's in here." She removed the bag of Starbuck's Italian Roast coffee, Drew's current favorite, from the refrigerator. She measured the coffee into the Braun Coffee Master that he insisted made the closest thing to a perfect cup of coffee next to using a French Press. She filled the carafe with water and added it to the machine. The coffee brewed quickly. "Here," she said, filling one of the mugs she had admired only yesterday morning, and handed it to her mother. "I made some of Nana's coffee cake. Let me cut you some of that."

"I don't suppose you have a Diet Coke?" Sofia asked. She had found Drew's fleece windbreaker with the Chayne logo on the pocket in the hall closet and was wearing it over her nightgown. She looked even more petite in the oversized jacket with the wisp of pink satin hanging beneath it.

"There's a case in the pantry," Franny answered. Her sister seemed to live on Diet Coke, Trident sugar free gum, and, she suspected, those weird diet pills you could buy over the counter. But Sofia was thin and she was not.

"Franny." Sofia studied her sister. "I know this is hard for you, but we have to get organized before the MacCulloughs get their hands in this. Drew always said they could screw up a two-car funeral."

"Somehow, I don't think it was his own that he had in mind though."

"Franny!" Her mother said, pretending to be shocked, but not quite able to hide her own smile, because she also remembered Drew saying it.

Searching for something, Sofia squinted at her BlackBerry. She refused to wear her glasses and had not yet put in her contacts. Her nails bitten to the quick looked sore as she moved rapidly from screen to screen. "Here it is," she said, sounding relieved, no doubt afraid that the BlackBerry had actually eaten one of her ever-present lists. "I made a list of everything we need to do."

"I need to feed the dogs before we start. They have to eat." Oliver chose that moment to begin barking to confirm this. He did not like to wait and no doubt felt that there had been entirely too much conversation already. It was time for his breakfast. Franny didn't bother to add that it was Drew who always fed the animals in the morning.

Bending down, she retrieved the dogs' dishes from the floor. Lucy and Oliver sat in a semi-circle watching her expectantly as she filled each bowl with kibble. Placing the dishes back on the floor, Franny realized that Thomas, who usually haunted her footsteps in the morning, was missing. She remembered him flashing past her on the stairs when she made her way down to the kitchen at dawn. He usually hung out there, hoping for something to eat. He liked the dogs' kibble better than his own food and Lucy didn't mind sharing.

"Mom, did you put Thomas out?" Her mother hated cats and whenever possible ushered Thomas out the door or down the cellar stairs. "It's freezing out," Franny opened the kitchen door. Thomas slipped past her, holding his tail straight up in indignation and jumped onto the counter where he sat pointedly in front of the can opener.

"You shouldn't let him on the counters, Franny. It's not clean," her mother said, her hands on her hips. Franny ignored her as she dumped a can of cat food into Thomas's dish. She silently counted to ten as she placed Thomas and his dish on the floor.

"Leave him in when he finishes. It's too cold for him to be outside today."

"Well, he's not walking all over these counters while I'm here." Marie decisively cinched the belt on her bathrobe. "People will be coming over, bringing food and things. I'm not having that dirty cat—"

"Just push him down, then." Franny's voice rose and she struggled to contain her growing annoyance. It was her house and her cat, after all. Seeing her mother's stricken look, she softened her tone. "Okay?" She looked over her sister, sitting on the rocker next to the cold wood stove, checking her BlackBerry. "I'm going to take a shower. When I come down, we can look at your list." Sofia began to protest about the time passing and everything they had to do, but Franny cut her off. "Drew's mother doesn't get up before ten on a good day. She may not get up at all today."

Thinking of her in-laws, Franny sent a silent thank you to Neil who made the sad trip over to the MacCulloughs to tell them that Drew was dead. It was one of the many small acts of kindness that he had done for her.

"Let me tell them, Franny. I've known them almost all my life," he said. She wanted him to call them from the hospital, but he convinced her that waiting another couple of hours until he could go over to the house wouldn't matter. "They're old. No parent should be told this news over the telephone." Struggling to remain composed, he added, "What difference does it make? They can't do anything more for him now."

Her father-in-law had driven up to Hiram's Forge last night, alone. The doctor, he told her, had prescribed Elaine a sedative and sent her to bed. He was a dignified man, very much in control of his emotions. Sitting stiffly in the living room, he remained so, but it was apparent that at seventy-six, he had never expected to outlive his only son. Removing a leather checkbook from his jacket pocket, he asked her quietly if she needed money. Neil had asked her the same question earlier in the day. I'd be a rich woman this morning, she thought, if I had taken all the money that was offered to me yesterday. She didn't need any money, she told him. There was money in several savings accounts and Drew had deposited the household money in her checking account last week.

"Is there anything else, then, that I can do for you?" Rod asked her. There was something she needed his help with, something that only he had the power to make happen. Somehow, she managed to explain to him what it was without breaking down. Blinking back his own tears, her father-in-law agreed to take care of it for her.

She thought about her mother-in-law. Elaine had never bothered much with her. Their paths crossed occasionally, usually at the country club where all four MacCulloughs were members. She and Drew put in an appropriate appearance at his parents for the holidays. She never felt that Elaine hated her. It was more like she was indifferent to her.

Her sister-in-law, Cynthia, explained it to her. "After Drew married another Catholic, Mother gave up."

In the beginning, Franny tried to make her mother-in-law like her. She had served on whatever committee at the club Elaine was chairing, going out of her way to be pleasant and open to the older woman's advice. It had gotten harder, the day she overheard Elaine, slightly tipsy, confide to a friend in the powder room at the club, "I don't know what I did to him to make him so taken with these girls. At least, this one wasn't raised over a saloon."

Elaine had become even more distant as the years went by without them having a child. After she lost the baby, Franny found it harder to ignore her mother-in-law's thoughtless comments, usually made when Elaine had too much to drink. Drew's way of protecting her from his mother was to visit his parents by himself. She had not spoken to her mother-in-law since Thanksgiving.

The thought of Elaine's predictable reaction to Drew's death was not something she wanted to think about this morning. Looking at Sofia sitting in the rocking chair, she said, "While I am in the shower, why don't you make a fire, so we don't all freeze to death."

As she started to leave the kitchen, her eyes fell on Drew's battered leather briefcase and overnight bag near the door where Neil left them.

"I am going to take these upstairs." Moving Drew's bag revealed a long white box with Cunningham's Florist written in its familiar slanting royal blue script along the side. The three women stared at the box in surprise.

"Where did that come from?" her mother asked.

"Maybe yesterday afternoon in all the confusion, someone slipped it in the door," Franny said as she opened the box to reveal the dozen long-stemmed red roses nestled in the waxed green florist paper. Holding the box in one hand, she slipped the card from an envelope simply marked "Franny" with the other. With a cry, she pulled the roses from the box, and slid down to sit on the floor. She rocked back and forth, keening an ancient cry of grief cradling the roses, her fingers oblivious to the thorns.

CHAPTER 7

The calling hours for Drew MacCullough were almost over when Desmond Sheerin, followed by Brid, made his way slowly up the brick walk toward the front door of the Thomas A. McKenna and Son Funeral Home, pausing as he went to say hello to many of the people who were leaving. He looked out of place without the worn leather apron he wore behind the bar. He was dressed to pay his respects to the deceased in a crisp white shirt and his funeral tie secured by an Ancient Order of the Hibernians tie pin. He wore an Irish tweed jacket that was too big. A relic from the days when he had been heavier, it hung off his wide shoulders, billowing slightly in the back as he walked. He nervously twisted a green tweed cap between his hands, the soft yellow light from the open door catching the gleam of the Claddagh ring on his finger. Brid, dressed in her red cape, followed behind him.

Jerry McKenna, son of the late Thomas A. and current owner, stood holding the door. He had gone to school at Our Lady Queen of the Angels with Brid and had known Des all of his life. Now, that will be a funeral, when Desmond Sheerin went to his glory, he thought as he watched the old man greeting people with the finesse of a politician running for office. With the second sense that came from years in his profession, he understood that this was a tough wake for Des. If Drew had died when he was still married to Brid, Des, as his father-in-law, would have been in the line of family mourners. Now, he was disenfranchised, which no doubt was why he timed his appearance at the end of the wake.

"Good evening, Des," Jerry said, extending his hand.

"A fine turnout it is, don't you think, Jerry?" Desmond answered. Looking around at the people filing out the door, he gripped the undertaker's smooth hand with his own.

"Yes, it is. It's been steady all evening and there was a crowd here this afternoon, as well."

"Drew was a grand lad. He'll be missed." Desmond seemed to steel himself. "I guess I'll go along in then to say a Hail Mary for him. Not that he'll be needing one, it's a bottle of Glenlivet he's no doubt sharing with the saints in Heaven right now."

Brid watched her father walk slowly down the hall, pause briefly at the door, cap in hand, before entering the room where Drew was laid out. She caught Jerry's eye and said. "Can't you see Drew now, in the big bar in the sky, knocking one back with St. Peter and the Angel Gabriel?"

"Not exactly dressed in mourning, Brid," Jerry observed, kissing her. "I hope you're not here to make trouble." He was smiling, but his tone was serious.

"Please try and remember that I sat behind you, while you smeared your gum into Angela Daley's hair, before you get high and mighty with me, Jerry," Brid answered, in a voice pitched for his ears only. "Don't look so worried, I'm not here to have the vapors in your fancy rose chair. I'm aware that I am not the widow." Every funeral parlor has a chair that stands apart from the others, closest to the casket, the chief mourner's chair. Always the chair used by the widow. In McKenna's, it was a high-backed wing chair covered in deep rose brocade.

"I wasn't expecting to see you here tonight," Jerry waited for her response. The ongoing feud between Brid and Drew was no secret among the Irish in Lynton.

"I actually came to pay my respects to Franny. Why should I bother to say anything to him now that he's dead? He never listened to a word I said when he was alive." She slipped the heavy cape off her shoulders and handed it to him. "Here, you take this if the color makes you nervous." She wore a black wool suit, somber enough, but at the same time unable to dim her luminous appeal. Two people across the foyer from where she and Jerry stood caught her attention.

"Who is that woman with Neil Malone?" She asked, indicating the tall, attractive red-head talking earnestly to Neil.

"That's Lorie Derouin. She introduced herself to me this afternoon. She worked with Drew at Chayne. Seems to be pretty broken up over his death, she's been here all day."

Brid studied the woman carefully. Lorie was dressed entirely in black. Even her stockings were black. Draped over her shoulders, she wore a black lace scarf shot through with gold thread. Around her neck, she wore an elaborate necklace also gold. Neil appeared uncomfortable with their conversation, whatever it was about.

"I think I will go rescue Neil. He doesn't look very happy. My being here will give him something else to worry about." She smiled wickedly and walked across the wide hall and insinuated herself firmly between Neil and Lorie.

"Hello, Neil," she said, kissing his cheek. "I am happy to see that you survived the wake Da held the other night."

"Hello, Brid." He appeared to be both relieved and dismayed to see her. He glanced nervously at the woman standing next to her.

"This is Lorie Derouin. She worked with Drew." He looked at Lorie. "Lorie, this is Brid Sheerin, she—"

"I know who she is. She shouldn't be here." Lorie said bluntly, her eyes frankly curious as she studied Brid.

Brid ignored her, giving no sign that the barb had found its mark. She slipped her arm through Neil's. "I need a breath of air." Brid began to walk toward the side door leading to the parking lot, firmly taking him with her.

"That was rude, Brid." He took the lighter she dug out of her purse from her hand and lit her cigarette.

"What do you mean, I was rude? She was rude first. Who is she? A tinker?" Brid took a puff of her cigarette and waited. Despite their surroundings, Neil burst out laughing. It was not a polite funeral home parking lot chuckle, but a braying guffaw that caused the couple getting into their car a few feet away to turn and look back at him with disapproval.

"A tinker? Very funny. Although, I do admit that outfit she has on is over the top." He struggled to regain his composure.

"Was that a rosary I saw around her neck?"

"No. She told me that was a host of angels, seraphim, in fact. She's into angels in a very big way. Jerry told me she showed up here this morning with four large ones that she wanted to stand guard around the casket. Franny said no angels."

"That's a pity, then. I would have loved to have seen that bastard laid out in his Louis Boston jacket and tie surrounded by four great big tacky plaster angels! All fallen, I presume?"

She deposited the cigarette butt in a can of sand next to the door. "I suppose I can't put this off any longer. How are they all doing in there?"

"I haven't actually been in there, yet." He looked down at his feet, suddenly fascinated by the Johnson and Murphy brogues he had worn in either black or brown for thirty-five years. Looking up, his eyes met hers. "I can't," his voice broke and he began again. "I can't bear to see him lying there dead. If I don't see him, then I can still believe he'll come around the corner and I can tell him that you called Lorie Derouin a tinker."

Her own grief, a complicated and forbidden thing, surfaced and was quickly banished. She put her arm around his waist. "Why don't we go in together, then? You can keep me out of trouble."

Franny was not sitting in the rose brocade chair. Several times, people had tried to maneuver her there, but she had refused, never moving from the side of the gleaming oak casket. Having been surrounded by people most of the evening, she was finally alone with her husband. The two families sat at the other end of the long room, divided into distinct camps, not quite hostile, but not friendly, either. Marie and her sister, Clare, sat quietly talking to Brendan in one corner, while surreptitiously watching the MacCulloughs in the other corner. Rod MacCullough sat rigidly on a folding chair, his expression unreadable, as he stared bleakly down the length of the room at the body of his son. On the sofa, next to him, Drew's mother was deep in conversation with Des.

Franny studied Drew, her fingers caressing the lapel of his black cashmere jacket, seeking comfort the way a child strokes the soft silk binding of its blanket. He looked peaceful, not as tired or stressed as he had the last few months. He also looked dead, very dead.

All afternoon, she had stood beside the casket greeting people, listening to their stories about Drew, accepting their condolences. Now, she was numb and her feet in her black pumps were swollen and hurt. She eased the left one out of her shoe. She wore a red dress piped in bands of black. She and Sofia found it yesterday by sheer luck, if anyone shopping for clothes for a funeral could be said to be lucky. The perfect dress, Franny thought, not too sad. He would be so angry if I spoiled everyone's Christmas. Many of the flowers that filled the room were also red. She selected the large poinsettia behind his head, herself. The card read: We miss you. It was signed: Oliver, Lucy, and Thomas. She smiled inwardly thinking of how much Drew loved the animals.

She slipped her hand into her pocket and took out a picture. It was one of two that the nurses had taken the night her little boy was born. Drew told her that at first he had not wanted them to take pictures of the baby. He thought that seeing him would break her heart. The nurses explained to him that there was a grieving process for a stillbirth and that she would want the pictures. And they were right. The pictures were her most cherished possessions. Now, she wanted to give one back to Drew.

Neil came up and stood beside her. He slipped his arm around her as they stood together, staring down at Drew.

"How are you doing, Franny? Are you all right?"

"I'm okay. He doesn't look scared, does he?" She asked, leaning against him for a moment.

"No. He doesn't look scared. In fact, he looks pretty smug to me, like he finally figured it all out."

"I want him to have this," she said, handing Neil the picture.

He glanced at it briefly. "I think that's a terrific idea. Shall I put it in his pocket?"

"Yes, please," she answered, nodding her head as she spoke. Neil leaned over and carefully slid the photograph into the pocket of Drew's jacket.

Standing in the arched doorway, Brid kept a close eye on Neil as he stood with Franny at the casket. She had never seen him so unsure of himself and she was worried. Out of the corner of her eye, she could see her father still talking with the MacCulloughs. Trust Da to be completely oblivious to the fact that they viewed him as being beneath them. She had no intentions of speaking to them herself. If her mother's ghost haunted her enough, she might send them a note. Elaine had been difficult to be nice to when it should have been easy. Tonight, it would be almost impossible. Straightening her shoulders, Brid reminded herself of the reason she was there.

Sofia had been talking with Drew's sister, Cynthia, in the corner of the room. Looking up to see Brid standing in the door, Sofia indignantly hurried over to where she stood, "How dare you show yourself here?" She hissed, glaring up at Brid who towered above her.

"I came to speak to your sister not to you."

Before Sofia could answer, Franny was there, a pale, mute presence. Her first thought whenever she caught a glimpse of Brid was of a night not long after she and Drew began dating. Two thirds of the way through a bottle of scotch, he told her mournfully, "My ex-wife is so beautiful."

"Stop it, Sofia," Franny's voice, hoarse from talking, was still able to convey how strongly she felt. "Please," she said, as Sofia began to protest again. "Please, leave this to me." Turning to Neil, who hovered anxiously behind the three women, Franny said, "Can you please get Sofia out of here?" He led the still protesting Sofia toward the foyer, shushing her as they went.

"I suppose you came to say good-bye to him," she swayed slightly, aware suddenly of how weary she was.

Brid shook her head. "I said good-bye to him years ago. I came to tell you if you ever want to talk or if I can be of help to you in any way, please call me." Franny stared at her, beyond words after hearing this extraordinary offer. "You see, I know something about surviving Drew MacCullough." Pressing her business card into Franny's hand, she turned, and without once looking toward the man in the casket at the front of the room, she walked out the door.

Desmond was waiting for her, standing with Jerry at the front door. Neil and Sofia were nowhere to be seen.

"I think we are the last." She added, smiling at Jerry. "I told you there was nothing to worry about. I will not be attending the funeral. So you can relax." Visibly relieved, he wished her and Des a good evening. On her way out the door, she turned back. "Jerry, keep an eye out for Neil tomorrow, will you now?"

He nodded. "I'll do that. Neil Malone is a strong man. He'll get through it." She smiled her thanks and followed her father outside.

On the sidewalk, Desmond turned to her. "The wake's moved on to Craic. Will you join us then, darlin'?"

She leaned up and kissed her father's cheek. "No, Da. I'm off to catch the end of the meeting at St. John's Hall."

CHAPTER 8

Neil stood next to Harry at the rear of the viewing room. They were the only pallbearers who were not employees of the funeral home. The cloying scent of too many flowers in too small a space was making him feel slightly sick. He watched as Franny, the last of the family to leave, kissed Drew good-bye. Jerry touched her arm and said something to her as she walked toward the door where Sofia and Brendan waited for her. Franny's fragile control shattered.

"No! Jerry, don't you dare bury him with that cross," she cried. Jerry glanced toward Neil and said something that he couldn't hear. "Fine, as long as you don't bury him with it," she answered him. Regaining her composure, she walked out of the room.

The undertaker beckoned Neil over to the casket. The two men stared down at Drew. "I ask that a member of the family be present when I close the casket." Jerry said. "Franny agreed that you could represent her. You okay with that?" Looking into the cosmetically serene face of his friend, Neil nodded. "She told me to give this to you." Jerry handed him the Celtic cross that Drew had worn since the day he and Brid were married. "They gave me this when I picked up the body." Neil slipped the cross into his jacket pocket, remembering that Drew had never taken it off not even when they played tennis.

Jerry hesitated for a minute before adding, "I see a lot of things in this business. People are either at their best or their worst. I know you were his friend, so I am going to ask you to make this call. I don't want to ask Franny. I have already upset her. Today will be hard enough for her." He took a step closer and lowered his voice. "This morning, before the family came in, that woman who worked with Drew, Lorie Derouin, came to me and asked me if she could put something in the casket. I told her that she would have to talk to Franny. She begged me to let her leave this with him." He lifted the right lapel of Drew's jacket and exposed a small silver angel. "This is Azrael, the Angel of Death. She said that Drew needed him to go on his journey to the other side."

Neil's broad shoulders started to shake uncontrollably, not from grief, but from suppressed laughter. Desperately, he tried to get control of himself. Drew would love it if I burst into hysterical laughter over his corpse, he thought. He couldn't help it. The absurdity of Drew being buried with the Angel of Death pinned to his jacket was too much for him.

"Jesus, Mary, and Joseph," he wiped the tears of laughter from his face. "It's a damn good thing none of us know what happens to us after we die." Reaching over, he tugged the angel pin from Drew's jacket. "Azrael, you said, this is?" Jerry nodded. Neil closed his fist over the angel pin and continued. "He was the classiest guy I ever knew. There is no way that he is going to his grave with the Angel of Death stuck in his jacket."

Jerry nodded sympathetically. "I need to close the casket now. I'll give you a minute." He stepped back, leaving Neil to say his good-bye.

Neil searched for some sign of the man, who had been his

closest friend for forty years, his finger unconsciously pricking the sharp end of the angel pin in his hand. *Drew, what mess have you left us with?*

Harry came to stand beside him. He didn't like funerals, and never attended wakes, calling them barbaric. The fact that he agreed to be a pallbearer attested to his own feelings for Drew. His eyes avoided the casket in front of them.

"Time to get this show on the road, Malone," Harry said, softly placing his hand on Neil's shoulder.

Jerry returned to Neil's side, reached down, and gently rolled the silk shroud over Drew's body. He looked at Neil and said, "I'm going to close the casket now." Neil nodded and the lid was closed. The funeral procession moved on to St. Peter's Episcopal Church where the MacCulloughs had worshipped for fifty years.

The music of Mozart's "Alleluia" followed the eight pallbearers out of the church as they prepared to carry Drew's body to the waiting hearse. Across from him, Neil saw that Harry was braced as he was, for the command to lift the casket from the wheeled cart on which it rested.

"One, two, three, and lift," Jerry said, counting softly. Grasping the silver handle tightly, Neil cautiously shuffled down the four wide granite steps, silently thanking God that the Episcopalians did not go in for the narrow, steep steps so often favored by the Catholics. Jerry positioned the casket on the rollers and they watched it slide soundlessly into the back of the hearse.

"You did a great job up there. I know it's not an easy thing to do. Your eulogy was one of the best I've heard in a long time," Jerry said, placing a comforting hand on Neil's arm.

Neil walked back up the four steps and joined Franny where she stood framed in the doorway of the church. He slipped his hand under her elbow and escorted her back down the steps to the black limousine waiting behind the hearse. Drew's family followed slowly behind them. At the door of the car, Franny stopped and looked up at him.

"Thank you for what you said about him. I knew you were the right person to speak today. He would have loved your eulogy."

"Well, thank you for the Mozart. The Catholics wouldn't have let you do that, you know. We have rules around funeral music."

Something that might have passed for a smile lingered briefly on her lips. "Yes, I remember from my father's funeral. That's probably why Drew never wanted to be one," she said. She climbed into the car, sliding down the long bench seat to make room for the MacCulloughs who were waiting to join her. Neil's eyes met those of Drew's father, but neither spoke. He simply nodded to the older man before turning away to blindly find his way to his own dark blue Mercedes in the long line of cars parked in front of the church.

Harry was waiting for him with the engine running. Neil's eyes narrowed and he felt a flutter of apprehension as Lorie Derouin, once again dressed in deep mourning, walked past carrying a curious dark-haired toddler in her arms. Jerry made sure that all the mourners were in their cars. The procession started to move, and they began the short ride to the cemetery.

"How about that music?" Harry asked. "The soloist was magnificent You have to admit that you never hear music like that at a Catholic funeral, even if you all do believe you have the fast track to heaven."

Neil chuckled and said, "You're right. You'll never hear Mozart at my funeral, unfortunately. The Church has a narrow view of what they consider to be funeral music. "Ave Verum" doesn't make the cut." Thinking of Drew, he added, "Drew loved Mozart. Remember how he used to call him 'the mad Austrian'?

Franny knew that he loved those particular pieces, especially the "Ave Verum." Do you remember hearing him play that?"

"Are you kidding me? I haven't heard Drew play the piano sober in thirty years. The last time I heard him play he was not playing Mozart." Harry thought for a minute. "I suppose I may have heard him play it at one of those recitals he used to make us go to when we were kids. Have you?"

"Actually, I have," Neil answered, his voice thickening. "Drew used to drop by the nursing home on Sunday afternoons to see my mother. He would show up with a big bunch of flowers for her. He would tell everyone that he was her secret boyfriend. She got such a kick out of it." Neil stopped for a minute, lost in his memories. "My mother thought the world of Drew. She used to say, 'that boy could charm a Jesuit.' He would push her down to the lounge in her wheelchair. There was an old upright piano there. I suppose they used it for sing-alongs and birthday parties. It was really not much of a piano, but someone kept it tuned. He would sit down and start to play and within minutes he would have an audience. You know how funny Drew could be about playing the piano."

"Yeah, which is why he usually had to be half in the bag before he would agree to do it," Harry answered, shaking his head.

"He was completely relaxed with those old people. I think he knew that no matter how badly he played it was a gift to them. They sure weren't keeping track of any missed notes. He often played Mozart. They loved whatever he played for them."

"Your eulogy was great, by the way. Drew would have approved." Harry said, after a moment, he added, "How the hell were you able to stand up there and deliver it?"

Neil kept his eyes on the rear of the car in front of him. "He would have done it for me. In fact," he added dryly, "knowing Drew, I am quite sure he would have preferred to have done it for me."

Harry laughed. "You've got that right. I don't think Drew was in any hurry to die. But then, who is?" He shifted in his seat. He eyed Neil thoughtfully. "On second thought, I can't imagine Drew without you at his back. I think if he had been given a choice, this is the way he would have preferred it." Neil shook his head, but didn't argue. Harry continued, "I guess we're finally going to see the inside of that damn mausoleum. It always gave me the creeps."

The MacCulloughs, as befitting their status as prominent citizens of Lynton, owned one of the large marble mausoleums that dotted the grounds of the cemetery. The ornate gate opened into a forecourt under a wide iron arch spelling out the name MacCullough. They had ridden their bikes to the cemetery as boys and sat around the small entry telling ghost stories. As teenagers, they had once gone there to smoke cigarettes and drink whatever liquor they managed to siphon from an unobserved bottle. Borrowing from Poe, Drew had called the place "The House of MacCullough." He often threatened to produce the key that unlocked the door to the tomb itself, but he never had. He had been inside for the internment of his grandfather. His stories, much embellished, of what it was like were enough to scare the other two witless.

"He's not going to be entombed in the 'House of Mac-Cullough'," Neil told Harry. "He is going to be buried up on the hill with the Chiesas."

Harry gave a low whistle to underscore his surprise. "You're kidding me? Elaine MacCullough agreed to allow her blue-blooded only son to rest for eternity with the Italians?"

"Franny told Rod that she wanted Drew buried near the

baby. He said he would take care of it, and he did."

"Good for the old man. Drew's mother must have thrown a fit. Drew would want to be buried near the baby."

They both fell silent as the cars slowed for the turn into Lynton Lawn. Most of the graves were decorated for the holidays with wreaths or memorial logs filled with holly and poinsettias. As the car began to climb the hill, his thoughts returned to the day when he had last visited the Chiesa plot with Drew. They had come here on a rainy summer morning to bury Drew's son.

Drew wanted to go alone, but Neil insisted on going with him. Franny was in the ICU, barely conscious, recovering from the birth that had almost killed her. He had gone to McKenna's with Drew to make the funeral arrangements. Jerry counseled them to wait until Franny could attend the burial.

"No," Drew had said in a voice that was not to be argued with. "I want it over with. Franny's not strong. The last thing she needs is to stand there and watch you put him into the grave."

There was no funeral service because the baby had been stillborn. The morning of the burial, Jerry took them into the room where the child lay in a tiny white casket. Neil marveled at how beautiful the little boy was with his head of dark hair so like his father's. Dressed in the lacy white dress Franny had intended for his baptism, with a stuffed lamb tucked next to his cheek, he looked like a doll.

"I thought that we would drive out in my car," Jerry told Drew. "The casket is so small you can hold him on your lap." Drew swallowed hard and nodded, unable to speak. The only sound during the short ride to the cemetery was the swishing of the windshield wipers. Drew sat beside Neil in the backseat with the casket on his knees, his hands wrapped protectively around it. His face was unreadable on the short ride to the Chiesa plot on the hill.

*Drew wanted the baby buried with his grandfather so that he
would not be alone. At the grave, he reluctantly handed the
small white box, not much larger than the boxes that roses are
delivered in, to the man from the cemetery waiting there. The
trio watched silently as the baby's coffin was gently placed at
the head of his grandfather's casket inside the cement vault.
Drew spoke only once on the ride back to the funeral home.
Neil was not sure if he was talking to him or to God when
Drew said in a low voice, "I really wanted a son."*

The brake lights flashed on in the car in front of him bringing Neil back from his thoughts. The procession halted in front
of the open grave. The bright green grave cover with the red
poinsettias banked on either side stood in sharp contrast to the
early winter drabness of the surrounding ground. He and Harry
joined the other pallbearers at the back of the hearse. "This part
is pretty simple," Jerry said in an undertone. "We just carry the
casket over to the grave and set it down on the metal frame."

Once the casket was in place, Neil returned to the limousine. The driver opened the door and Drew's mother and father
gingerly stepped out, Elaine grasped the hand that Neil extended to her. Cynthia and Steve and their two children followed.
Cynthia, her eyes red-rimmed, had obviously been crying in
the car and clutched her husband's arm for support. Following them, Franny ignored Neil's hand and stepped out of the
car unassisted. She hesitated, stunned by the sight of the casket
positioned over the open grave. The wind was more noticeable
here on the hill and whipped her hair back from her face, expos-
ing the depth of her grief. She straightened her shoulders and
reached for his arm.

Reverend Goodwin, the rector at St. Peter's Church, took
his place at the head of the grave and began to read from the

Book of Common Prayer.

"O God, whose mercies cannot be numbered: Accept our prayers on behalf of thy servant Andrew, and grant him an entrance into the land of light and joy, in the fellowship of thy saints; through Jesus Christ thy Son our Lord, who liveth and reigneth with thee and the Holy Spirit, one God, now and for ever. Amen."

Behind him, Neil heard someone begin to wail, the sound growing in volume and intensity. Instinctively, he turned to Franny who stood to his left. But Franny was mute, her lips moving soundlessly. Next to her, Drew's mother wept softly. It was only then that he realized that the cries he continued to hear were those of a child. The Derouin boy, he thought, I knew she never should have brought that child here.

Franny reached down and pulled one of the long red roses from the spray that had covered the casket. They were her flowers, the ones from her to Drew. Carrying the brilliant red blossom, she walked the short distance to her father's grave and laid it in front of the stone engraved:

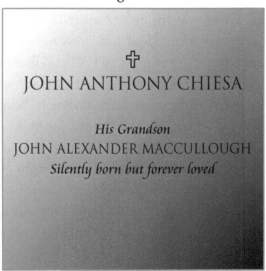

✠

JOHN ANTHONY CHIESA

His Grandson
JOHN ALEXANDER MACCULLOUGH
Silently born but forever loved

She turned and walked with purpose back to where Neil stood. Her eyes locked on his. "Please take me home, Neil."

CHAPTER 9

Franny sat in her car, staring at the four large wreaths decorating the front of the Chayne Communications building. They offended her, as any sign of the holidays had this year. It had felt wrong to her to celebrate without Drew.

The day after the funeral, Sofia put up the Christmas tree while Franny was resting. The sight of the tree, standing in the corner of the living room in the spot where it had stood every Christmas had upset Franny, but she knew that Sofia was only trying to help.

The following day, she took it down, dragging the poor tree out into the back yard. She didn't bother to coil the ten strings of white lights around the green plastic reels that Drew bought to hold each one. Instead, she tossed them tangled together into a black plastic trash bag and stuffed them into the back of the hall closet. The delicate ornaments they had collected over the years from antique stores and boutiques did not fare much better. These, she put haphazardly back in their boxes. She did not bother to wrap them individually in bright green and red tissue paper as she had in the past. She didn't care if she ever saw them again.

The Chayne parking lot was almost empty. Many people took the last two weeks of the year as vacation.

Franny shivered. She was cold even though she was dressed warmly in woolen pants, a turtleneck sweater, lined boots, and a navy peacoat. She had lost weight and her clothes were too big. Someone, usually her mother, was constantly approaching her with food, and begging her to eat it, to "keep up your strength," but nothing appealed to her.

It was ironic. Drew spent their entire marriage trying to get her to lose weight with little success. Now that he was dead it was finally happening without her even trying. Another one of God's little jokes, she thought as she opened the car door and stepped into the glare of the late December sun.

"There are some forms that have to be filled out," Lorie explained apologetically when she called and asked Franny to meet her at Drew's office.

Walking up the circular drive to the lobby, Franny slowed her pace as she was engulfed with memories. She had dropped Drew off here when his car was in the garage for service. No matter how rushed, or who might be watching, he would kiss her good-bye. Kisses I mistakenly believed would go on forever, she thought. I should have savored them, every one. She shook her head to clear the images from her mind and moved quickly across the tiled entryway into the building. The lobby was empty except for the large Christmas tree in the corner. One of the security guards approached her from the glass booth filled with closed circuit television monitors and other equipment. He was about twenty, dressed in his official uniform, importance and acne warring on his face.

"Can I help you, Miss?" he asked.

"I have an appointment with Lorie Derouin," Franny answered. "Her extension is 6709."

The guard smiled at her as he pushed the numbers on the phone in front of him. "Hi, Lorie, this is Brian in the lobby. You have a visitor." He handed her a visitor's badge. "Please sign the Visitors' Log," he said, indicating the binder in front of him. "She'll be right down."

Waiting in the silence of the deserted lobby, Franny thought about Lorie — Lorie and Drew. She stood as Lorie came down the stairs towards her. Lorie wore jeans ripped artfully across one knee and thigh topped by a long electric blue sweater with a deep cowl neck that emphasized her slenderness. When she moved, the bells on the bracelet she wore on her right ankle tinkled invitingly. Drew must have hated that bracelet, Franny thought. "Dress the part, Franny, and you're halfway there," he lectured her as she watched him inspect himself in the bathroom mirror.

Lorie, her large green eyes brimming with tears, pulled her into a hug. "How are you doing?"

Awkwardly, Franny extracted herself from Lorie's arms.

"I'm okay, somehow the days go by. Each one seems to bring one more thing that I don't know." Picking up Drew's briefcase from the floor beside her, she added, "This place is empty."

"Everyone is on vacation. Most people take off the week between the holidays."

"Well, I hope that you didn't come in here just to meet with me. We could have waited until next week to do this."

"Oh, no," Lorie answered, shaking her head. "I have plenty of stuff to do." She headed back toward the stairs.

Franny climbed the stairs behind her. Lorie stopped at her cubicle. A collection of crystals in varying sizes and colors decorated the top of one of the bookcases. A pink quartz angel, wings unfurled, stood in the corner of her desk.

The walls were covered with framed samples of art work

from projects that Lorie had worked on. Franny took a closer look. "These are terrific. Drew told me that you were doing some exciting things. He was really impressed."

"Thanks. I try to do things that pop." Lorie shrugged. "Sometimes it works and sometimes it doesn't. What you're looking at are some of my wins, and Drew...he was always encouraging." Franny picked up a picture in a Winnie the Pooh frame of Lorie's son, Alex, a laughing dark-haired little boy determinedly clutching a red truck.

"He's so cute. And so big! How old is he now?" She asked, her finger tracing the child's jaw line.

"He's almost two. I had that done a few weeks ago to give as Christmas presents." Lorie smiled down at the image of her son.

Franny looked closely at Lorie and again at the picture in her hand. "He must look like your husband. I don't really see any of you there."

Taking the picture from her, Lorie studied it. "I do think he looks like his father. But you know how it is with kids, people see different things." She laughed. "Steve's mother thinks he looks just like her."

Looking at the picture now firmly in Lorie's grasp once more, Franny said, "He must have been fun this Christmas."

Lorie smiled. "Yes, he was." She set the picture back on her desk. "Of course, what he really liked were the boxes and the wrapping paper. He pretty much ignored the pile of toys that Santa brought." Crossing the small hallway, she opened the door of Drew's enclosed office opposite her cubicle. The nameplate that should have been to the right of the door was missing.

Franny stood in the doorway and looked at the neat space almost empty of anything that indicated Drew had spent his days here. His pictures were stacked against the wall. On the desk was a cardboard box used to ship copier paper. An Aran sweater spilled out of the top of it. "What's this doing here?" Picking up the sweater, she examined it closely. It was a cardigan, and judging by its size, definitely a man's sweater. She had never seen it before. What made it unusual was the color. It was brown with flecks of white and blue rather than the solid cream-colored yarn commonly seen in commercially made Aran sweaters. She counted the number of different stitches, aware that the variety increased the value of the sweater. There were eight different stitches; the knitter was not a novice. Turning the sweater inside out, she looked for a tag or some other sign that it had been purchased, knowing even as she did so, she wouldn't find any.

"Drew had that sweater for as long as I have worked here. He wore it sometimes when he was cold or if he thought he was coming down with something."

Franny let the sweater slip back into the box. She realized that they both knew who had knit it for him. Franny refused to think about it now, couldn't bear to think about her dead husband wrapped up against a chill in a sweater Brid knitted for him. She didn't want to discuss Brid with Lorie. She couldn't think about Brid right now or about the extraordinary offer she had made to her at Drew's wake.

"Why don't we sit down," Lorie took the chair that would have been Drew's, leaving the one next to the desk for Franny to use. "I have some forms that Johanna asked me to have you fill out." She removed several papers from a blue slash folder with Drew's name on it. "Ann Trianni from HR should be the one meeting with you, but," Lorie faltered, "she's on vacation until the seventh of January. Johanna was anxious to get this done, so I told her that I would do it with you." Lorie seemed to be expecting some response from her and when none came, she went on to say, "I told her that we are close."

Close? I would never describe us as close. Franny thought, focusing on the paper in Lorie's hand. Certainly her relationship with Lorie was cordial, but rarely social. She learned early that Lorie could be counted on to know where Drew was and to get him for her if she needed him.

Drew had told her a lot about Lorie's personal life in that way that spouses gossip about their co-workers. She knew that Lorie's marriage had been shaky. Lorie and her husband, Steve, had separated once. Drew was sure that Steve slapped her around, although Lorie had denied it, when he asked her, explaining away the bruise that sparked the question. Lorie adored children, but had not been able to have any. She was shocked when, at thirty-six, she found herself pregnant with Alex, but both she and her husband were thrilled and doted on him. This last year, her fascination with angels had become an obsession. Lorie offered angel card readings to a growing number of regular clients. Drew told Franny that he had warned her that it had better not be at work.

Together, they went through the forms that were more appropriate for an employee who was leaving the company than for one who had died. They both cried over number 30: What is the impact of the loss of this employee on Chayne Communications?

"I told him," Franny sobbed, brushing angrily at her tears, "that this job was going to kill him. All that traveling! Last month, he was here all night working on that long range plan. He laughed when I told him that he was killing himself!"

"It was her. That witch, Johanna," Lorie said, grimly. "She had it in for him from the first day she got here. He could have done her job in his sleep and she knew it." Lorie lowered her voice to a conspiratorial whisper. "They had an emergency staff meeting the day after Drew died to figure out who would take over what he was doing. They realized then that he was working on seven major initiatives. Seven!"

Franny thought about Johanna Caras, Drew's manager. She had come to Drew's wake. Taking both of Franny's hands in her own, she said, "He was one of the last of the old guard at Chayne. He'll be missed." Squeezing Franny's hands slightly, Johanna added, "Mrs. MacCullough, if there is anything we can do for you, please don't hesitate to ask." She paused in front of the casket, Franny recalled now, but she had not knelt and said a prayer.

Drew rarely talked about what he did at work unless it was something either especially amusing or annoying about the people he worked with. When she complained, telling him she felt left out of a major part of his life, he had replied, "You're the major part of my life. I live my job all day, I don't want to bring it home with me and sleep with it." They did not socialize with the people from Chayne beyond the mandatory company functions, preferring a small circle of friends they had met in Hiram's Forge along with Neil, Harry, and Sofia. She was aware that there was tension with Johanna, if only from the fact that Drew never called her anything but, "The Wicked Witch." She knew he felt that Johanna took advantage of his knowledge of the business and his wide network of contacts throughout the industry.

Franny also knew something had been bothering him. Consumed by her grief, she had barely functioned after she lost the baby. Battling clinical depression, all she did was pop pills, eat, and sleep. She had been in a deep hole and everyone, even Drew, was on higher ground beyond her reach. Finally, she made her way back into the world only to discover that she and Drew seemed to have lost touch with each other while she was gone.

Without being aware of it, she had been waiting for something to happen. And now something had.

Lorie looked up from the papers in front of her. "I think the only thing that I need from you now are his corporate credit cards. His laptop was here in his desk. There were no personal files on it. I checked to make sure."

Franny lifted the briefcase from where she placed it next to her chair. Snapping it open, she reached inside and removed the two credit cards she found in Drew's wallet: Corporate American Express and Diners Club. She handed them to Lorie. Her fingers lingered over the white business envelope in the front pocket. For a moment, she debated asking Lorie about its contents. Making her decision, she closed the briefcase and stood up.

"I know that we've been over this before, but are you sure he never told you why he was staying at the Sheraton?"

Lorie was checking her list to make sure that they hadn't missed anything. "I told you," she said without looking up, a hint of impatience in her voice. "He called me the night before and asked me to meet him the next morning at the hotel for coffee. He said he had something important he wanted to talk to me about and he wanted to do it outside the office."

"But, if he came home early and was here in the office that afternoon, why didn't he call me? Did something happen? Was he in some kind of trouble?" Franny asked. Lorie leaned back in the chair, clearly uncomfortable, trying to distance herself from Franny and her questions.

"Look, I know this must be driving you crazy, but I don't know. Alex was sick. He had another ear infection and I had to take him to the doctor. I wasn't here when Drew got back from Seattle. I didn't even know he was back until he called me that night. I'm sorry, I really am. I wish I could tell you something that would make this easier for you." She pushed a form across the desk to Franny. "You need to sign and date this where the yellow 'sign here' stickers are." Franny signed where Lorie indicated; officially signifying that she was confirming that due to his death, employee number 43, Andrew MacCullough, was formally terminating his employment at Chayne Communications.

Lorie reached for Franny's hand. "Let me read the cards for you. They can help you. We can do it now. I have some in my office."

"I…no…." Shocked, Franny struggled to find her voice. "Thanks, but I am not comfortable doing that. I don't mean to hurt your feelings, but, no, thank you anyway."

Lorie sighed. "Okay…but think about it, the cards really do provide insight. Your angels are there for you even if you don't believe in them." She slipped the forms back into the blue folder on the desk. "I'll help you carry his things down to the lobby." She lifted the two pictures leaning against the wall. Franny picked up the box and the briefcase. This time, Lorie led them to the elevator. They rode down in silence, nothing left to say to one another. In the lobby, she handed the visitor's badge back to the security guard who initialed the time of her departure in the binder in front of him.

Slipping the briefcase onto her shoulder, she reached for the pictures; managing to avoid the hug she knew was coming. "Keep in touch, will you?" Franny said, forcing herself to smile.

"I will," Lorie answered, sadly. "You take care of yourself. And think about doing a reading." Lorie started toward the stairs. She stopped, turning back to Franny, she smiled apologetically. "I forgot to ask you for his badge. I need to turn it in."

Franny shrugged. "Well, I hope you've got a shovel. I buried it with him." She smiled, oddly pleased with herself. Hitching the briefcase higher on her shoulder, she turned and walked out the door.

CHAPTER 10

Neil Malone was thinking about skiing. Methodically, he reviewed in his mind the fall he had taken the last time he skied at Gunstock on a black diamond trail labeled, appropriately, "Hotshot." This season he had finally given in and bought himself a pair of new skis. He hated doing it, seeing it as a concession to aging. But he also knew if he wanted to continue skiing, he had to acknowledge the fact that he was closing in on fifty. He no longer had the strength in his long legs to ski all day. His right knee injured in the game against Holy Cross his junior year in college, protested at every turn. He wasn't as sure of himself on the new skis as he had been on the old Raichles. Maybe if he had leaned into the turn more—

"So, you agree, then, that it makes sense for me to be there?" Sofia asked, studying him carefully. The wide gold bracelet she was never without clanged on the edge of his desk, emphasizing her point. Neil recoiled slightly from the fruity smell of her perfume. She had been trying to convince him that she should be present at the reading of Drew's will for the last fifteen minutes.

Neil had directed his mind elsewhere and as a result had not heard a word she had said. It was a talent he had perfected through eighteen years of Catholic education when first, the nuns, and later, the Jesuits, stood in front of him, hammering away, like Sofia was doing now. It could be a problem because occasionally he missed something important. This time he knew it didn't matter. He had no intention of allowing her to be present when he went over Drew's will with Franny.

Looking across his polished mahogany desk at her waiting for his answer, he remembered the day that Drew had asked him to hire her.

They had gone to Craic for a nightcap after their weekly tennis game. Drew, dutifully on the wagon, that night anyway, drank tonic water and lime. They were sitting outside at one of the wrought iron tables under the green and yellow striped umbrellas so that Drew could smoke. Never a smoker, Neil enjoyed the smell of a freshly lit cigarette, or even better, a cigar. Now, he thought, wryly, they say even that can kill you.

"Don't you need some young blood in that Mick bastion of yours, Malone?"

"You can never have too many sharp young lawyers, Drew."
He took a sip of his gimlet. "You have anyone in particular in mind?" Knowing that, of course, Drew did.

Drew picked up the Marlboro again. Neil waited. Drew would get there, when he felt like it. "I was thinking of my sister-in-law." His eyes met Neil's. "Sofia Chiesa."

"I thought she was down in Boston at one of the big name firms, I knew which one it was once, but it's gone now." He remembered the story in the Ledger when she passed the bar. The girl certainly had the right credentials: undergraduate Dartmouth, law school at the University of Virginia, Editor of the Law Review. She had gone into one of the old Yankee firms. Mentally, he retrieved the news clipping and saw the name. "Wait, she's at Winthrop, Symthe, Shippen, and Cornett isn't she? Why would she want to leave a firm like that to come

to, what was it you called us? A 'Bastion of old Micks'?" He looked at Drew over the top of his drink. "She wouldn't make anywhere near the money that she is making now."

"Not much gets by you, does it?" Drew chuckled. He took another drag on his cigarette. "She's worried about her mother. She wants to be closer to Lynton."

"Boston's only an hour away and you and Franny are closer than that." He was a good lawyer. One of the first things he had learned was never to accept something at face value. Twenty-five years of practicing law and it usually paid off. Now, he stared into his old friend's eyes and asked softly, "What's the deal Drew?"

Depositing his cigarette in the small glass ashtray in front of him, Drew took a sip of his drink and leaned back in his chair, narrowing his eyes thoughtfully. "You don't know Sofia, do you?"

"I know her as well as I know anyone who I turn around and give the Sign of Peace to at Christmas. She asks me how I'm doing when she sees me, but she says it in a way that makes me feel like Jerry McKenna's standing behind me, with a shovel in his hand and his hearse idling at the curb."

Drew laughed. "Don't take it personally. I'll bet she feels the same way about me, or anyone over forty. I don't think she trusts Franny to keep on top of the situation, not with the way Franny's been since she lost the baby. They had a funny chemistry to begin with. If you didn't know it, you would think that Franny was the younger sister, not Sofia." He seemed about to say more, but decided against it. "Sofia needs to be in charge. She has to have her hands on everything."

"Nice that she has something in common with you."

Drew grinned and saluted him with his glass. "I wouldn't ask you, if I didn't think she knew her stuff."

"How is she on corporate law? Things like mergers and acquisitions? As it happens, we could use someone there." Neil checked his watch and drained the last of his gimlet. "I'm getting too old for this. It may be time we found a couple

*of other old farts and started playing doubles." He knew
they never would. "Tell Sofia to give me a call and we'll set
something up. Make sure she knows that she won't get the kind
of cases nor the money that she gets in Boston. I don't have
time to waste."*

*"Of course you don't. I would never want to cut into your
billable hours." Drew answered, smiling into the glass he held
in his hand.*

"What time is Franny coming in?" Sofia asked, a hint of impatience in her voice, bringing him back to the reason she was
standing in his office not quite tapping her foot. The conversation with Drew had taken place two years ago. Neil had never
fully understood the reasons why Sofia decided to come into
the firm. They both had known it was not a career-enhancing
move. That, coupled with the fact that she had taken a significant pay cut, made him wonder about it occasionally; usually
when she did something that made him aware of what a good
attorney she was.

He had offered her an associate position in corporate law,
working with his partner, Mike O'Shea. She had proven herself
to be a strong negotiator, one who was not afraid to use a red
pencil when going over a contract. He had no regrets and she
certainly hadn't voiced any, at least not to him. Drew had been
right, she knew her stuff. Sofia Chiesa was an asset to the firm.
But she didn't like being told 'no.' He braced himself as he prepared to do exactly that. He had a hunch she was expecting it.

"Have a seat," he said, pointing to his client chair, a Windsor embossed with the seal of Boston College, placed squarely
in front of his desk.

"I don't need to sit, Neil," she balked, "I need to—"

"Sit." He repeated, emphasizing the word. He was by nature a conciliator not a fighter, an odd trait in an Irishman. The angrier he became the quieter and the more slowly he spoke, leaving enough space between his words to make his listeners wonder if he had stopped talking in mid-sentence. He rarely lost his temper. When he did, there was no doubt that he could trace his lineage on both sides directly back to County Roscommon. He lost it now.

She was a small woman, viewed from the rear, she was often mistaken for a child, a fact she knew and despised. Looking at her now with her hands clenched, and her mouth set in a stubborn line, that's what he saw – a stubborn, spoiled child. Rising from his chair, he loomed over her.

"God damn it! I said, sit down." Neil roared. Her mouth hanging open, Sofia stumbled backwards in surprise and half fell into the chair behind her. "Now, you listen to me. You're a damn good lawyer, but you've got one serious flaw." Her lower lip began to quiver. "You have no sense of how to read people – none. Until you learn that, you'll never be a great one." He turned away from her, walked over to the window, and stared out at the choppy waters of the Merrimack River visible beyond the sloping back lawn. "I was his lawyer, not you. I drew up this will, not you. And I did it before he ever met your sister." He turned to glower at her. "I make it a practice not to have anyone present for the reading not mentioned in the will. You," he said pointedly, "are not." He knew, even as he said it, if Franny asked for Sofia to be there with her, he wouldn't refuse her. Instinct told him it wouldn't happen.

His attitude softened as he looked at Sofia, her eyes brimming with furious tears. Lowering his voice he continued, "He was my closest friend. I met him when we were in the third grade." Remembering the little boys they once were, he smiled.

"He trusted me. Surely, you're not suggesting that I would do anything to betray that trust?" Chastened, Sofia shook her head.

"Good. If Franny wants to show you the will after the reading, she can do so with my blessing." The phone on his desk rang. "Neil Malone." He paused to listen. "Fine, Erica. I'll be right out." He nodded at Sofia. "Let's go, Franny's here."

Franny sat in the waiting room, staring at the Childe Hassam print of the Boston Common hanging across from her, an unopened People magazine on her lap. Drew's death, Neil thought, has aged her ten years. He felt Sofia stiffen in disapproval, as her eyes examined her sister.

"God, Franny," Sofia said. "You've got your coat buttoned wrong. You look like a street person."

Franny looked down and hastily unbuttoned the offending coat. "I was in a rush when I left Chayne. I suppose I wasn't paying attention."

"You went over there by yourself? I told you I would go with you."

Franny ignored Sofia's comment and smiled up at Neil. "Hi, Neil."

"Let me have your coat and we'll go into my office and get started." He took the coat from her hands. Handing the coat to Erica, he turned to Sofia. "I'll send her your way when we finish." Before Sofia could reply, he took Franny firmly by the elbow and ushered her into his office. Franny carried Drew's briefcase with her.

The law firm of Maguire, O'Shea, and Malone was housed in an old white Victorian in the north end of the city of Lynton. Five years out of Boston College Law School, Neil and his classmates Tom Maguire and Mike O'Shea had hocked their futures, and in his case, his widowed mother's as well, to establish the firm and buy the aging building. Originally, they used only the ground floor, renting the two apartments on the floors above. The firm had grown to include five associates, four paralegals, and three administrative assistants. The law offices were now spread throughout the building. Neil still used the small space on the first floor that he had moved into twenty years earlier.

Once the back parlor, Neil liked it because it had a distant view of the river and a fireplace that worked. The refurbished offices on the second floor, where the two other partners moved to after they renovated the place, were larger, the furniture running to teak and chrome. Neil used a mahogany desk that came from his grandmother's house in Jamaica Plain. The walls of his office were painted an ivory color and hung with his diplomas from Boston College. Two framed photographs stood on the mantle over the fireplace. They were of his parents: his mother, smiling serenely, and his father in his patrolman's uniform. Hung unobtrusively on the wall across from the desk was a small ebony crucifix with an ivory corpse of Christ. It had been a graduation gift from his mother. "Hang this in your office, Neil," she had said, devout to the bone. "Let it remind you that the law is never bigger than Our Lord." It was an old-fashioned office, but it suited him.

"You have a fire, how nice." Franny walked over to warm her hands in front of the flickering flames.

"It's why I keep this office. The ones upstairs are definitely more upscale, but I like my fireplace. This time of year, I usually do have a fire. This fireplace draws better than most of the new ones I've seen in some of these million dollar homes they're building today." Pointing to the Windsor chair, he said, "Have a seat. Can I get you anything? Coffee? Tea? Water?"

"No, thanks, I'm fine," she said, settling herself in the chair.

"How are you really doing, Franny? Are you eating?"

She laughed. "Do you realize that I am asked that question at least five times a day? Of course, three times it's by my mother." The laughter left her face, leaving weariness in its wake. With a catch in her voice, she said, "Drew was always trying to get me to stop eating. I can see him up there in heaven cringing every time someone asks me that question."

Neil opened a long manila folder that lay on the desk in front of him, removing from it two copies of the will. He slid one across to Franny who took it reluctantly.

"This isn't complicated. The first page indicates this is the Last Will and Testament of Andrew Roderick MacCullough. Item One and Item Two state that he wants his debts and his taxes paid. Item Three refers to the Marital QTIP Trust of which you are the beneficiary and Item Four names you as his executrix. Your house is held in joint tenancy with right of survivorship and according to my notes the cars are in both your names, as are the checking and savings accounts. Put in simpler terms, Drew left all his worldly goods to you." He looked over his bifocals waiting for Franny to confirm what he said. But she sat there mutely watching the fire, apparently finding the flames licking at the hardwood more interesting than the reading of Drew's will.

Slowly, her gaze returned to meet his. "Did you know that there is a life insurance policy on the loan for the Lexus?"

"No, I didn't, but that's great." He said, making a note on the yellow legal pad in front of him. "That's one less bill that you have to worry about paying each month." He consulted his notes. "Drew took out a life insurance policy specifically to pay off the mortgage, so the house will be paid for, too."

Franny's mind was on the car loan not the house. "Right after we bought the car he walked in and tossed the life insurance policy in my lap. He laughed and said, 'If anything ever happens to me, your car is paid for.' We financed five cars. When we bought the Lexus, it was the first time he ever got a life insurance policy on the loan." She leaned forward. "Why this car? Why then?" Her eyes filled with tears. "Do you think that he knew he was going to die?"

Neil put the pen down, folded his hands, and looked at her solemnly. "Drew was the most vital guy I know. I don't think he really believed that he was ever going to die, certainly not ten days ago. I think that he was just hedging his bets as he did with the mortgage on the house. He loved you and he wasn't about to leave your future to chance." His eyes scanned his notes. "You said you were over at Chayne this morning. Did you meet with the person from Human Resources?

"Not today, but this woman, Ann Trianni, from HR called me last week. She said that he carried the maximum life insurance available to him. She said that I was 'golden'." Franny's smile was bitter and, for a moment, she looked much older than she was. "I bury my husband the week before Christmas and she tells me I'm golden. Can you believe that?"

He answered her smoothly, although inside he cringed. "It's certainly less than sensitive, but some people are at loss with how to deal with a death. Chayne is a small company; she probably never handled an employee's death before. I suppose she was trying to reassure you. Put it out of your mind." Clearing his throat, he consulted the legal pad. "Now," he began once more on familiar ground, "the last time I met with Drew about his estate, he said the life insurance from the company was for one million dollars. Is that what this woman told you?"

"Yes. She said the policy would pay out at a million dollars. She said that he also had a 401K with two hundred fifty thousand dollars in it. I am the only beneficiary."

Looking up, he asked gently, "You sound surprised that you're the only beneficiary. Did you think there might be someone else?"

She shrugged. "He could have left money to Cynthia or her children, or even to Sofia." A smile played around her mouth fleetingly. "For all I knew, Brid Sheerin could be in his will."

"She's not. I'm not surprised at all that you are the sole beneficiary. Drew was first and foremost concerned with taking care of you." The other people you mentioned were not his responsibility." He hesitated for a moment, uncomfortably aware of the letter in the back of the manila folder on the desk in front of him. He continued, giving nothing away, "And Brid was history. They've been divorced for a long time." Looking at her, he tried to gauge the impact of his words, but her wan expression betrayed only sadness.

"I think that we're about done for today," he said, smiling to reassure her. "As I said, Drew named you as the executrix of the will with his father as the alternate, although I don't see any reason to involve Rod. You and I can do this without any problem. I'll open a checking account for the estate. Don't pay any bills or funeral expenses until we have that in place. Let me know when you get the check for the life insurance and we'll go from there. I want you to meet with Ken Fine. He is my financial advisor. Talk with him about investing that money. You have to be careful, especially in this market." Neatly ripping off the page he had been writing on from the legal pad, he carefully slipped it into the manila folder. Rising from his chair, he waited for Franny to stand, but she remained seated.

"Neil, do you think that Drew was in some kind of trouble?"

"What makes you ask that? Did he say something to you about being in trouble?"

"No, nothing specific, but he was so tense this past year. He always seemed to be looking over his shoulder."

"Things start to change in a man when he realizes he's facing fifty, believe me, I know. A lot of things that you're able to bury with work and by keeping busy start to bubble to the surface." Neil hesitated. "I don't mean to cause you any more pain, but I don't believe Drew ever came to terms with the loss of the baby. I think it ate away at him."

"Oh, I know that. He couldn't even talk about it with me. Isn't that sad?" She bent down and opened Drew's briefcase. Reaching inside, she took out a white business envelope. Handing it to him, she said, "I found this when I went through his things."

"Mother of God," he said, after giving it a quick read. "Have you shown this to anyone else?" She shook her head. "Discussed it with anyone else? Sofia? Rod MacCullough? Your mother?" Again, she shook her head, no. Neil leaned toward his carefully tended log fire, the letter in his hand. Behind him, he heard her strangled protest.

"You're right," he said, turning back to her, placing the letter on the desk in front of him. "Now, you listen to me, this letter never existed. Do you understand me? Drew never wrote it." Neil paused to let this sink in, to make sure that his message was clear. "I can't stress to you how crucial this is. If he formally resigned, and it was accepted, it could change everything. It might, and I am only saying might, impact the life insurance paid out by the company. Let's hope he was indulging in one of his fits of pique." He rose, paced the room, and turned. "You were over there today. Who exactly did you see?"

"I met with Lorie Derouin to fill out some forms. Ann Trianni is on vacation until January and Johanna Caras wanted them taken care of before that. I picked up his personal things from his office. You know, pictures, the things in his desk. The place was deserted."

"Did Ms. Derouin say anything about this letter? Give you any indication that she knew that Drew had written it?"

Franny shook her head. "The only thing that she was upset about was his boss, Johanna Caras. She seems to think that it's Johanna's fault that Drew is dead."

"The point is that he is dead. We both know that he didn't like Johanna. It would come as no surprise to me, if she, in turn, didn't like him." He paused for a moment, letting her think about what he said. "But she didn't kill him. Drew would want you to go on with your life. The only way, and I mean this, the only way you can do that, is to let the past go."

He came around from behind his desk and reached down to help her from her chair. "Do you need any money? You have enough cash until we get this insurance settled? I can write you a check now, if you need money." He reached into his jacket pocket and took out his own checkbook as he spoke.

She remembered Drew telling her, "If anything were ever to happen to me, you go to Malone. Oh, I know he can be a little too starched. What else can you expect from someone who had the snot beat out of him by those nuns? But, bottom line, he will take care of you."

"I'm fine, Neil. There are several savings accounts that I can go to if I need money."

"That's good, then. Why don't you go and see Sofia? No doubt, she'll want to talk to you." Neil thought about hugging her as he would have hugged Brid without hesitation, but in the end he took her hands in his, holding them for a moment, struck by how cold they were. There was something reserved, almost secretive about Franny, something that seemed to say, "Come this far and no further." She opened the door to leave when he stopped her.

"Franny, there's one more thing. That woman who worked for Drew, Ms. Derouin. Stay away from her. I'm not sure she's playing with a full deck."

Franny smiled. "I suppose Drew told you about her thing with the angels. That really made him crazy. But as I tried to tell him, a lot of people are into that now. It really doesn't make her some kind of a nut. We were raised on guardian angels, weren't we?" Not waiting for a response, she added, "Thank you. I'll call you when I get the insurance check."

He smiled at her. "Make sure that you do."

As soon as the door closed behind her, Neil dropped into his chair and raked his fingers through his hair. What the hell was Drew up to? Neil turned and stared into the fire. He sighed. Was the letter Franny found one of several? All they could do was wait and see if Drew actually had submitted his resignation to someone over at Chayne.

He closed his eyes and thought about the half empty bottle of Glenlivet, safely hidden in the trunk of his car, that he found in Drew's room at the Sheraton. There was no question Drew had been in some kind of a mess. But what was it?

Franny, on her way out, asked Erica for her coat. She put it on, being careful to button it correctly, and said, "Please tell Sofia that I needed to leave. I'll give her a call later." Knowing all the while that Sofia would be furious with her.

It was dark as Franny drove down Boston Post Road even though it was only four o'clock. Inside the houses she passed, she watched various family tableaus unfold, women moving about their kitchens, children running back and forth chasing one another. Everywhere she looked – Christmas trees, flickering lights, and Santa Claus. It's the season, she thought. She was conscious of the lump in her throat that had started in the waiting room at St. Luke's and continued to grow larger with each day. Turning up her driveway, she stopped the Lexus in front of the garage. She could hear the dogs barking. She was glad that the porch light was on a timer. Fumbling for her keys, she saw the plate and the note left by someone on the table next to the back door.

More ham, she thought, the official funeral meat. Her neighbors had been very thoughtful, dropping off meals for her since Drew's death. The plate was plastic, cheerfully decorated with candy canes, the kind that she used to buy for cookie swaps and pile with butter cookies shaped like reindeer and Santa. The ham was carefully arranged in the center, a sprig of holly on top. Mounded around it were slices of cheesy potatoes au gratin. Suddenly, she was starving, her appetite returning with a vengeance. Dropping Drew's briefcase and her keys, she peeled back the plastic wrap and began to eat the potatoes with her fingers, no longer conscious of the biting cold or her barking dogs.

CHAPTER 11

Franny ran her company, Francesca's Foundlings, from the third floor of her home. Standing at the entrance to her workroom, she smiled, remembering that when Drew was asked what kind of work she did, his answer was, "She plays with dolls." Foundlings had started as a hobby left over from her childhood love of dolls. She had continued to collect them through her teens, bringing boxes of dolls with her when she married Drew.

He was charmed at first, diligently searching for what he determined to be the perfect doll for her Christmas and birthday gifts. He helped her hunt for dolls at the flea markets and antiques shows they browsed through on the weekends. After her second miscarriage, he stopped buying her dolls. They never discussed it, but she believed he found it too painful to buy baby dolls, when they couldn't have a child of their own.

The idea of being a doll broker came to her after she realized that while many people were interested in collecting dolls; few people had the patience or the interest to ferret them out of the attics and cellars where they usually ended up in a mildewing cardboard box or an old suitcase. These were the dolls that Franny loved, not the ones carefully preserved in tissue paper in their original boxes. She enjoyed the challenge of discovering the dirty half-naked dolls, often in need of repair. She had begun her business casually, advertising with a whimsical poster drawn in crayon hung in the local toy shop. Later, she placed a small ad in the paper.

She started going to doll shows, setting up a table with her latest finds. While she was still at Chayne developing training, she began taking orders to locate specific dolls for interested buyers. She thought of her doll business the way her father had characterized his weekly poker game, she was happy if she broke even. She wasn't doing it to make money. It was the dolls she loved, delighted by how they were made and what they wore. She was happy to put them in the hands of a fellow collector who appreciated them as much as she did.

Most of her inventory consisted of baby dolls or character dolls like Amy, Beth, Jo, and Meg from *Little Women*. Occasionally, she bought and sold antique dolls, but her expertise was in the Madame Alexander, Suzanne Gibson, and Ideal dolls she had played with herself.

The business had grown slowly and come to a halt after she lost the baby. It had taken her all summer to recover physically from the traumatic stillbirth and subsequent hysterectomy. Long after she should have been able to physically, she found herself unable to get out of bed, held there by a depression as black as a night without stars.

She would lay in bed, tracing the rosebud pattern of the wallpaper over and over in her mind. It was only through a teeth-gritted effort of will that she was able to get up late in the afternoon and sit mindlessly in front of the television, still dressed in her nightgown. It was a good day when she made a half-hearted attempt at fixing a meal; usually haphazardly assembled sandwiches or reheated slices of a pizza that Drew had picked up on his way home the day before.

Her disability insurance ran out and she turned in her resignation from Chayne. She had no desire to return to the work she had been doing. Developing corporate training and writing marketing strategy seemed pointless to her. They had planned for her to stay home after the baby was born, her salary, so much smaller than Drew's, made little difference to them.

It was Drew who pushed the idea of expanding Foundlings. He spent the second summer after the baby's death renovating the attic of the house. He buried his grief among the sawdust and the blue board, patching his broken heart together as surely as he taped and mudded the drywall seams. He would rush home from Chayne, eat without comment, and go upstairs to work until midnight or later. The results had been magical, at least as far as the room he had built. Her healing took longer, but it had begun on the third floor in the space he created for her.

After climbing the stairs to the attic, Franny stepped into the large open room. The two dogs crowded in behind her. They missed Drew. Lucy carried around one of his black leather gloves in her mouth. Franny wondered what the dogs thought about the fact that Drew was no longer here. Poor puppies. They were sleeping with her now. She needed their warm bodies next to her own. Tears welled in her eyes when she remembered that Drew was no longer there to object. Well, he wasn't sleeping with her either, not anymore.

Looking around the room, the pleasure she felt surrounded by the world Drew created washed over her. She remembered the night he first cajoled her up the stairs, walking behind her, his hands covering her eyes. "No peeking," he ordered as he led her blindly into the room. Truly, it could have been the doll room in Santa's Workshop at the North Pole.

He had lined the long back wall with shelves inhabited now

by all manner of dolls and their accessories. On the right side of the room under a bright rainbow, with the words "Francesca's Foundlings" painted over it, was a dolls' nursery. It held the doll furniture they had found on their antiquing trips: two cribs, a playpen, a walker, a bassinet, high chair, several doll carriages of different vintages, and a small swing, all sized for a baby doll.

There was a child's table painted gaily to look like Peter's pumpkin shell set for four with a miniature Victorian tea set. Dolls of all shapes and sizes slept in the cribs, sat in the high-chair, posed in the playpen, and waited for their tea. Her customers, who came by appointment, were enchanted. When she was alone, she fussed over the dolls. She made sure that each doll was positioned to advantage, their dresses and overalls displayed invitingly.

The other side of the room served as her workshop and of-fice. There was a built-in work surface extending the length of the wall under long, multi-paned windows that let in the afternoon sun. The computer she used to run her business sat on the far end. Drew created a website for Foundlings, so that she could sell the dolls online and answer questions from potential customers.

Her sewing machine stood at the other end of the work sur-face surrounded by bolts of muslin, colorful calicos in crayon colors, and soft pastel ginghams. Oak shelves held clear plas-tic boxes filled with baby shoes: white leather boots; small red, blue, and brown double buckle sandals; and blue and white saddle shoes; all carefully polished to look almost new. Under-neath the shelves were four colored plastic bins labeled with the names of doll manufacturers containing restored doll clothes.

This year, she expanded her inventory to include a toddler-sized doll made from cloth. She designed the doll to wear the clothes mothers tucked away to remind them of their babies now grown. The doll was customized according to gender, hair and eye color. If someone wanted to buy only the doll, Franny insisted she be sent the clothes. Once she had dressed the doll to her own satisfaction, she would return it.

Some customers sent her baby pictures and requested that she recreate the outfit the child in the picture wore. She kept an ever-growing collection of clothes she found at yard sales and flea markets, carefully laundered and repaired, in three wooden steamer trunks nestled under the eaves opposite the stairs. In some cases, working from the picture the customer sent, she made new clothes for the doll to wear.

Two large Raggedy Ann and Andy dolls sat on the end of the shelf. Her mother made them for her baby shower. Once, they had been downstairs in the nursery.

Drew had dismantled the nursery while Franny was in the hospital, removing the crib, the white wicker changing table with the blue gingham pad, and the bassinet decorated in white eyelet that had cradled all the Chiesa babies born in the last sixty years. Franny had no idea where it was now. She had never asked.

In a final effort to convince her that the room was never meant to hold a baby, he covered over the mural they painted together with a soft white paint, returning it once again to the extra bedroom it had always been. They had such fun designing that mural. Franny wanted the animals willy-nilly, but Drew, pencil in his mouth and a tape measure in his hand, insisted they be the same distance apart, gaily marching in a parade around the room.

He was a fool if he thought that she could ever forget what the room looked like the night the paramedics rushed her out to the ambulance. The thick white terry towels wadded between her legs in an attempt to staunch the blood that wouldn't stop coming, blossoming with deepening splashes of scarlet. She could walk into that room tonight and see it in her mind exactly as it looked as a nursery, the colorful animals lining the wall, waiting in anticipation for the baby that never came home.

She reached for the Raggedy Andy, hugged it tightly, and remembered the night her son was born.

Her baby was a dusky color, splashed with blood mixed with chalky white vernix, nothing like the pinky peaches and cream she expected him to be. She saw that much as he was lifted over her head. The baby was passed swiftly to a waiting pair of hands gloved in white latex. The room was hushed in expectation; there was a sense that time had stopped, waiting for her son's first cry. Her obstetrician issued terse commands tinged with panic. Her ears strained to pick up the low conversation in the corner of the room where the pediatrician and two nurses hovered over the baby. Drew, having fought his way into the room, stood behind her head. Please God, please let the baby cry, she thought. The eerie silence continued until mercifully she lost consciousness, spiraling down into blackness.

When she opened her eyes, Drew was sitting next to the bed, her hand held firmly in his own. He brought it to his lips and held it there, his bloodshot eyes bravely meeting hers.

"Tell me." She demanded fiercely, the tears leaking out of the corners of her eyes and coursing down the sides of her face. "Tell me."

"You had something called placenta abruption. It—" Drew groped for words. "The placenta pulled off the uterine wall, causing a hemorrhage. That was where all the blood came from." She shivered, wanting to stop him from continuing. "The baby," his voice broke and he fought for control. "He was born dead." Letting go of her hand, he lowered his head against the side rail of the bed and sobbed, his shoulders shaking, her fingers caressing his cheek.

Lucy whined, probably sensing Franny's sadness. The sound brought Franny back to the present. Now, Drew was dead, too. Her mother was convinced they were together up there in her tidy version of heaven. Franny wasn't so sure. God, who she relied on less and less, had never seemed so remote or so cruel. She had come upstairs to work on the four Christmas orders she hadn't finished. She was grateful they had been for "Dress Me" dolls. Everyone was very understanding when Sofia called to explain the dolls would be delayed until after the holidays.

Franny made a point of getting her Christmas dolls, the ones that Santa would bring, boxed and shipped by the fifteenth, making sure that she was not responsible for ruining some little girl's Christmas. She was glad that most of her business was with adults, women like herself who simply loved dolls. "Silly women," Sofia had said once, "with money to burn."

Franny opened one of the four folders stacked neatly on top of the desk and removed the picture of a cherubic blond boy who appeared to be about sixteen months old. She studied the clothes on the child in the picture: red corduroy overalls with a blue train appliquéd on the front, blue jersey, and blue sandals with red socks. She walked over to a large wicker baby buggy crammed with muslin "Dress Me" dolls waiting to be clothed. Selecting one with short yellow curls, she sat the doll on her hip, its legs dangling like a real child's and walked over to the long shelf where she kept the shoes. Picking out a pair of well-worn blue sandals, the soles scuffed by some child's scampering feet, she carefully fitted them on the doll. She studied the bolts of cloth piled on the desk, going back to check the exact shade of red the child in the picture wore. As she stared at the face of the smiling toddler, the nebulous feeling of dread that she had carried away from Chayne that morning began to crystallize into an actual image and she shivered.

"No." She spoke the single word aloud, causing Lucy to lift her head and look up at her questioningly. The dog thumped her tail twice against the hardwood floor, as if to reassure her. Franny sat the doll she was holding on the desk next to the bolts of cloth.

"Come on, let's go," she said to the dogs. Standing and stretching, they followed her, running down the stairs. Franny moved rapidly through the dark house until she stood in the formal living room. She loved this room and rarely entered it without pausing to experience a wave of satisfaction at the way the colors and furniture blended together. The room "worked" as her sister-in-law, Cynthia, once told her approvingly. Cynthia seemed to be surprised in that haughty way she had inherited from her mother, that Franny was capable of managing such a thing. I may have been unable to give Drew the child he so desperately wanted, but I was able to create a charming place for him to read the newspaper, Franny thought bitterly, as she had surveyed the room.

A small lamp burned next to the long chintz sofa. In the corner, shrouded in shadows created by the light from the lamp, the grand piano seemed to crouch like some large benign animal. Franny moved across the claret-colored Oriental rug and stood facing the mantel over the fireplace. Her hands were shaking as she reached for the small picture in an ornate gold frame, the only one she kept there. She stared down at the picture, her eyes filling. It was a black and white studio portrait, artfully lit, of Drew, taken when he was eighteen months old. He was dressed in a style popular with the mothers of little boys in the sixties, in a romper with a ruffled collared pleated blouse and attached shorts; his feet, stretched out in front of him, were neatly shod in polished high, white, leather shoes. She traced the shape of the lantern jaw already firmly in place. The child laughed up at her through wide thickly lashed eyes, the black and white of the old photograph effectively masking their blue-green color. As she stared at the side part carefully taming the shiny cap of dark hair, she remembered with a stab of pain the thick mop of dark hair on the head of the child she had briefly glimpsed but never held.

She felt oddly detached, almost like she was watching herself through a lighted window much as she had watched the families she had driven past on her way home from Neil's office. It wasn't possible, was it?

Clutching the picture in her hand, she retraced her steps, more slowly this time, lost in thought, climbing back up the stairs to her bedroom. Dropping the picture on the bed, she walked over to Drew's dresser. She reached for his cell phone. Neil had given her Drew's wallet and his phone when he returned from the hotel. For some reason she couldn't quite explain to herself, she kept the phone charged.

Climbing onto the high bed with the dogs leaping up to settle in next to her, she studied the baby picture of her husband. He smiled up at her. The only glimpse she had of her son had been during that brief moment in the delivery room. She was bleeding to death, they told her later, and only the skill of the medical team had saved her. It was Drew who had sat in the rocking chair in the small room off the nursery and said goodbye to their dead son. It was Drew who marveled at the shape of the ears and the downy softness of the thick black hair that had covered his small head.

"Perfect," the nurse told her when she had given her the two pictures taken of the baby before Jerry McKenna took him away. Perfectly dead, Franny thought as she had stared at her son's picture. Drew made the decision to bury the baby before they let her come home from the hospital, her recovery hampered by severe loss of blood and a stubborn infection. It was only afterward that she had discovered the formal photograph of Drew she now held in her hands. She was convinced that had he lived, her son would have grown to look very much like the sturdy little boy in the picture.

Today, she had seen another child whose picture this could have been. Or had she? Leaning back on the fluffy pillows, her fingers blindly stroking Oliver's curly ears, she shut her eyes and wondered if she might be losing her mind. How many times had she read about a woman going mad with grief? Had she perhaps, slipped into madness? Babies looked alike. She knew that better than most people from studying the pictures people sent her for the dolls. If only she had the picture of Lorie's baby. Surely, if she could put the two next to each other, she would see that there was only the most superficial resemblance.

Unless Drew had a picture. The thought dropped unbidden into her mind and with it, she was off the bed and reaching for his wallet on top of the dresser. Her frantic fingers pulled the small plastic sleeve of pictures out: Sofia smiling in cap and gown at her graduation from Dartmouth; school pictures of Owen and Meri, his sister's kids; a picture of her taken not long after they were married; and at the back, a small, much creased black and white snapshot of three boys in Lynton Little League uniforms, their bats crossed in front of them. Franny smiled: Drew, Harry, and Neil. Could a man sentimental enough to carry a forty-year-old picture of his boyhood friends in his wallet have a secret family, a hidden life?

With Lorie? What was it she had said today about her little boy? Franny racked her brain, willing herself back into Lorie's office. "I do think he looks like his father." Did he? Franny struggled to transpose the long, sallow face of Steve Derouin over that of the happy little boy she remembered from the picture.

The photograph in her lap and the one she had seen this morning had become one and she couldn't do it. She bit her lip hard to keep from screaming. When had Lorie's baby been born?

"March," Franny said, aloud. "He was a year old last March." She remembered because Drew asked her to get a birthday present for him. She bought a stuffed elephant. He was conceived then in June, three years ago in June. Where had Drew been then? Had he been traveling? Three years ago, she thought, when I was numbed to the point of living a life that was a slow-moving blur buffered by antidepressants and too much sleep.

Opening Drew's phone, she searched the contact list and scrolled down to Lorie's name before her nerve failed her. Her heart raced as she listened to the ringing of the phone. On the third ring, it was answered.

"Hello." Lorie answered, sounding rushed.

Franny swallowed in an effort to moisten her dry mouth. "Hi, Lorie. It's Franny." Who else could it be? Franny thought, remembering she was calling from Drew's phone.

For a moment there was only silence, slowly, the woman on the other end of the phone replied. "Yes, I saw it was you. Is everything okay?"

She had no idea how to begin. She knew that once she allowed herself to walk through this door, everything would change. There would be no retreating. For a moment, she was tempted to snap the phone shut and let the other woman chalk it up to weird behavior by the widow. But no, it was too late. Perhaps some women could have done that, but she was not one of them. The silence stretched between the two women, becoming more charged with each moment that passed.

Franny sunk back against the nest of pillows stacked at the head of the bed, holding the phone loosely next to her right ear almost to suggest to herself that this was a casual call after all. That she didn't really need to hear the answer to the question she was about to ask. Across the room from the top of her dresser in a silver picture frame, her husband appeared to beam at her encouragingly. Go ahead. Ask her.

"Today, when we were talking, I had the strangest feeling that you were trying to tell me something." On the other end of the line, she thought she heard Lorie sigh, but she might have imagined it.

"Did you and Drew have a thing going on?" Franny asked. "Did you hook up with him?"

"He told me that you knew." It came out in a rush, the relief in Lorie's voice making her almost breathless. "He said you didn't care."

Franny's body lurched forward, reacting as to a blow from behind, arching up from the pillows where she lay to curl into a ball. Her voice became jagged and hoarse and sounded to her like it belonged to someone else. "How could I have known? He was still living here wasn't he? We were married."

"He said you never had sex anymore, that you were too depressed after losing the baby."

Franny and Drew had gone riding once and the horse, bored and no doubt tired of her inept attempts to tell him where she wanted him to go, had thrown her. She remembered the way she felt after she hit the ground, shocked, and uncertain that she would ever take another breath. She felt that way now.

"I'm sorry Franny. I took something that was yours. I knew it was wrong, but it happened and then..." Lorie stopped. Sighing, she continued. "We fell in love."

Franny's heart raced, her mind recoiling in horror from Lorie's words. "No, I don't believe you." Even as she spoke, she was shocked by the terrifying realization that she could kill this woman. She could walk up to her, shoot her straight through the heart, drop the gun, turn around, and walk back the way she had come. And not look back.

"We were in love," Lorie repeated. "Drew loved me."

"He was drunk." It wasn't a question. She looked across the room at Drew's picture smiling at her, remembering.

She snuggled against his bare back, feeling decidedly decadent, and enjoyed the novelty of waking in the crisply sheeted bed of an unfamiliar hotel room. Too drunk to drive home after a night of drinking and languidly dancing cheek to cheek □ in truth, they had been having sex with their clothes on □ so closely had they moved together across the polished dance floor. The ice in the glass of Scotch he held in his hand was cold against her flushed cheek. They had decided to be smart and spend the night at the inn where they were having dinner. Drew rolled over to look at her, smiling, as his eyes met hers. "Thank God it's you," he said.

"Who else could it be?" She asked in wonder. Drew continued to smile as he pulled her toward him.

Lorie's voice in her ear brought her back. "Maybe he was the first time, but not after that." Her tone changed. Lorie was angry now. Franny heard it and tried to close her mind to the images that began to form – Lorie and Drew in bed, Lorie and Drew making love. She racked her brain trying to figure out when this had taken place and where? Why? "He loved me, why won't you believe me?" Lori insisted. Underneath the anger, Franny could hear the other woman's desperate need to be believed. "Neil Malone knew about us," Lorie said. "Ask Neil, if you don't believe what I am telling you. We talked about it at Drew's wake."

"Did he say he would marry you?" Was I so out of touch that I had no idea he was going to leave me?

"We talked about it, but he said, 'You'll never be my wife. I love my wife.'" The indignation was there.

A scrap of validation, but it was enough. Franny felt the anger begin to seep away from her, leaving behind exhaustion and a profound sense of sadness. In her mind, Lorie's words echoed: he had said, "I love my wife."

Franny's voice was a whisper now, barely audible even to herself. "I just don't understand why he would do this. And now I can never look into his eyes and ask him." Her voice broke into fragments.

On the other end of the phone, she could hear Lorie breathing fast the way the dogs did during a thunderstorm. "I need you to tell me that you forgive me. I need you to promise me that you won't tell Steve. He would kill me."

Franny didn't answer. She closed the phone, ending their conversation.

CHAPTER 12

Brid was barefoot when she answered the door to find Neil Malone standing outside. His hair was wet and the shoulders of his topcoat sodden from the January sleet. The water on his cheeks created the illusion of tears.

"For the love of God, come inside. You look half drowned," she said, moving aside to let him pass her into the warmth of the large room, brightly lit by a wood fire. "This coat is soaked," she said, sliding it off his broad shoulders. "Do you not own an umbrella?" She draped the wet coat over the tall, ornate steam radiator that stood hissing against the far wall.

"Go and sit by the fire. I'll make you a cup of something hot. What will you have? Tea, coffee, hot chocolate?" She called over her shoulder as she headed down the hall leading from the large living room. Returning from the depths of the flat, she handed him a thick white towel to dry his hair.

"Tea would be great, but don't go to any trouble," he said. "I'm sorry to bother you at home, but I needed to talk to you about a few things. I thought it would be better to come here instead of having you come into the office."

"Protecting me from Sofia Chiesa are you, Neil?" she asked him. Before he could reply, she added, "It's no bother. I

was about to fix myself a cup. Here. Wrap yourself up in this."
She tossed him one of the quilts stacked at the end of the sofa as
she left the room.

He hesitated for a minute, shivering. Making up his mind,
he wrapped the quilt around his shoulders. Slowly, the raw-
ness of the wet night melted from his bones and he began to
relax. Closing his eyes, he listened to the music playing softly
in the background. Bach, he was certain – "The Goldberg Vari-
ations"– he thought. He allowed himself to wonder for a moment what it would be like to come home to a room like this
and to a woman like Brid. He supposed that the men who did
took it for granted, the way contented people do. He wondered
for a moment, if Drew had.

Neil had always planned to marry and he had dated several very nice women. When he graduated from law school,
he moved back into the house on Wisteria Street where he was
raised. During his first years learning the law, at a firm in Lynton, he had been grateful for the home his widowed mother
made for him. By the time he lifted his head from the work,
he discovered his mother had become an old woman and himself nearly forty. Maybe it was as simple as never having met
the right woman, or having the right woman beyond his reach.
Some days he felt he should have become a Jesuit. He was, after all, living like one

Brid returned, bearing a tray carrying a creamy Beleek teapot dotted with shamrocks, a sugar bowl, creamer, and two
cups. Along with the tea, there was a small plate with brown
bread and smoked salmon, a glass dish with shortbread cookies, and two linen napkins. She placed the tray on the low oak
coffee table, pushing aside a stack of magazines and books, including, he noticed with interest, a volume of Yeats.

"Now, how did you put all this together?" He asked, humbled by her hospitality.

Kneeling opposite him on the other side of the coffee table, Brid poured a cup of tea and handed it to him. "I keep most of this in the kitchen, except for the brown bread, which I made this morning before I left for the gallery." Seeing his look of astonishment, she laughed. "You should see yourself. Never forget that I was raised over an Irish pub. My mother did teach me to cook you know."

He helped himself to a thick slice of brown bread upon which he piled a generous serving of salmon. "Of course I know you can cook. You've fed me before, haven't you? It's just such an unexpected and undeserved treat," he said, gesturing toward the tray. "All of this, I mean. Thank you."

Brid smiled and poured herself a cup of tea. "You would no doubt prefer something a bit more bracing than tea, but I don't keep it in the house. So this is what you get."

"Well, I tell you," he said, reaching for another slice of bread, "this is perfect."

They sipped their tea in companionable silence; the only sounds the snapping of the kiln-dried logs, the ticking of the mantle clock, and the Bach. His eyes roamed the spacious room. He had never been here before, his loyalty having gone to Drew after the divorce. He admired the effect that seemed to be so carelessly achieved. On either side of the fireplace, two wing chairs, upholstered in a tiny check pattern, sat waiting for someone to drop into them. The golden oak of the hardwood floor beautifully framed the deep rose and muted green of a worn Oriental carpet. In the far corner of the room, the prancing carousel horse stood watch.

"I see you still give a home to old Bucephalus," he said. "Will you ever forget how obsessed Drew was with that horse?" After Brid and Drew bought the horse at the outdoor market in Brimfield, Drew set about meticulously restoring the old charger to its past glory. He spent long hours sanding the wood and replacing the missing leg with one he made using an assortment of expensive woodworking tools bought only for that purpose. He also researched the colors of the original paint and carefully matched it. He and Brid had thrown a party when the restoration was complete. Pouring champagne over the horse's head, Drew christened him Bucephalus, after the warhorse of Alexander the Great, the Greek king who had been one of his heroes.

"I've been offered a fortune for that horse," Brid said, thinking of the customers and artists she had entertained in the flat who had fallen in love with it. "He and I have grown accustomed to one another after all this time. I tell people he is my pet when they tell me how much I need a cat. I often use him to hold my hats." When she and Drew had separated, she offered the horse to him. His feelings hurt, he replied, "I brought him back to life for you, Mick."

With a sigh, Neil reached reluctantly for his briefcase. Unsnapping it, he looked over at her and said, "It's because of Drew I'm here to see you. You know that I drew up his will?" She should know it, he thought, she was there in the room when Drew made the first one.

For the first time that evening, Brid seemed annoyed. "I hope to God that I have nothing to do with Drew MacCullough's will. We've been divorced for seventeen years. Please don't tell me that he neglected to make a new will." Her eyes flashed at him. "Don't tell me that you didn't insist that he make a new will."

He smiled gently, taking no offense. "Calm down, Brid. Of course, I made sure that he made a new will. You don't figure in it all. After the renovations on the bar were finished, he left this with me." Reaching into the briefcase, he handed her a long white envelope. Printed on the front, was her name, Brid Sheerin. She hesitated, unwilling to take the envelope, finally reluctantly accepting it with limp fingers.

"Wait until you're alone to open it, if you want," Neil said, trying to unscramble the puzzle of emotions crossing her expressive face.

"Don't be ridiculous," she said, ripping open the envelope. She held in her hand, a single sheet of stationary and a life insurance policy for two hundred and fifty thousand dollars taken on the life of Andrew MacCullough. The beneficiary named was Brid Sheerin. "Did you know about this?" Neil could see that the contents of the envelope disturbed her.

"About the insurance policy, yes, about what is in the letter, no. Drew told me that he wanted you to pay off the note on the bar."

She unfolded the letter and read aloud:

Mick,

If you're reading this, then I have actually, as they say, expired. Please use the money to pay off the note on Craic. It will give Des peace of mind to know the place is finally his at last. The only thing I ask is that you don't tell him where the money came from. We both know Des can't keep a secret to save his soul. Within no time he will have it all over Lynton. Just tell him that the gallery is doing really well.

I know you, and you will worry that this takes something away from Franny. Believe me, I have made sure that she will be fine, at least financially. And this is really for your father, not for you. I know you want nothing from me. Oddly, while I have found that to be a source of intense frustration, I have always admired you for it.

It would hurt Franny if she knew about this. She has always been jealous of you. This is the reason I have asked Neil to take care of it for me and have not included the bequest to you in my will. The happiest days of my life were spent in Craic with you, Des, and Rosie. This is my way of saying thank you.

Please know that no matter where I am when you find yourself reading this and I guess only God knows where that may be, you will always be "a ghrá mo chroí."

Drew

Angrily, Brid brushed at the tears streaming down her cheeks, a ghrá mo chroí — Irish for the love of my heart. "Even dead he's maddening, do you know it?" Defiantly, she looked up at Neil. "He says that he has taken care of Franny. Is that true or is it more of his blather?"

Neil reached over with his handkerchief and wiped the tears that slid down her cheeks. "Obviously, I can't divulge the contents of his will to you, but I can tell you that he is telling you the truth. Financially, she should be fine."

"Funny, you say it that way, that's exactly what he says in his letter." She got up and restlessly paced the length of the room. Turning, she asked him. "And how is Franny?"

Neil stared into the fire. "I don't know. Franny's always been hard to read. If I had to sum it up in one word, I guess I would use lost."

Carefully, he folded his napkin and placed it on the tray. Having delivered Drew's letter, he had accomplished what he had set out to do. It was time that he was on his way, reluctant as he was to leave the comfort of the room and the woman in it.

Rising from the sofa, he said. "Drew was everything to Franny. I think she is finding it very hard to cope without him."

Brid made no effort to reply to what she viewed as a scripted answer. She thought he was being deliberately evasive. Knowing him as she did, she supposed he felt that it was none of her business how her ex-husband's widow was dealing with his death. She reached behind her and retrieved the topcoat from where she hung it over the radiator. "Almost dry," she said with a smile, holding the coat out for him to slip on.

"Thanks for the wonderful tea. I haven't had brown bread that good since my mother died." Buttoning his coat, Neil reached for the door.

"Neil, what were you talking to Lorie Derouin about at Drew's wake?" Brid was no longer smiling. She waited, watching for his reaction to the question. She wasn't disappointed. His hand froze on the doorknob. The color drained from his face. He slid his tongue over his lips before he spoke, in an obvious effort to delay answering her.

"I don't recall. I am sure it was nothing important." She watched while he warily pulled himself back together, feigning ignorance as he answered her.

"You're a true Irish liar," she said, the honey gone from her tone, her anger flaring. "Jerry and I watched her back you into one of those conveniently placed alcoves that night. We both commented on how unhappy the conversation seemed to be making you."

"I must have spoken to fifty people that night." Neil answered. "Certainly you don't expect me to remember what I said to them all."

"If I were a gambler, I would wager you remember what you said to her."

He stood like a stone in front of her, his jaw set obdurately.

At that moment, he embodied everything about the Irish male she had grown to despise. "Fine. Go!" She pulled open the door, "Leave." Looking him straight in the eye, she delivered her final thrust. "I know something was going on with Drew. He told me so himself." She waited for his reaction and was not disappointed.

He shifted from one foot to the other, clearly uncomfortable. "When did you talk to Drew?" Brid didn't answer, waiting to see what would come next. "I mean, I guess I was not under the impression that you talked to Drew on any kind of a regular basis. Did you?"

"He came to see me about four months ago. Just turned up here one morning around 1:30 and—"

Accurately reading the horror in his eyes, she lost her temper. "Get out," she snapped, placing both hands on his chest and shoving. He was a big man, but she caught him off guard and succeeded in pushing him into the hall. "And no, I did not – do you hear me – did not take the drunken fool into my bed." Without another word, Brid slammed the door in his astonished face.

CHAPTER 13

Brid stared at the door. Retreating to the sofa, she gathered the quilt around her, suddenly cold despite the warmth of the room. She reached again for Drew's letter. Clutching it tightly in her hand, her thoughts returned to the night in October when he had turned up at her door.

Someone was singing "The Wild Rover." The realization that it was Drew together with the pounding on her door brought her upright, wary and completely awake. Not bothering with her robe, or the light, she groped her way to the door and wrestled with the locks. Flinging it open, she found herself facing her former husband clutching a vase with a rose in one hand and a bottle of Glenlivet in the other.

"Good morning to you, Mick," he said, slurring his words. "I come bearing gifts. This," he offered her one of the Waterford bud vases from the dining room at Craic, "is for you." He grinned, obviously delighted with himself, eyes crossing slightly, his normally crisp features, rubbery, his mouth like a clown's. The palm of her right hand itched to slap him. Instead, conscious of what it had cost, she relieved him of the vase he was waving at her. She placed it gently on the oak sideboard behind her.

"What in the name of God and His angels are you doing here, you drunken ejit?" She demanded, her Irish accent surfacing with the word ejit. Tentatively, Drew planted one foot across the threshold.

"I thought we could have a drink, like we used to." He smiled at her, gesturing with the bottle of scotch.

"Get out." Once, when they were still married, she had horrified him, when, after reading a newspaper story about a woman who shot her husband, she told him that was precisely why she would never keep a gun in the house. She gave silent thanks that she did not own one now, because, by Jesus, she would be sorely tempted to use it.

Her less than gracious welcome did not seem to discourage him. Bringing the other foot into the room, he moved closer to her. "Come on, Mick, you be nice." As she neatly side-stepped the intended kiss, he lost his balance and stumbled. The bottle, slipping from his hand, shattered at his feet. The distinctive bouquet of single-malt scotch perfumed the room as the amber liquid formed a puddle on the oak flooring. Taking advantage of his fascination with the spreading mess, she shoved him back through the door not concerned in the least that he landed sprawled in the foyer. Slamming the door shut, she slid the dead bolt home.

"Feckin, feckin, feckin, FECKIN, Drew MacCullough!" She switched the overhead light on before cautiously picking her way barefoot through the broken glass to the kitchen. In a rage, she grabbed a dustpan and brush, returning to kneel cautiously amidst the scattered shards of glass, glittering like carelessly discarded gems on the floor around her.

Outside her door, she heard Todd, her neighbor, asking Drew what the hell he thought he was doing.

"Go back to your boyfriend, pretty boy." Drew sneered in return. Todd threatened to call the police. Trust Drew to unleash his homophobia, Brid thought as she flung the door open, her eyes taking in the scene before her. Drew was slumped on the floor, leaning arrogantly against the wall, oblivious to how ridiculous he looked. Todd was halfway up

the stairs, apparently having changed his mind about waiting for the police.

"Todd, it's okay," Brid smiled her most disarming smile. "I know the drunken fool. I'll bring him in and sober him up. I'm sorry he woke you."

"Are you sure, Brid?" he looked dubiously at Drew. "I can kick his sorry ass out of here if he's bothering you." To prove to her that he meant what he said, he advanced two more steps up the stairs.

"Really, it's fine. Go back to bed." She extended her hand to Drew and hauled him to his feet. He fell heavily against her, leaving her no choice but to shuffle backwards into the flat.

"Right where I want you," he murmured in her ear.

Reaching her arms around him in a reluctant embrace, she pushed the door shut and steered him toward the sofa. When she was fairly certain that at least his head would land softly, she shoved him away from her.

"Not so fast, Mick," he said, taking her with him as he tumbled backwards onto the thick cushions. She sprawled across him, their legs entwined. As she struggled to get up, his hands, with a familiarity that made her ache, snuck under the long tee shirt she wore to sleep in, to rest possessively on each of her slender hips.

"Where," she demanded between clenched teeth, "is your wife?" The smile disappeared. He sighed, removing his hands from her body, his inane grin replaced by a look of sadness so profound that it was palpable. Taking advantage of this, she scrambled quickly off him. She wrapped her arms around herself for both warmth and protection. It was not Drew she was afraid of; it was herself that she feared. How can I still be attracted to this man? She thought as she stared down at him.

"Where's Franny? She's not sitting there waiting for you is she?" How many times had she herself done that? Curled up on the sofa, watching for the headlights to light the driveway, finally letting out a breath seemingly held for hours as his car turned in, weaving its way to an abrupt stop. How many times had she whispered a silent prayer of thanks to the God she had

an uneasy truce with at best, as she listened to him fumble with his key in the lock?

"She's at a fancy spa for the weekend. It's out in the Berkshires somewhere." He leered up at her. "Unlike you, she needs to lose a few pounds." He reached out and cupped his hand around her right thigh.

"You and your sexist idea that all women should be built like Barbie." His eyes travelled to her small, high breasts, the nipples clearly visible beneath the thin fabric of her tee shirt.

"Don't worry, mo mhuirnín, no one can accuse you of looking like Barbie."

It was clear to her now how the evening had unfolded. His wife out of town, he had spent the evening at Craic, eating at the bar. The meal would appear without him having to ask for it: escargots, salad with the blue cheese dressing Craic was famous for, tenderloin cooked medium rare, and a baked potato, no dessert. This was accompanied by glass after glass of Glenlivet served over ice followed by Drambuie. The place and the liquor fueling his thoughts of days long gone.

"Don't talk to me in Irish, Drew. I hate it. And I am not your sweetheart. I'm going to put some clothes on, I'm cold."

He had learned all the Irish terms of endearment and whispered them accordingly: a stór, darling, a ghrá mo chroí, the love of my heart and her favorite, the one that could still unleash a kaleidoscope of poignant memories, a chuisle mo chroí, the beat of my heart. He had wooed her in Irish, and made her fall in love with him in Irish. It pained her beyond words to hear him speak it to her now. It felt obscene; like being caught making love in public. She much preferred his other name for her, "Mick," the name born of everything Irish about her that annoyed him.

As she headed into her bedroom, she heard him say, "And I was hoping you would take your clothes off." She bit her tongue to keep from answering him.

Returning to the living room, dressed in leggings and her Boston University sweatshirt, she found him prowling around the oak sideboard, pulling open drawers and doors, searching for something to drink.

"You won't find what you're looking for. I don't keep it in the house." He looked so woebegone, that she relented. "Look, I can make you a pot of coffee."

"I would love a cup of your French press coffee, but only if I can have it with one of your Waterford balloons filled up to here with Courvoisier." He used the fingers of his right hand to make his point. "I don't suppose you keep any of that around for your lovers?" She refused to be drawn; she had sparred with him too many times to be caught so easily in one of his traps.

"All I have is coffee." She hoped her tone warned him that her love life was not up for discussion.

"Thank you, but no. Why ruin a perfectly good buzz?" He rose unsteadily to his feet. "I'm out of here." He promptly collided with the low table in front of the sofa. He hit the floor with an alarming bang and would have one more mysterious bruise to explain to himself in the morning.

Gazing down at him wedged between the sofa and the table, she was filled with the bitter despair that she usually succeeded in keeping at bay. "Damn, damn, damn," she cursed aloud. There was no way she could let him leave. Not this drunk, he would surely kill himself or even worse, someone else.

"Drew." She shoved the table out of the way. "Let me help you back to the sofa." She knew that if he was not able to assist her, he would spend the night on the floor. She couldn't lift him. She knew this because she had tried. Grabbing her hands, he managed to lift himself onto the cushions.

The tears began to slide from the corners of his eyes. He clung to her the way a child would. "I fucked it all up, didn't I, Mick?" She didn't bother to answer. As he closed his eyes, she thought that she heard him say, "I can't lose my son."

Not the baby again. Des had told her that on those rare occasions when Drew drank now, this was what he talked about when he made that final turn into melancholy before passing out. That poor, dead little boy, the babies Franny *would never have and the babies she, Brid, had refused to give him. Each drunk has his own story; they were all victims of something, something that justified drinking themselves blind. As the years passed, the stories continued to get worse like bad soap operas with familiar villains who grew older and more tired looking. For her, it had been her painting, her illusive, unpainted, but much mourned masterpieces.*

Covering Drew with one of the quilts stacked at the end of the sofa, she shivered, not from the cold, but because she was afraid. Instinctively, she knew that his presence in her life, here on her sofa – for God's sake – threatened everything she had worked so hard to leave behind. Looking at him sleeping, his expression unguarded, she understood how easily he could pull her back to the emptiness she had managed to escape. She had loved him, and hated him. She had fought desperately with limited success to be indifferent to him. What she felt for him now, she knew, was the most dangerous emotion of all – pity. "No, I can't go back there. I won't," she said, aloud, and turned toward her bedroom wanting only to sleep.

She was sprawled across her bed after a restless night when the irresistible smell of freshly brewed coffee woke her. Opening her left eye, she focused on the digital clock next to her bed. It was after nine o'clock. The previous night came flooding back to her. She rolled onto her back and sighed, thinking damn Drew MacCullough. Rising from the bed, she paused to twist her body into the yoga stretch called Half Moon, gracefully bending first left and then right, finishing with a fast Breath of Joy, the yogic breathing guaranteed to promote calm. She had a feeling she was going to need it.

Wrapping herself in her long cashmere robe, she followed her nose to the kitchen. Through the open French doors, she could see Drew on the deck, pensively smoking a cigarette.

Hearing her come into the kitchen, he turned and smiled. Her guard up, she did not smile back at him. He was freshly showered and shaved. She wondered if he had used her razor, realizing that he must have unless he now carried one around in his pocket. "Good morning. I was just getting ready to bring you some coffee." Putting the cigarette out in the saucer in front of him, he rose from the chair, walked back into the kitchen, and poured her a cup of coffee. "Do you still drink it black the way I taught you to?"

"Yes, thank you," she answered, thinking it was true. He had taught her to drink coffee. Her parents used tea as an answer to every thirst not satisfied by Bushmills or Guinness, never acquiring the American habit of drinking coffee. Drew had introduced her to the finer points of freshly brewed coffee. He refilled his own mug and sat down across from her. They drank in silence. Looking at her, he said, "You're the only woman I have ever known who looks beautiful first thing in the morning."

She took another sip of coffee before answering him. "Coming from you, I suppose I should take that as a compliment, given the sample that you no doubt have to pick from." He scowled and she knew that her comment had found its mark.

"Listen, lady, I didn't come here to fight with you. I know you must be furious about last night and you probably have every right to be. I apologize." He sighed. "I needed someone to talk to and I thought of you. Obviously, I made a mistake." He stood up, walked over to the sink, dumped out the coffee, and rinsed the cup. She knew that he was angry.

"You have a wife. Why not try talking to her?"

He answered her without turning around. "She is still pretty fragile." He turned from the sink, carefully drying his hands on a towel. "I feel like my job is to keep her safe, not to upset her."

"Well, you've always wanted a child." The moment the words left her mouth she regretted them. Silently, she cursed her vile tongue. His reaction surprised her. Instead of the anger she expected, she saw only sadness. Putting down the towel, he took a step toward her.

"Brid, why didn't we have kids?"

"Mother of God!" Springing up from her chair, she crossed the room and stared blindly out at the garden. Without

looking at him, she asked, "How many times have we had this conversation, drunk and sober, both?" Her voice thickened with unshed tears. He was behind her in two strides, his lips on her neck, knowing fingers caressing nipples already stiffening with desire.

"Bríd, mo mhuirnín," he whispered as his lips began to nibble with growing insistence along the side of her neck. "We would have made such beautiful babies."

Carefully articulating each word, she turned and answered him, "As I have told you before, I didn't want them." He stepped back from her, his hands held rigidly at his side. She marveled at his control, instinctively knowing how much he wanted to slap her.

They stared defiantly at each other before he moved past her toward the door. His hand on the doorknob, he glanced back at her and said, bitterly. "Mick, you don't ever change. You're still beautiful and you're still a bitch." Before she could answer, he walked out, slamming the door resoundingly behind him.

Standing in the middle of the room, she breathed deeply, concentrating on the simple acts of inhaling and exhaling to slow her racing heart. "I need," she said, aloud, "to move." She grabbed her running shoes from the deck next to the table where Drew had been sitting. The sun shining on the silver cigarette lighter, on top of the pack of Marlboros, caught her eye. Dropping her shoes, she snatched up the cigarettes and deliberately shredded them into the saucer he had used for an ashtray. Looking at the lighter, monogrammed with the initials ARM, she wondered how many lighters he had left in his wake, thinking of the four she had bought for him herself. This one, made of sterling silver, was expensive. Heading toward her bedroom, she dropped the lighter into the trash can by the door.

She changed into her running clothes and pulled on her sweatshirt to ward of the early morning chill. On her way out, she stopped and retrieved the lighter, setting it on the corner of the oak sideboard next to the door.

The crashing of the smoldering logs into the fire brought Brid back from the past. She stared down at the letter in her hand, debating whether to toss it into the glowing embers. Deciding against it, she walked over to the sideboard and slipped it into one of the drawers.

CHAPTER 14

Neil's weekday mornings never varied. After shutting off his alarm at 5:30, he got out of bed and shaved, lathering his face with the ivory handled badger-bristled brush that had belonged to his father. He then showered and dressed. If he was going to court, he wore a suit. If he wasn't, then he preferred a more casual jacket. His closet contained six such coats because he kept them forever, custom tailored of imported Irish tweed. In addition to these, he owned a black cashmere blazer he reserved for weekends.

He was in his place in the fourth pew from the altar at Our Lady Queen of the Angels by 6:10 for the 6:30 mass. He spent the twenty minutes waiting for the mass to begin saying the rosary. He did this every morning, his fingers slipping over the worn black beads he had received after making his First Communion forty-four years earlier in the same church.

He was devout in that quiet solid way certain Irish men are. He had a horror of being mistaken for one of the "Rectory Rats," the term he used to describe the small army of hard-working laity that seemed to be everywhere at Our Lady's these days. Willing to offer his back or his checkbook, he had demurred when asked if he would like to serve as a Lector or Eucharistic Minister. "If I had wanted to be on the altar, I would have granted my mother's dearest wish and become a priest," he had responded when asked. The truth was he had almost become a priest, deciding finally, he was too fond of life's comforts to make a success of it.

This morning, despite his good intentions, his mind refused to stay focused on the ageless prayers he learned as a toddler sitting on his mother's lap. His thoughts kept returning to his disastrous visit to Brid the night before. He could see her face, all the more beautiful when she was angry, as she shoved him out the door. Threw my ass right out the door, was what she had done, he thought, chuckling, until he saw that he was attracting the attention of Agnes Hurley who sat in the pew across from him. So Drew went to see her, not that it really surprised him. He had long suspected that his friend was still in love with his first wife. Deep in his cups, Drew had confirmed it in that tearful way common to drunks, more than once.

On the altar, the priest said the prayers over the gifts, changing the water and the wine into the body and blood of Christ. Automatically, Neil sank to his knees, wincing as he connected with the kneeler. He missed the tinkling of the three bells he had rung so vigorously as an altar boy. Rather than Christ's sacrifice, he found himself wondering if Brid returned Drew's feelings. She had told him often enough in no uncertain terms how she felt, rarely placing Drew's name in a sentence without modifying it with, "that bastard," or worse. Hard to say, Neil thought, remembering her tears last night, as she read the letter Drew left for her. Guiltily, he lined up behind Agnes to take communion, knowing he had given short shrift to this morning's liturgy.

Before leaving the church, he took the bucket of rock salt mixed with sand from where it stood in the corner of the vestibule, and liberally sprinkled the steps, slick from last night's sleet and glittering in the cold morning light.

Conscious of his aching right knee, he eased himself behind the wheel of his dark blue Mercedes, taking a moment to savor the smell of the leather interior. The Mercedes was typical of his view of the things in life that money bought. It was five years old, purchased new after a significant amount of research, coupled with no small amount of guilt on his part from its sticker price. The car was meticulously maintained. He planned on keeping it for a long time.

Unlike Drew, who always needed the latest and the most expensive toys, only to then easily discard them, Neil was far more discerning. He was careful how he spent his money, the things that he owned were few, but fine. The soft caramel colored vicuna topcoat he wore had been purchased his first year out of law school at Louis Men's Store in Boston. His clever Korean tailor, Keong, made sure that it still fit him.

He parked the car neatly between the two white lines of his parking space, lining it up in front of the sign that read: Mr. Malone. The reserved parking spaces for the three senior partners had begun as a joke.

"Why not?" Mike O'Shea said when they had first put the firm together. "If we're not gonna get all the perks we would get with a white-shoe firm on Wall Street, the least we can have is our own parking spot."

Laughing, Neil and Tom Maguire had gone along with it. And now, Neil thought, chuckling, as he climbed out of the car, I really enjoy it. I am getting old.

Newspapers tucked firmly under his arm, instead of entering his office, he walked swiftly across the parking lot and headed back toward the heart of Lynton, striding forward at a good clip. Alone now in the house on Wisteria Street, the much pampered son of a doting Irish mother, he rarely cooked a meal. He was able to manage a small selection of dishes that kept him alive: eggs of any kind with scrambled his specialty, fried bologna sandwiches, and when all else failed, day or night, large bowls of Irish oatmeal.

Every workday morning, he ate his breakfast at Caroline's Kitchen across from the Presbyterian Church on Main Street. He walked the mile and half from his office in thirty minutes, a time that he felt to be sufficiently respectable. He credited this effort, which he often made twice a day, eating his lunch at Caroline's if he had no business lunches scheduled elsewhere, with keeping his waist under forty inches. He and Drew had tried to keep a weekly tennis date and he skied as often as he could, which to his way of thinking was never enough. He viewed this walk, which he made regardless of the weather, as his daily exercise. He had no interest in the current passion for working out, telling his two overly enthusiastic partners, "I did enough of that in the gym at Boston College to last me for the rest of my life."

"You can set your clock by Mr. Malone," Caroline Nealy, the owner of the small restaurant, told the other diners. It was a rare morning that didn't find Neil sliding across the sticky red vinyl in the second booth from the back next to the window fronting on Main Street at 7:35 a.m. The table was always waiting for him, the other regulars having seats of their own. If an unwitting stranger approached the booth, Caroline would find them another seat, shooing them away from "Mr. Malone's table."

He engaged in no idle chatter beyond the initial "Good morning," and "Have a great day," offered upon arrival and departure. He never bothered to look at the menu. He ate the same breakfast every morning: orange juice, oatmeal with brown sugar and raisins, accompanied by a small pitcher of whole milk, English muffins, and tea.

He read two papers in the same order from front to back each morning: *The Boston Globe* and *The Lynton Ledger*. *The Globe* was a relic left over from his days as a student in Boston. While sports were certainly covered in *The Ledger*, only *The Globe* could evoke the appropriate level of pathos required to report the triumphs and tribulations of the Boston Red Sox adequately. Much to Drew's amusement, he remained a stubbornly loyal member of the Red Sox Nation, always optimistic no matter what was happening on the field.

He read *The Lynton Ledger* to keep his finger on the pulse of what was happening in the city. Munching on the second half of his English muffin, he was reading the obituaries when someone slid into the booth across from him. Putting the paper down, he scowled across the table at Sofia Chiesa.

"I hope I'm not interrupting you," she said, chewing nervously on her right thumb.

"Just reading the paper," he answered, trying his best to conceal his annoyance. He didn't like to talk to anyone in the morning, before entering his office, beyond the most banal of pleasantries. He never invited anyone to join him at Caroline's, not for breakfast.

"I was on my run and I knew that you ate here. I thought we could, you know, talk for a few minutes." Even more aggressive gnawing of her thumb followed this pronouncement.

It explained why she was dressed the way she was, in black tights, a black fleece jacket, and a UVA baseball hat. What the hell is this now? He thought as he attempted to coax his expression into a semblance of a smile.

"Have you talked to Franny?" Sofia asked, nervously.

"Not since she was in the office." Something about the clandestine nature of this conversation made him uncomfortable, but then he had been uncomfortable since Drew died. "I was thinking that I should call her this morning to find out if she's received the insurance check." His eyes narrowed. "Why? Did something happen? Is anything wrong?"

Before Sofia could answer, Caroline, curious, no doubt about his companion, appeared, pad in hand, and asked Sofia, "Can I get you something?"

"I'll have a Diet Coke, please."

Caroline turned to Neil. "Can I get you anything else, Mr. Malone?"

"Just the check, please. Put the Coke on it."

She was back in two minutes with a tall glass of ice and a can of Diet Coke. Sofia poured the soda into the glass and took a sip. He couldn't keep himself from shuddering as he watched her.

"How do you think that a guy like Drew ever put up with my sister?" she asked, putting her glass down and staring at him intently.

"What?" Neil snapped, just shy of speechless.

"Oh, I don't know – he was such a great guy – I mean no one knows that better than you – and my sister, I mean I love my sister, but God she has to be like the most narcissistic person on the planet."

"Okay, Sofia, what's this about?" He reached for his wallet, pulling out a ten and three ones. His usual tab including tip was $11.00. He figured he had covered her drink and if he hadn't Caroline would let him know tomorrow.

"On second thought, don't tell me. Not here. I'll see you back in the office."

Before she could protest, he gathered up his newspapers, shrugged into his coat, and left the restaurant without a backward glance, ignoring, the chorus of "Have a great day!" following in his wake. Leaving Sofia sitting there, he left the restaurant and marched past the window.

All the way up Main Street, he fumed. He was still preoccupied when he arrived at his office, walking brusquely by Erica with hardly more than a grunt in response to her cheery, "Good morning, Neil." Seated at his desk, he sighed wearily and rubbed his temples, his head in his hands. Damn you, Drew, what in God's name is this about? Squaring his shoulders, he pressed the button on his phone.

"Erica, when Sofia comes in, tell her I want to see her right away. Please."

He began reviewing the estate documents he had been working on the day before. He found it difficult to concentrate, his mind returning to his earlier conversation with Sofia. How was he supposed to know how any man put up with his wife, never having had one himself? Glancing down at his watch, his annoyance increased. His hand was on the phone to find out where the hell she was, when a soft tap sounded at his door.

"Come in," he barked.

Dressed for work, Sofia wore a trim black suit with a silk scarf, comprised of dramatic splashes of red and gold, looped jauntily around her neck.

"Where did you go this morning? I expected you to run past me."

She seemed surprised by the question. "I ran back to the Y. I shower and change there every morning after my run."

"What did you mean when you asked me how did Drew put up with Franny?" He glared at her. "He loved Franny."

Sofia recoiled and answered indignantly, "I love Franny, too. She's my sister. But she can be so wrapped up in herself, you know?"

"No, I don't. The woman's husband dropped dead last month. I think that she's entitled to certain amount of self-absorption."

"I guess we had what you might describe as a fight."

He sighed, resigned to hear about it. "Why don't you describe it to me?"

"Well," she began, not as self-possessed as she usually was. "Last night, Franny called me and she asked me what I thought of Drew's relationship with Lorie Derouin."

"And? What did you think of it?" He asked, watching her closely, conscious that he was sweating even though the office was chilly.

"I know Drew liked her work. He thought she was a great designer. He was her boss and they were friends. That's all."

He looked at his watch. "Tell me more about this fight you think that you had with your sister."

"She asked me if I knew that Drew had an affair with Lorie." Her eyes widened and she spoke slowly. "With Lorie Derouin! Somebody better go up to Lynton's Lawn and see if he's still in his grave. Can you imagine Drew involved with someone like Lorie? He thought she was way out there with that obsession she had around angels and the rest of that fantasy stuff."

Neil sighed and answered her truthfully. "No. I really can't. But you still haven't told me what the fight was about."

"I told her she was crazy, that Drew would never do that. Never!"

"What made her think that Drew had an affair with Lorie?"

"Oh, that's the best part. Franny called Lorie up the other night and asked her." She shook her head in disgust. "Lorie told her that Drew was in love with her."

He said nothing. The only sound in the office was the ticking of the clock. Sofia continued. "What did she think Lorie would say when she asked her that? Of course, Lorie said he loved her. She's probably had a thing for Drew for years. And Franny believed her."

He sighed. Somewhere in his neatly ordered mind he was beginning to feel an unexpected flair of anger toward Drew.

"Franny's not stupid. It was inevitable that when the numbness wore off she would start to ask questions like: Why did he lie to her about when he got back from Seattle? Why did he spend the night at the Sheraton and why didn't he call her the next morning?"

Sofia nearly bounced out of her chair; she was on her feet so fast. "You're not suggesting any of this could be true? Are you? You knew him better than any of us."

"Think like a lawyer and revisit the facts, Sofia. He lied to his wife about when he was coming home from his trip. He left work and spent the night at the bar in the Sheraton. Instead of making the twenty minute drive home, he spent the night there. Although, that may have been the only smart thing he did. We only have Lorie's word that she didn't spend the night with him. I wouldn't say that Franny's conclusion is wildly off the mark, would you?"

"Yes!" He could see she was close to tears. "You knew him. He would not risk everything to have an affair with someone who worked for him. He was too smart. You know that! Not someone who reads angel cards!" Sofia was begging for Neil to believe her. "He was always on Franny to lose weight. I told her that if he had had an affair – and if he did it would not have been with some flaky hippie-type like Lorie Derouin – it was her own damn fault the way she let herself fall apart the last few years!"

"You said that to her?" He asked, stung by the girl's cruelty to her sister. "The last few years haven't exactly been kind to Franny, you might remember."

"Oh, yeah, I know she lost her baby. She can't have another one." She clenched her hands into two white-knuckled fists.

"Why is it that no one ever seems to realize that it was his baby, too, that maybe he was grieving, too? Oh, no. He was a man, so he could never feel what a mother feels, right? Drew was supposed to hold Franny together, the hell with his own pain."

Neil brought his hand out to stave off any more information. "Enough. Where has it been left? Are you two still speaking?"

She seemed to deflate in front of him. Even though it didn't seem possible, she looked even smaller than she was. Slowly, she brought her hands down to her sides. She bit her lip nervously and shrugged. "I don't know." She hesitated. "I guess the answer is no. She hung up on me. I called her back several times, but I kept getting her voicemail. I asked her to pick up, but she wouldn't." The side of her thumb was back in her mouth. "I don't know what to do."

"I'll call Franny. I had planned to call her about the insurance money anyway." He looked at Sofia sternly. "You leave her alone."

"But I feel like I should—"

"Let this cool down. Franny must feel that her life has been shattered. I think you should leave her alone. I'll handle it."

Nervously, she played with the gold bracelet on her wrist and squared her small shoulders. "Okay. Maybe you're right." She started out of the office, but turned back at the door. "You will make sure she's okay? I don't think that she would ever do anything, but..."

"I'll check on her, I promise."

She hesitated in the doorway. He waited, sure of what was coming. She didn't disappoint him.

"Neil, do you think that Drew did have an affair with Lorie?"

"It would have been an act of sheer stupidity, if he did," he answered.

A relieved smile replaced her scowl. "You're right. He would never have hooked up with her."

Funny, he thought as he watched her close the office door, she isn't quibbling about him screwing around, only with Lorie. Sighing, he decided he didn't want to examine that thought any closer, and picked up the phone to call Franny.

CHAPTER 15

Neil arrived early for his dinner with Franny. Making his way across the crowded room to a spot near the corner of the bar, he ordered a vodka gimlet and settled down to wait.

Even though it had been ten years since Craic had been remodeled, he still experienced a sense of displacement. He remembered the bar the way it was when he was a young man whose main occupation on a Saturday night was the pursuit of his next beer. In keeping with the character of the neighborhood, it was a working class bar, patronized by the mill workers and others like them who lined their metal lunch boxes up inside the door. Hard drinkers, they were mostly men, although on the weekends, couples, like his mother and father, wandered in for a game of darts and a pub supper.

In those days, Craic had consisted of one large room scattered with small tables, covered with yellow plaid oilcloth. The tables could be pushed together to accommodate a crowd when the occasion called for it. The bar, running along the length of the back wall, was the focus of the room. An upright piano stood in one corner and a dartboard hung on the wall in the other. Behind the bar was a montage of faded photographs hung haphazardly, proudly sharing wall space with cheap prints of the Sacred Heart and Our Lady of Perpetual Help. Many of the faces in the pictures were immediately recognizable to anyone who knew their Irish history: James Connolly, Eammon Ceannt, Michael Hanrahan, Padric Pearse, and Joseph Mary Plunkett. Among those famous Irishmen, in the back row of a group picture, cap twisted nervously in his hands, stood Francis X. Sheerin, Des's father.

The food had been typical pub fare: thick sandwiches, brown bread, and Irish cheddar, and on Saturday, if you were lucky, Rosemary's shepherd's pie or corned beef and cabbage. The clientele came to drink, to gossip, and to sing along with Des while he played the old Irish ballads on the battered piano. There were many nights that ended in a brawl, not that it mattered. Half the cops in Lynton were Irish and willing to turn a blind eye to what went on at Craic.

When the mills first closed, the neighborhood declined further and Craic became seedier. By then, Rosemary was dead of lung cancer, the result of a cigarette habit begun in Ireland when she was in grade school. The food dwindled to baskets of stale popcorn and dishes of peanuts, more often empty than full.

Then, the fortunes of the neighborhood changed. Dock Street was suddenly the place to be in Lynton. The abandoned mill buildings with their long windows and softly muted brickwork were converted to expensive residential condominiums and prime office space. Stavros's Shoe Repair Shop next to the bar and the pawnbroker across the street were bought out and replaced with a French bakery and an upscale florist. Business at the bar declined even further. As the streets turned from potholes to cobblestones, the regulars, with a few exceptions like Des's cronies, Shanahan and Mahoney, stopped coming, no longer feeling comfortable in the old neighborhood. The new neighbors viewed Craic as a dive and avoided the place. Craic, and Des along with it, were in real danger of going under.

Reflecting on the way the place once looked, Neil slowly sipped his drink. In the corner, a young man in a tuxedo softly played the refurbished piano. Neil nodded to several young lawyers he knew, sitting together on the green velvet love seats. It was inevitable that his thoughts turned to Drew and to Brid.

Neil stood at the bar, no longer gleaming the way that it had when Rosemary was alive, nursing a beer. At the far end, an old geezer with a porkpie hat on his head slouched on a stool, giving a pretty good imitation of having already been embalmed. The only other person in the place was the bartender. A young guy with greasy black hair tied in a ponytail with a leather bootlace, he was polishing glasses; no doubt some relation to Des. The old man himself was nowhere to be seen, which was odd on a Saturday afternoon.

Neil was waiting for Drew. "Meet me at Craic at 2:15 on Saturday. I need to talk to you," Drew said when he called, refusing to divulge anything more. Ordinarily, Neil would have begrudged the day away from the ski slopes. Fortunately for Drew, who was late, he had heard the ski report – it was sleeting in the mountains. Prompt to the minute himself, he was annoyed, even though Drew was never on time. He glanced at his watch for the second time, when Drew came through the door.

"I'm sorry to keep you waiting, Counselor. I got tied up with Franny," Drew said, sliding onto the stool next to him. "Glenlivet on the rocks," Drew yelled to the bartender. Turning to Neil, he said, "The joint's jumping isn't it?"

"I think the guy at the end of the bar is dead," Neil answered with a straight face.

Drew laughed. "I think you might be right." Nodding his thanks, he picked up the glass the bartender put down in front of him.

"What's the deal, MacCullough? Why are we drinking in a morgue on Saturday afternoon?"

"That's the point of this meeting, but we have to wait until—"

At that moment, the door opened to reveal Brid standing there fighting impatiently with her umbrella.

"Then again, we don't," Drew said, as he slid off the stool onto his feet, a gesture not lost on Brid.

"Oh, if you please, don't bother being gallant," she snapped, putting a French accent on the word gallant. Closing the umbrella, she deposited it, along with her raincoat and hat, on a table near the door. She ran her hands through the cloud of curly black hair surrounding her face, joined the two men at the bar, and kissed Neil on the cheek.

"Hello, Neil. How are you?" Brid smiled.

"I'm fine, completely mystified as to why I'm here, but fine, and yourself?"

"I'm grand, thanks. It's good to see you. It's been a while."

"I don't suppose the old ex-husband gets a kiss, does he?" Drew asked as his glance took in Brid's black sweater and tight jeans.

"Don't be a pig, MacCullough. This is business." She smiled at the bartender, "Hey, Tommy, I'll have some black coffee, please."

Drew drained his drink. "Actually, that sounds like a great idea, only chase mine with Courvoisier."

"Thanks," Brid said to the bartender when he handed her the coffee. "Why don't we sit at a table, we'll have more room." They moved to a table in front of the windows looking out onto Main Street. She addressed Neil, her chin in her hands.

"It was my idea to ask you to be here today. It's not really that we have need of an attorney, I think rather a referee. I need someone sane about me, when I am engaged in conversation with Drew."

Not offended in the least, Drew laughed. "Awh, Mick, that's so completely unfair."

Brid ignored him. "We need to get started. We only have about an hour. Da's over at McKenna's for Margaret Callahan's wake." She reached into her purse and pulled out a pack of Marlboros and took out a cigarette. As she groped for her lighter, Drew took his own from his pocket and lit her cigarette. Their eyes met and held. Brid took a drag on her cigarette and Drew snapped the lighter shut.

"Look around you, Neil, the place is dying," Drew said. "Even I don't come in here that often and when I do, the bar is empty. Like this." He paused to light his own cigarette. "It seems our little student here," he grinned at Brid, "has a grand plan for the old place."

If Drew's sarcasm bothered her, Brid didn't react to it. She opened a leather portfolio and removed a neatly printed document. By reading upside down, a trick he learned in law school, Neil read the title: Business Plan for Refurbishing Craic. She placed a set of architect's drawings on the table next to the business plan.

"I decided to use renovating the bar as the final project for my MBA. As much as I hate to agree with Drew, the bar is dying. I am afraid if we don't get some customers in here soon, Da will die right along with the wretched place."

"I'm amazed that Des hasn't been offered a fortune for it. It's a prime piece of real estate located here on the corner of Dock and Main Street," Neil said.

"Ah, but you see, that's the curse of it, he has." Brid shook her head. "Da, of course, says, he'll never sell. 'It's carrying me out they'll be, feet first.'" Her imitation of her father was uncanny.

"Come on, Neil, where the hell would he go? To Florida to play golf? Des?" Drew stubbed out his cigarette in the ashtray in front of him. "Or better yet, back to the 'auld sod' to sit in some thatched hut and piss in the back yard?"

"My God, Drew, you're a bigot! Ireland is a beautiful country and not everyone pisses in the damn yard." Brid sighed. "But you're right. Much as it pains me to admit it. There's nothing

left in Ireland for Da. His home is here." She looked around her glumly. "Unfortunately, right here."

For the next twenty minutes, the two men silently sipped their drinks while Brid outlined her plans. The bar would be completely remodeled, saving only the actual oak bar itself and "the damn pictures on the wall because Da will never part with them." She proposed a full service dining room along with the bar. When she finished her pitch, she waited for their reaction.

"Sounds like a solid plan. Given the location and the gentrification this neighborhood is undergoing, I think you've got a great chance of it being a success." Neil smiled at her encouragingly. Preening slightly, she smiled back.

Drew picked up the business plan from the table and flipped through to the last page. "You got an A, on this? I'd have given you a B." He handed it back to her.

"You're such a conceited bastard, Drew. Who asked you to grade me?"

"I thought you wanted my help, but if you don't..." Drew reached for his lighter and cigarettes and prepared to stand up.

"All right," she said, exasperation lacing her voice. "What's wrong with it?"

"You tell me. What's the hook?"

"Hook? What the hell are you blathering about, MacCullough?"

Drew raised his hand and signaled to the bartender for a refill. By Neil's count, it was Drew's fourth cognac. "Why do I come here? I mean, why choose Craic instead of the Inn, Les Haricot, or Poppies?" Drew waited for her answer.

Brid wrinkled her nose in concentration. "Oh. You mean what's the draw?" She tapped her pencil on the table. "The food, the atmosphere, what you would no doubt call, 'the ambiance', Da?" She waited for his reaction.

Drew smiled. "Well, you get one right." Removing a gold pen from his breast pocket, he turned the business plan over and began to write. "To make this place fly, it has to be unique. We start with Des." He grinned at them both, like a small boy about to embark on an adventure. "The old reprobate will love it. Then, we cut the size of the dining room in half. You make your money on the bar, not the food service. The trick is to fill the bar by making the customers yearn to get into that exclusive, reservations only, dining room so they, too, can enjoy the new Irish cuisine."

Printing neatly on the back of Brid's business plan, Drew itemized his ideas: exclusive dining room, two dinner seatings, the freshest food going far beyond potatoes and cabbage, Irish linen tablecloths, a harpist, the servers to be men only, dressed in black tie, the finest wines served in Waterford crystal. At this last, Brid could no longer contain herself.

"You're mad! Who do you think is going to wash the Waterford? It can't go in the dishwasher. Little old ladies are the only ones with the patience to take care of that stuff."

"Ah, Mick, and to think we couldn't get along. Those are my thoughts exactly. Rosie's friends would love to do it. After church in the morning, they come in and have a cup a tea and wash the crystal. It would give them a renewed purpose in life and some money to play the Megabucks. We can get Agnes Hurley and Mary Maher to do it."

Brid shook her head in disbelief. "And you think the Board of Health is going to go along with that?" Drew smiled and took a sip of cognac.

By this time, Neil, too, had switched to coffee, without the cognac. "How do you plan to finance the place?" he asked.

"My mother left me some money. For the rest, I'll have to take a second mortgage."

"Your mother will turn in her grave if you put that money into this place. She wanted you to have that so you could get away from all this," Neil said. "I know because she told me so when she made her will."

"She would be a fine one to talk." Reaching for Drew's lighter, Brid lit another cigarette, and sat for a moment lost in thought.

"*She put her life into this place. I'm only doing what she taught me to do – keeping Da afloat without him knowing it.*"

"*No second mortgage, Mick.*" *Drew removed a checkbook from the inside pocket of his jacket and pushed it across the table toward her. "There's over a hundred and fifty thousand dollars in this account. It should cover what you need." Brid stared at him, speechless. She opened the checkbook. The names on the checks were: Andrew R. MacCullough and Brid M. Sheerin. She held the checkbook out for Neil to read.*

"*You never closed this account?" she asked, in amazement.*

"*No. As I said, there's over a hundred and fifty thousand dollars in there. I put it in there the day we signed our divorce papers. It's yours. It's always been yours. Use it. However, I do have one condition. I don't want anyone besides Neil to know where it came from.*"

She had wanted nothing but her car, her clothes, and her paintings, refusing any money. Neil remembered they had fought bitterly over a small self-portrait she had given Drew as a birthday gift. If his memory wasn't faulty, Drew prevailed and kept the painting. Neil wondered where that picture was now, hardly imagining it being cherished by the second Mrs. MacCullough. Concerned about the legal ramifications of the deal, he said, "I'm not sure–"

"*Shut up, Malone. You're not here as an officer of the court. You heard her. She wanted you here as a referee." Drew looked across the table at Brid, all levity gone. "Don't be a fool, Brid. Take the damn money. Leave the note on the place, as it is. You don't need to add to it.*"

Brid took a deep breath and let it out slowly, her fingers reluctantly closing over the checkbook. "I'll do it, but I have one condition, too." She turned to Neil. "You're a witness to this. When Da goes, the bloody place is yours, Drew, including the Waterford crystal."

"*Let's not worry about that right now. Besides, the last time I saw your father, he didn't look like he was in a hurry to give Jerry McKenna any business. On second thought, I do have one other condition." Drew's eyes twinkled at her. "Make sure that the Waterford pattern is 'Colleen.'"*

"I hate that pattern and you damn well know it."

"It'll all be part of the spin, Mick. Charming widower Desmond Sheerin, rebuilding the place after mourning these last few years for his dead wife, Rosemary, his beautiful daughter, Brid, as lovely a colleen as you will find in all of Ireland, at his side, the crystal pattern chosen in her honor. I can see the write up in the Lynton Style pages of The Ledger now." Drew grinned at her. "It's called marketing. Remember that's what I do for a living. And I am damn good at it."

Brid stood, returning the business plan and drawings to her portfolio. "I need to go. Da will be back soon. I don't want him to know that this is my idea. You're the one who is going to have to sell this to him." She turned toward the bartender. "Tommy, you haven't seen me in here today, right?"

"Sure, Brid. Not a word to Himself." Tommy winked at her.

"Leave it to me. I can sell anything, when I put my mind to it." Drew tipped his glass towards her.

"Yes, I know, especially to Da. Thank you for your help. I really do appreciate it." Brid turned to Neil. "Good-bye, Neil. It was so nice to see you." She kissed him on the cheek. Before he could reply, she was out the door.

"She never changes," Drew said, slurring his words slightly, raising his empty glass to indicate he was ready for a refill as he gazed toward the door Brid had disappeared through. Neil decided not to point out to him that she wasn't the one who never changed.

"I hope you haven't been waiting long? It seems to take me forever to get myself out of the house." Pulling his thoughts back from the past, Neil focused on Franny, who was standing next to him. He rose to his feet, trying to decide if he should hug her or shake her hand. His social instincts were usually sound, coming as he did from a race of backslappers and baby kissers, but there was something about this woman that unnerved him. He settled on taking her elbow and gently steering her toward the hallway leading to the Snug. The Snug had been Brid's idea. In the old days, bars in Ireland had a room where the ladies could drink in private, sequestered away from the men. Drew had been delighted with the idea.

At Craic, the Snug contained seven groupings of tables surrounded by high back wing chairs, upholstered in supple leather and rich damask stripes that enhanced the sense of being away from both the bar and the dining room. A gas fireplace glowed invitingly in the corner. A portrait of Constance Gore-Booth, Countess Markievicz, painted on a whim by Brid hung on the wall. "A snug was for the women wasn't it? Let's put one up on the wall worth looking at," she said of the woman who was second in command on St. Stephan's Green the day of the Easter Rising. If you knew to look for it, you would find the block lettered, Sheerin, blended into the lower right corner of the painting. At this time of night, people were seated in the dining room or drinking in the bar and the room was empty, as Neil hoped it would be.

"I thought we would have dinner in here tonight, if that is okay with you." He selected a table near the warmth of the fire.

"In here? I didn't know that they served dinner in this room, only appetizers." Franny dropped wearily into the chair he held out for her.

"They don't as a rule, but as the Irish say, I had a word with Des."

She laughed. "Of course you did. I keep forgetting that you're like Drew, one of them."

Neil caught a hint of bitterness in her voice. "Maybe I should have chosen another place. We could go to the Inn if you would be more comfortable."

She seemed confused for a moment. "Oh, you mean because of Drew's relationship to the Sheerins? You are too late for that. We came here all the time." She smiled and it transformed her face. "Drew loved this place. It was his favorite place to eat. Although we never did eat dinner in here," she looked around the room. "I'm not sure it ever crossed his mind. He loved to come in here for after dinner drinks and coffee." Des walked into the room carrying two menus and a basket of Irish brown bread. Neil rose to take the old man's hand.

"Ah, now don't be getting up, Neil." Solicitously, Des turned to Franny. "Mrs. MacCullough, how're you coming along? I'm sure that you're missing him. I can only tell you when I lost my Rosemary – God rest her soul – it took a long time for me to be able to turn my face forward. Neil can tell you that's the truth of it." He handed them each a menu. "We have a lovely baked stuffed lobster in a whiskey cream sauce as the evening specialty. We call it Lobster Uisce Beatha." He winked at Franny. "*Uisce Beatha* is Irish for whiskey. Literally translated it means the 'water of life.' I'm afraid that's what it is for far too many of the Irish."

To Des's delight, Franny ordered the lobster. Neil had the beef tenderloin. As they waited for their dinners, she steadily ate the warm brown bread from the basket Des had placed in front of them. For the first time since she had arrived, Neil took a close look at her. He was startled at the changes that were apparent since he had seen her in the office for the reading of Drew's will. Her features seemed blurred and her figure thicker. She had never been a small woman, but it was clear even to him, never the most observant of men where a woman's appearance was concerned, that she was gaining weight. "How are you really?"

She finished eating the piece of bread in her hand before she answered him. "I suppose Sofia told you about Lorie."

She went silent as the waiter arrived with their dinners. Neil tested the wine Des sent to the table with his compliments. Assured that it was excellent, the waiter left them to enjoy their meals.

"I warned you to stay away from Lorie Derouin. This is hard enough for you without having to deal with her fantasies about Drew."

Franny went on as though he had not spoken, her brown eyes accentuated by the dark circles under them. "She told me that you knew about them, that you knew they were having an affair." Franny paused to eat a piece of lobster swimming in the whiskey-flavored cream sauce. "She said you were the only one Drew talked to about it. He said Harry couldn't keep his mouth shut, so of course, it would have been you. Lorie said that she talked to you about it at the wake." Neil took a sip of wine, studying her, knowing the importance of how he answered her. "She did speak to me at Drew's wake. It was nonsense – utter nonsense. I paid no attention to her, and nor should you."

Franny said nothing. It was clear from her stony expression that she was not convinced by his argument.

Speaking slowly to make his point, he continued, "Lorie Derouin is living in a fantasy, Franny. Death does that to some people. Believe me; in my business, we see it all the time." He watched as she reached for another piece of brown bread, spreading the soft creamy butter across the top like nothing was more important than covering the bread with the butter. He continued to press his point. "For God's sake, the woman is obviously unstable. Look at this obsession with angels. It doesn't take a shrink to see that Drew's death has unhinged her."

Franny remained silent; her eyes wandering around the room until they came to rest on the portrait of Countess Marki-evicz. "She painted that you know."

"Who? Painted what?" Neil asked, blinking in confusion at the abrupt turn in the conversation.

"That portrait. Of that woman who fought in the Easter Rising. Brid Sheerin, she painted it." Franny sighed. "Drew told me that she painted it."

He was nonplussed. Cautiously, he asked her, "I thought we were discussing Lorie?"

Her eyes drifted back to him. "I thought if Drew ever cheated on me, it would be with Brid, or some sexy Harvard MBA. Not someone like Lorie." Her shoulders shook as she began to sob.

Neil, never at his best around crying women, was at a loss for words. Awkwardly, he reached across the table and took her hand. "Look at me, Franny." When she refused to meet his gaze, he repeated himself, more sternly, "Look at me."

Slowly, she raised her brimming eyes to meet his. "I thought losing him was the worst thing that could happen to me. But I was wrong. Not knowing if he loved me is tearing me apart. Please tell me," she begged him. "I know that you know the truth. Drew told you everything. I know that he did." Her voice dropped to a whisper. "I have to know if he loved me." She gripped his hands with more strength than he would have thought she possessed.

"You saved him, Franny. When he met you, he was killing himself, drinking himself to death and you saved him. You gave him something to live for."

"Please tell me the truth, did he ever tell you he was having an affair with Lorie Derouin?"

"Drew loved you. I swear to you on my mother's grave. He never mentioned Lorie Derouin's name to me."

CHAPTER 16

B rid sat in the corner of her bedroom that she used for her office, squinting at the computer screen. Stretching for a moment, she shifted in her chair and made a conscious effort to refocus her tired eyes as she looked again at the liquor inventory for the restaurant. Compared to last year, there was a notable increase in the bottles of vodka and gin the bar was using. Martinis, she supposed. The GenXers drank these drinks that they called "tinis" like water. They had better be careful, she thought as she stood to execute a yoga twist, or they might find themselves flat on their asses.

Martinis could be lethal. She had never liked them. Her drink of choice would be beer, the darker the better. If I were still choosing, she thought regretfully. "At heart, you remain an Irish peasant," Drew had told her. He, on the other hand, she grimaced at the memory, loved martinis. He usually drank single malt scotch, but when he started drinking with the sole purpose of getting drunk, he relied on martinis to do the job. Martins, he had called them, like he was talking about an old friend. Thinking about it, she realized he was. God knows she had seen him flat on his ass after drinking them.

She curled her bare feet under the rungs of her chair and picked up the pack of Marlboros next to her laptop. She tapped a cigarette out, studying it for a moment before running it under her nose and taking a long sniff. God, it smelled good. Holding it over the ashtray, she broke the cigarette into three pieces, shredding each onto the pile of tobacco that was already there. I'm winning, she told herself smugly. She regretted that she had started smoking again the night Drew died, but she had reached the point where she was shredding more cigarettes than she smoked.

Getting up from her chair, she moved restlessly over to the windows overlooking the snow-covered garden. The shrouded bushes appeared almost spectral hidden in the shadows created by the soft light spilling out from the back of the house. Her reflection stared back at her from the cold glass of the window. She felt empty as if Drew had taken a part of her with him.

Why do I feel like a great hole has been torn in the fabric of my life?

She had rarely seen him. His disastrous visit last October was the first time he had ever shown up at her door. He had come into the gallery only once, the first year she was open. She remembered that he bought a pale blue shawl for his sister. Knowing Cynthia, Brid doubted she would like it and told him so. He, of course, had delighted in telling her she was wrong. Every so often they exchanged terse e-mail regarding the bar or Des, who Drew made a point of keeping track of, but that was it. He had not been a part of her life. And yet, she felt bereft.

Bereft, she thought, shaking her head, an old-fashioned word to be sure, but there it was. It was how she felt. Next to her, the phone rang. She looked down at her watch. It was almost midnight. Da, she thought. Des often felt chatty at this time of night and depending on who was sitting at the bar, he sometimes called to talk.

"Hello." She answered not bothering to see who it was. She wished for the second time she had that cigarette, sure she would be stuck listening to him go on for a while.

"You win, Brid. But you always do. Prettiest, sexiest, smartest, best in bed, and now best able to cope with his death. You are clearly the winner." The words were thick and sounded like it cost the speaker something to say them.

"Who is this?" Brid demanded, trying to place the voice.

"I can't do this. Do you hear me? I can't live without him." The speaker's tone became insistent. "Do you hear me? I can't do this! You win again, always the better wife."

"Franny!" Understanding dawned on Brid.

On the other end of the phone, Franny began to cry. "There's no point to anything anymore. Everything I believed was a lie. It was all lies. Everything he ever told me was a lie." Her voice sounded flat, her words slurred. Suddenly, like the unexpected flare of a match in the dark, Brid heard the rage. "I won't live without him."

"What have you done? Have you taken something?"

"I decided this time I would be the one to get drunk. And it doesn't help. It doesn't help," Franny wailed. "I want to die."

"NO YOU BLEEDIN' WELL DO NOT!"

"I have some pills."

"Franny! Listen to me! Don't be stupid." Brid waited and when no answer came from the phone, she exploded. "Don't touch the pills! I'll be there as soon as I can."

"It doesn't matter, Brid. Nothing matters. Not anymore." There was a click followed by the persistent drone of the dial tone.

Brid's hands shook as she punched in the number for directory assistance on her phone. Impatiently, she listened to the automated voice ask its questions. "Malone. Neil F. Malone," she snapped into the phone. Her heart began to slow down as the number began ringing. Despite the time, he answered on the second ring.

"Neil Malone." He sounded the same as always did, pleasant and completely in control. She had a ludicrous vision of him, lying fully clothed on top of his bed dressed in a tweed jacket and one of his conservative ties with his shiny brown brogues neatly tied, toes pointing up at the ceiling.

"Neil, it's Brid. Meet me at Drew's. Franny just called and there's a problem." This last was muffled, as she bent over to pull on her boots.

"She called you? Now? In the name of God, why?"

"She's in trouble. I am afraid that she's going to kill herself. Just get over there." She slammed the phone down, wrapped herself in her cape, and was out the door.

The temperature was in the twenties and the roads were slick when she turned the Jeep up the long driveway leading to the MacCullough house. She found it easily because Drew had told her once that it was a stone's throw from the historic old forge for which the town was named. The wheels spun for a moment and slipped free as she gunned the engine up the slight incline in front of the garage. The house was dark with the exception of a single light in one of the upstairs rooms.

Inside, she could hear the dogs barking hysterically. Of course, there would be dogs. He couldn't live without a damn dog, she thought, as she opened the screen door leading to the porch. The dogs hurled themselves at the door leading from the porch into the house, their frenzy increased by her presence. She rang the bell and waited. No one appeared to let her in or to quiet the dogs. She tried the door, not surprised to find it locked.

"When you want to hide something, Mick, put it in plain sight." How many times had Drew told her that? Where then, had he hidden the damned key? Her eyes scanned the porch: oak table, white wicker chaise and rocker, an empty planter, and on the door, forgotten after the sad Christmas this house had endured, a Santa holding a brown burlap sack. There, nonchalantly nestled between a candy cane and a miniature teddy bear, the bronze tip of a house key.

Cautiously, she opened the door to be greeted by what at first glance appeared to be a pack of wild dogs. It was only after she curtly told them, "Stay back!" and then ordered them into a down/stay that they sorted themselves out into a grinning black Lab and a liver and white Springer spaniel who stared up at her reproachfully. People assumed that she was afraid of dogs. They were wrong; she wasn't. She knew that Drew would never keep a dog that was vicious and that any dog he owned would have been trained to follow obedience commands.

"Stay," she reminded them again. The dogs didn't move as she crossed the threshold into the kitchen but she sensed them watching her in the dark.

She groped along the wall nearest to the door until she found the panel of light switches. Light flooded the room and her jaw dropped as her eyes took in the chaos surrounding her. She was standing in a gourmet kitchen with cherry cabinets and black granite counter tops that were almost completely covered with dirty dishes and pans. Scattered among the dishes were several empty containers of Brigham's ice cream and bags of Hersey's kisses. The pan nearest to her held the crusted remains of what appeared to be macaroni and cheese. A large bag of dog food sat in the middle of the granite island, pushed back out of the dogs' reach. The dogs whined but didn't move. She began to make her way through the house calling Franny's name.

"Franny? It's Brid. Where are you?" She ran up the stairs in search of the light she could see visible at the top. Following the glow to the master bedroom, she stopped. A sense of relief flooded her as her eyes met those of Franny MacCullough. Distraught, as the younger woman obviously was, she was not lying unconscious. She was not dead. Thanks be to God, Brid thought automatically.

"I can't believe that you actually came." Franny spoke slowly, slurring her words. Taking a closer look, Brid saw that Drew's widow was drunk. A half-empty quart of scotch lay abandoned next to her. A brown pharmacy bottle stood on the night table next to the bed.

"You called me, remember?"

Franny said nothing, continuing to stare drunkenly at her guest.

"What in hell has been going on here? Those poor dogs are frantic." Franny flinched, a guilty look passing over her face.

"I've been feeding them and I made sure that they had fresh water. They've spent a lot of time in bed here with me. I haven't had the energy to walk them much this week."

"Well, they seem pretty upset. I think they know that something's wrong." Moving slowly, so as not to startle her, Brid edged over to the nightstand. Her fingers closed over the bottle of pills, which appeared to be full.

"Those are mine." Franny reached her hand out for the bottle.

"So they are." She answered, squinting at the prescription on the front of the bottle made out to Francesca MacCullough: Nortriptyline, 50mg. To be taken in the morning and the evening.

A heavy car crunched its way up the icy driveway and came to a stop.

"You didn't call the police?" For the first time, Franny seemed worried.

"I called Neil," Brid answered, relieved to hear the slam of the car door.

Franny smiled that endearing, lopsided grin common to drunks. "Sweet Neil to the rescue. Like Drew always said he would."

"I'd better go down and rescue him from those dogs."

Turning to leave the room, Brid slipped the bottle of Nortriptyline into the pocket of her cape.

She found Neil peering through the door at the dogs leaping at the pane of glass. "I thought I told you," she said to the dogs, "Down." At this, both dogs dropped to the floor. She unlocked the door and Neil stepped into the kitchen.

"Hello, Oliver and you, too, Lucy," he said politely. Lucy searched for something to present to him as a gift. Finding one of her toys, she returned his greeting. He nodded toward Brid. "Brid."

"Thanks for coming. I'm going to need your help."

"She's okay?"

"She's drunker than a tinker, but otherwise she seems okay."

He gave her his lawyer look. "You told me that she was going to kill herself. We can't take that lightly."

"I understand that. But I think what she really is and doesn't quite know it yet, is angry. So angry, that she could set herself ablaze with it." Brid shrugged. "It's a feeling I'm familiar with where Drew MacCullough is concerned." She stood aside so that Neil could enter the kitchen.

"Sweet Mother of God!" He said, whistling softly as his eyes took in the room. "What was she trying to do? Drown herself in food?"

"So it would seem." Brid picked up an empty ice cream container. "Death by pistachio nut. I can think of worse ends."

"Should we take her to the hospital?"

"No, I don't think she needs that. She didn't take any pills. She's only drunk and I'm the living proof that it doesn't kill you that quickly." She laughed as she made this small joke on herself. "We'll take her to my place to sleep it off. I think she needs to get away from here for a night. I can go in late in the morning. I'll see how she is then. But before we leave, I'm going to try and get her into the shower, if I can. I don't think she's been out of bed except to come down here and eat in days."

Neil looked down at the dogs. "I'll let these two out in yard while you're doing that." The dogs looked at him expectantly, Lucy's tail thumped on the floor.

Franny was close to passing out when Brid returned to the bedroom. She made no effort to resist as Brid pulled her to her feet. Removing her boots, and tossing her cape on the bed, Brid maneuvered Franny toward the bathroom. Bracing the younger woman, she pulled the food-stained nightgown, stinking of stale sweat and spilled Scotch, over Franny's head.

"Leave me alone! I don't want to take a shower. I want to go to sleep."

"You stink. It's disgusting. You need a shower."

Brid was none too gentle as she guided Franny through the door into the spacious bathroom. A Jacuzzi large enough for two people, surrounded by candles, stood under the window. She steered Franny backwards toward the corner shower. Keeping one hand on Franny's shoulder to make sure she stayed upright, Brid reached beyond her to turn the water on in the shower. After testing it to make sure it was not too hot, she pushed Franny in, not quite stepping in behind her. Franny sputtered in outrage but she picked up the bar of soap in front of her. When she stepped out of the shower ten minutes later, Brid wrapped her in a thick terry cloth robe she found hanging on the door. Drew's. The smell of Polo still clung to it.

As Franny stumbled into clean clothes, Brid, dressed once again, hastily packed a small canvas bag hanging from a hook in the closet with what she thought Franny would need in the morning. Franny was clearly feeling the effects of the Scotch despite having been momentarily revived by the shower. She swayed precariously as she stood up.

"Neil? I need your help up here." Moments later, he appeared in the bedroom door.

Franny smiled tearfully at him.

"Drew promised me you would take care of me, Neil. You – not her," she said, scowling at Brid.

Cautiously, they made their way down the stairs in an awkward shuffle that had Franny sandwiched between Neil in the front and Brid in the rear. They paused in the now clean kitchen, the dishwasher humming, to figure out the best way to get Franny back to Lynton.

"I can't believe you cleaned this up so fast." Brid said, looking around her.

"It went pretty quickly. I tossed most of it into garbage bags. The pans were the worst. I left a couple soaking." Neil said, indicating two pots full of soapy water in the sink.

"You're a saint," she said admiring the gleaming kitchen.

"Franny, you ride with Neil, and I will follow with the dogs."

Neil opened the garage door and the dogs rushed in circling Franny in their excitement. She dropped to her knees pulling them into a hug. Neil hooked a leash to each dog's collar and helped Franny to her feet. "Okay. Shall we go?"

"You be good, Thomas. I know you're not hungry. I put lots of food in your dish this morning." Franny told the cat who had materialized from somewhere and eyed them all reproachfully.

Franny slipped into the front seat of the Mercedes as Neil held open the door for her. Closing it firmly, he asked Brid. "You're sure that you want to bring the dogs?"

"I don't believe you want them in your car, do you?"

"Well, no, not really," he hedged, "but why don't we leave them here? They'll be okay for one night."

"No," she said, looking down at the dogs waiting patiently at their feet. "They've had a terrible time. You can see how anxious they are by looking at them. If we leave them, they'll feel abandoned for sure, especially since Drew has just disappeared. It's not like they can hurt my car now is it?"

Looking at her battered Jeep, front bumper slightly askew, door panels bubbly with rust, parked in front of his Mercedes, he answered. "No, I can't say they'll do much damage, at that."

Brid followed the Mercedes back to Lynton. Oliver was curled on the rear seat in a tight brown and white ball, but Lucy sat with her black nose lodged firmly against the back of Brid's neck. The smell of dog and the sound of Lucy's panting brought back the memory of another dog on an icy road.

They were on their way to the Holly Ball held ever year at the Lynton Country Club. Brid was in a rage as she told Drew the comment his mother had made earlier in the day about the way she dressed. He laughed it off, which inflamed her even more.

"Did you hear me, you bastard?" Flawlessly mimicking her mother-in-law's Smith College articulation, "She said, 'I do hope that you will buy a suitable frock for the Holly Ball, my dear. You look like one of those Irish gypsies – I can never remember what they are called – whenever you go out. I would think my darling son would be mortified. You have to think of Drew and try not to embarrass him.' She actually called it a frock! Do you believe that? A feckin' frock!"

"Why do you listen to my mother? How many times have I told you that she lives in her own world? By the way, her darling son thinks you look very fetching in your feckin' frock. He wouldn't mind feckin' you in it." Grinning, he mimicked her Irish accent, pleased with his cleverness.

Out of nowhere, in a blur, an animal appeared in front of them racing across the road, the car clipping it with a sickening thud. "Damn! I think I hit a dog!" Drew said and stopped the car at the side of the road, its headlights revealing a large black dog, struggling without success to stand. Drew was out of the car before Brid could say a word. She watched him squat next to the injured animal. He unwound the white cashmere scarf from around his neck and gently wrapped it around the dog's muzzle. Removing his camel hair topcoat, he draped it over the dog like a blanket.

"You drive. I'll hold the dog," he called to her over his shoulder. Obediently, she moved into the driver's seat.

Drew gathered the limp dog in his arms, the blood in sharp contrast to the snowy white of his formal shirt and scarf. Rising to his feet, he staggered slightly from the dog's weight, before catching his balance. "It's okay, pup. You're going to be fine." Drew comforted the whimpering animal. Much to his mother's annoyance, they never made it to the Holly Ball. After leaving the dog at the emergency vet, they opted instead for a bottle of brandy in front of a roaring fire to which Brid wore nothing – nothing at all.

Up ahead, the stoplight changed from green to red. Brid's eyes registered the change, but it was another second before her brain grasped the facts that she had to stop and that she was driving too fast. Instinctively, her foot stomped on the brake pedal. The car skidded to a halt with a loud squeal of tires. Lucy hit the back of the seat, her nose driving Brid's head forward.

There was a startled yelp from Oliver who suddenly found himself on his back on the floor. After a wild thrashing of legs, he righted himself and scrambled back onto the seat. When he saw Brid looking at him in the mirror, he gave her an indignant "woof."

"Not as mad at me as you were the last time I was here?" Neil smiled at Brid after they had tucked Franny into her bed.

"Hardly." Yawning, she stretched, arching her back like a cat. "I couldn't have managed without you tonight. I really appreciate you giving up a night's sleep."

Neil glanced down at his watch. "Ten after three. It's almost not worth going to bed." He laughed. "I wouldn't have thought anything of it once. But now, I think I'll go home and steal a cat-nap before mass." Opening the door, he started to leave.

"I don't suppose you're going to tell me what she was going on about tonight?"

"Ask her. She called you, not me. Maybe she'll open up to you in the morning. She's having a rough time, and maybe what she needs is an older sister to confide in. I suspect that Sofia has been less than a comfort and rather more of a nag." He hesitated for a moment longer in the door. He smiled, telling Brid, "Get some sleep. I'll give you a call in the morning." He left, quietly closing the door behind him.

Brid stared at the door. "Older sister my, ass, Malone," she muttered at the ludicrous thought.

"She hates me with a passion."

Someone ironed these sheets, Franny thought before she opened her eyes. She spread her fingers and moved them around on the mattress top to absorb more of the crisp, sweet-smelling Egyptian cotton. Her mother ironed sheets along with everything else. Smiling, she remembered the feeling of waking up in her maple spool bed, the twin of the one Sofia lay sleeping in next to her, in the small ranch house on Gosling Road on sheets that felt like these. Things had seemed so simple then, before she met Drew.

Drew's dead. The thought slipped into her brain, dividing time from then to now and from pleasure to pain. I must be getting used to it. It took me at least ninety seconds to remember.

Grudgingly, she opened her eyes. She had no idea where she was. She studied the room in which she had been sleeping. It was a long room with tall multi-paned windows and pale green walls. A scattering of pastel Oriental rugs in various shapes and sizes covered the satiny honey oak floors. The bed in which she slept filled the room, making the statement that one's purpose for being there was either to sleep or to make love. Her eyes fell on a white tee draped over the Bentwood rocker by the window. Emblazoned on the front was the circular Celtic design inlaid in the ceiling over the bar at Craic. Underneath it was written in flowing script: Enjoy the Snug at Craic.

Brid. Sighing, she shut her eyes and let herself sink down into the nest of fat pillows. Slowly, the events of the night before began to replay themselves in Franny's brain with painful clarity. Along with the realization of where she must be and how she must have gotten here came a pounding headache. She needed a drink of water and a bathroom with about the same degree of urgency. The room did not seem to have an attached bath. With a growing sense of dread, she realized that she had no choice but to venture outside its refuge in search of one.

There was a stabbing pain behind her left temple as she stood up and reached for her bathrobe which someone – Brid? – had left on the end of the bed. Gingerly, she made her way out the door and down the hall. She paused briefly to admire the photographs hung gallery style along the white walls, until she found herself in the living room.

"And how are you feeling this morning?" a voice asked, making her jump.

She turned as rapidly as her pounding head would allow and saw Brid dressed in a yoga pants and a tee shirt, lying on a mat on the floor in front of a large carousel horse. She had been hidden by the sofa. Her arms were stretched out from her shoulders and her legs were bent up toward her body, the soles of her feet touching.

"Yoga." She replied to Franny's unspoken question. "It helps keep my damned blood pressure down. It seems I've a foul temper." She grinned impishly. "This pose is called the Goddess, although I never feel like one when I'm laid out like this." She unfolded herself into a sitting position. "You'll be wanting the bathroom. You've passed it there on your left."

When Franny returned to the living room, Brid handed her a glass of milk and three aspirin tablets. Her stomach lurched.

"I can't drink this. It will come right up."

"That's what these are for," Brid said, reaching for a small plate with crackers on it. "Trust me. My family has been in the business of drinking too much since before you were born. Ma swore by this. And from the look of you, you could use it."

Reluctantly, Franny drank the glass of milk Brid held out to her, gagging slightly as she swallowed the aspirin. From somewhere behind her she heard a low whine, both plaintive and familiar. Turning, her gaze met the four watchful eyes of her dogs. They lay with their noses on the threshold of the oak floor that defined the kitchen from the living room, having obviously been forbidden to enter.

"Oh, you've brought my dogs." Dropping to her knees she opened her arms and called them. The dogs whined, but didn't move, their watchful gaze on Brid.

"Okay." Brid said, releasing them to race across the room into Franny's outstretched arms, the spaniel's head thrown back, joyously woo-wooing as he went. Brid watched them, an indistinguishable bundle of brown hair, arms, legs, and tails rolling on the floor.

"I thought you hated dogs?" Franny asked. The pair in question was now happily glued one on either side of her.

Brid snorted. "Ah yes, 'The Gospel According to Drew MacCullough.' I believe there is a chapter entitled, 'Brid Hates Dogs.'"

Franny hesitated. Brid had driven through the cold winter night to bring not only her, but also Oliver and Lucy to her home. Would she…could she have done the same had their situations been reversed? She chose her words carefully. "He made it sound like you hated the dog you two owned together."

"I finally came to understand that Drew created pictures with words the same way I do with paints. When I am painting and I want to leave out a particularly ugly tree, or building, or even a person, I do. If I want to make something beautiful when in fact it isn't, I do. Drew was like that with facts. I believe he invented his own reality." She reached for the pack of Marlboros and popped a cigarette into her hand. She walked over and opened the door to the deck. Lighting the cigarette, she took a puff, blowing the smoke outside and said, "It's a filthy habit." Holding the lit cigarette behind her, she answered Franny's question.

"I'm sure he has told you this story. He bought me a dog the first Christmas we were married. He decided I needed an Irish wolfhound." Shaking her head, she took another drag, "Home the fool comes, drunker than a lord, with a puppy the size of your Lab, a big red bow around his neck. Talking about how every Irish bog maiden needed a wolfhound. Drew named him Boru, for Brian Boru, the Irish King. We lived in a third floor walkup in Somerville. I was in school and working part-time and Drew was traveling constantly in his job. To make a long story short, we gave him to the owner of the gallery where I worked. The guy had a big place in Beverly Farms. The dog loved it – the place, the two kids, and the wife who, by the way, was home during the day. He lived out his life there happier than he ever would have been with us. Drew never forgave me, hence: Brid hates dogs."

She stubbed out the cigarette in the ashtray that was sitting outside the door on the deck. "I know what I can and what I cannot do. Drew never understood that, I suppose, because he believed that he could do anything." She reached for her sweatshirt hanging from a coat tree by the door. "Get dressed. When you're ready, I'll drive you home."

Franny was quiet on the drive to Hiram's Forge. As they turned onto the exit that led to the village center, she asked suddenly, "Did Neil tell you what happened?" She waited.

"You would be more likely to get information from one of the stiffs at McKenna's than from Neil Malone. Mind you, when Neil does tell you something pay very close attention to the words he uses to tell you."

Franny absorbed this information without comment. "The woman who was the lead graphic designer at Chayne told me that she and Drew had an affair. Her name is Lorie Derouin." She took a ragged breath and seemed to steel herself to continue. "She told me that he loved her."

Brid said nothing. She made the turn into the MacCullough's driveway, parking by the porch door. "You need to call whomever it was that prescribed those pills for you. I think it would help you to talk to someone who understands the impact of dealing with the kind of stress you've been under."

Franny climbed out of the car and opened the rear door, releasing the two dogs who immediately charged off after a squirrel. "I don't know how to thank you for last night. I feel ridiculous. I don't expect you to believe me, but—"

"Please, you don't have to thank me. A lot of people reached out a hand to me when I needed it. I'm glad that I was able to do the same for you. Promise me you'll call your doctor."

"Yes, I'll call him. Thank you again." Franny was reluctant to end the conversation.

"Do you think that Lorie was telling the truth? Do you think that they were lovers?"

For a moment, Brid didn't answer. Then, pushing in the clutch, she shifted the Jeep into reverse. She licked her lips and said, "Yes, I do."

Franny nodded without a word and shut the car door.

CHAPTER 17

Standing in the crowded workroom behind the main gallery, Brid unpacked a crate of paintings from Grainne Fallon. She gently leaned each painting against the wall behind the long table she used for staging. She picked up and examined each new addition like it was a small treasure, which in a way it was.

Grainne Fallon was one of a group of young artists she had discovered on her last buying trip to Ireland. Grainne worked almost exclusively in watercolors, Brid's own first love. Ironically, it was the medium in which she was least accomplished. She had been told that she was a competent artist in oils by one of her teachers at the Massachusetts College of Art. He had gone on to say, sadly, that, unfortunately, her work had no spark.

No spark, Brid thought, as she studied the small painting in her hand. Grainne's whimsical flock of sheep seemed to be standing on top of each other, so sheer was the hill they were grazing on. The splotches of bright blue paint the farmer used to mark their wooly rumps made them look like a fluffy checkerboard as they clustered together. No one would ever accuse Grainne of having no spark, she thought, as she admired the "Dingle Ewes."

"There's someone here to see you, Brid." Lilah, her assistant, or, as the girl jokingly called herself, "dogsbody" said, lounging languidly in the doorway leading into the gallery. People thought that Brid had hired her for her looks or to be more accurate her "look," which was perfect for working at the gallery. In fact, Brid hired her because she was articulate, smart, and shared Brid's eclectic view of art. She was also a genius at building websites. Looking at the girl leaning against the doorframe, it occurred to Brid that it was possible she had never actually seen Lilah stand up straight. There was a liquid, almost feline quality about her that created the impression that she wound herself around things or melted into them as she did now with the doorframe. Lilah was small in a way that was compact and supple rather than petite. She gave off the slightest hint of menace, her demeanor suggesting that she could handle herself in any situation. This effect was enhanced by the tattoo of a sinewy spotted snake wound around her left calf and disappearing into the top of her black patent leather Doc Martin and by the piercings in her lip and right eyebrow.

"Oh, damn. Be a sweetie and get rid of them, will you?"

Lilah shrugged. "Sure, but she said it was like important. She said to tell you that it was Franny."

Brid almost dropped the painting in her hand. Handing it to Lilah, she entered the gallery to find Franny admiring a display of blue glazed pottery.

"Franny?" Brid's tone was tentative.

"This place is fantastic. I knew it would be. I used to peek in the windows when you were closed." Franny said, carefully placing the bowl she was holding back on the shelf. Brid took in the younger woman's shiny hair and subtle make up. Dressed in pants and a sweater from Ann Taylor, a Coach bag slung over her shoulder, Franny looked like the affluent young suburbanite she was. The drunk, dirty, half-crazed woman might never have been.

"I've wanted to come in here for years." She grinned sheepishly. "But, of course, I couldn't, until now." Until Drew died, the words unspoken hung between them.

"Well, now you've come, and I'm glad." Brid said quickly to fill in the awkward silence.

"I was wondering if you would have dinner with me tonight." When Brid didn't immediately answer, Franny continued in a rush. "What I mean is that I would like to take you to dinner to thank you for what you did the other night."

"Look, you don't have to buy me dinner. I told you I was glad that I was able to help you, thankful, in fact, that you called me before doing something foolish."

"I would really like to have dinner with you. I want to talk to you." Whatever joy was in Franny's face, as she had examined the pottery, was gone, banished by an emptiness emphasized by the shadows under her eyes.

Brid's heart, the same heart that Drew had accused her of not having, went out to Franny. "All right, but I've got to finish a few things before I can leave. Perhaps you would like to look around while you wait?"

"I would love to. Everything is so unique."

"I try. I vowed there would be no shamrock clocks, ceramic Irish cottages, or grinning leprechauns, although Da thinks it's a shame. He says I don't appreciate my Irish heritage. You would be amazed at how many people come in looking for exactly that. I try to showcase the best of what Ireland's contemporary artists have to offer. As you can see, it's both considerable and fine. Can I offer you some tea?"

"Actually, I think that I would like that." Franny said, pointing at the painting that Lilah was holding.

"The Dingle Ewes?" Brid glanced at Lilah, who, sensing a sale, was holding the painting upright on the counter so Franny could get a better look.

"Is that what it's called?" Franny said, laughing. "How absolutely perfect."

"Isn't it? I just unpacked it," Brid agreed, warming to her subject. "It's an original not an artist's proof or a serigraph, so it will be expensive. Grainne Fallon is up and coming and her paintings are highly collectable. Her work will only increase in value. It would be a good investment at that, but not cheap."

"Please tell me how much it is," Franny said, rummaging through her bag, dropping her gloves in her haste, and finally bringing out her checkbook. "I assume you will take a check?"

"You really don't have to buy anything, Franny," Brid said.

"I want the painting, Brid," she said fiercely, softening her voice. "It will be the first positive thing, the first happy thing, I have done in weeks."

"Fine, then. As I said, it's a good investment." Using the calculator on the counter, Brid quickly figured out the markup after paying Grainne. "What do you say to forty-five hundred?"

"I should make the check out to the Sheerin Gallery, right?" Franny asked, setting her purse on the counter so she could write the check. "I have nothing but money, did you know that?" She shook her head. "No, I suppose Neil would never have told you, would he? The woman from HR at Chayne told me I was 'golden.'" She looked at Brid. "Do you believe that? She said, 'Mrs. MacCullough, you're golden.'" Franny handed Brid the check. "I can have anything I want, anything except my husband or my baby."

Brid was at a loss for words to respond to Franny's anguish. "This is for the wrong amount," she said, reading the check with a frown. "You've written it for five thousand."

"I figured you shaved the price. Sort of a 'Wives of Drew MacCullough' discount." She smiled bitterly. "Besides, I can afford it." Seeing no point in arguing, Brid rang up the sale.

"Wrap this for Mrs. MacCullough, Lilah."

While Brid finished unpacking the rest of the paintings, Franny wandered through the gallery. She was engrossed in the case where the jewelry was displayed when Brid appeared at her side.

"Ready to go?"

"You've got such unusual pieces here. They are really exquisite."

"All Irish made, mostly of eighteen carat gold." She pointed out various pieces. "That's by Fiona Mulholland and those two were done by Nuala Jameson. Their work is quite well known in Ireland."

"Do you sell it? I mean, here? In Lynton?"

"Actually, I do. It was a bit of an uphill trot at first, but now people come out regularly from Boston and even New York and there are mail orders from the website that Lilah created. The write up in *Around New England* magazine a few months ago didn't hurt either. Lynton itself is seen as a very "in" place to be. It's one reason Craic is booming. Speaking of Craic, shall we go there for dinner?" She asked, as she hooked the toggle at the neck of her cape.

"Sure, unless you think the shock of the two of us showing up together would be too much for your father."

"Not likely. Da's a tough old bird. They've a new entre there he's been raving about, a salmon dish that Jim Kilbride, the chef, found in a little pub in Connemara on his last trip home. The truth is I rarely go there for dinner. Da will be delighted to see us. Besides, we can eat there for free." She raised her hand, as Franny started to protest. "Ma taught me to seize luck when it presents itself, rare as that is. You'll find plenty of other things to spend your money on."

They walked the four blocks up Main Street to the restaurant, past the specialty boutiques selling clothing, tobacco products, and jewelry. Brid stopped to admire a splashy display of tulips in the big bay window at McGonagles.

"Tulips are survivors," Brid said. "No matter how hard the winter, back they come, in all their glory, year after year. I think that's why I love them."

Tucked between McGonagle's and O'Hanlon's News and Tobacco Shop was a small store front with a "For Rent" sign in the window. "It used to be an antique store," Brid said as they walked past. "But the owner died. His kids had no eye for the business and it went bankrupt."

Suddenly, Franny turned around for another look at the empty store. She felt a strange attraction to it – after all they had a lot in common. Both of them had had the life sucked out of them by death. An idea began to take form in her mind. Why not? She thought, if Brid could give life to an empty building with art, then my dolls could do the same for this one. She grinned, "Come on, I'm starving."

Desmond's jaw dropped as Brid came through the door. When she came, which was not often, it was in the morning before the place was open for business. His expression made it clear that he was even more shocked when Franny came in behind her.

Recovering quickly, he said, "Brid, darlin', how grand to see you." His voice grew serious as he turned to greet Franny. "And you, Mrs. MacCullough, you're looking a bit better, and it is better I'm hoping you are. I admit it's surprised I am to find you girls here together tonight, though."

"Yes, well, 'God is good' as Ma used to say." Brid answered her father, her tone completely devoid of the irony behind her words. "I thought we would slip into the Snug and have a bite."

"Lovely, darlin'. Ronan, set these two pretty girls up for dinner in the Snug," Des called to the waiter standing in the door of the dining room.

They followed Ronan's straight back down the narrow hall and into the Snug. There were three other parties talking and sipping their drinks while waiting to be seated for the early dinner.

"Ronan, I think tonight we might enjoy the privacy of the actual Snug itself," Brid said, as her eyes swept the crowd in the room.

"Ah, there's a treat for you then," he said and led them to the back of the room where he opened a door, the top half consisting of ornately frosted glass to expose a tiny room big enough to comfortably accommodate two people. There was a table in the center and on either side was a small bench with a high back. Set in the wall behind the table was what appeared to be a sliding panel.

"I'll be right back with your table settings."

"Have a seat, Franny," Brid said, indicating the bench opposite her, as she slid onto the one on the left side of the table. Franny obeyed, aware that conversation in the room behind them had momentarily ceased since the two women had stepped through the door in the wall.

"But what is this?" Franny asked looking around her. "Has it always been here? I've never noticed that this was here."

Brid thought, I wonder what you would say if I told you your husband loved this hole in the wall, that it was his idea to incorporate it within the larger Snug. He had flown over and met Neil, who, on vacation in Ireland, had actually found the little room in an abandoned pub in Kinsale scheduled for demolition. Delighted, Drew bought it on the spot and made arrangement to have it crated and sent to New Hampshire.

"This is a real snug taken from a bar that was about to be knocked down in Kinsale. Around the time that Da was restoring this place, Neil decided he needed a trip to Ireland. He found this and a lot of the other things we've used. The truth is not a lot of people know it's here. We include it in the advertising, but most people think that the bigger room is the Snug. I suppose, to be fair, we call it that, and they don't ask to see this. It's a secret. Once or twice, someone who needed a private place to have a conversation and knew it was here has asked Da to eat in here and he has accommodated them. His rules are arbitrary, a holdover from Ireland where the bartender's word is law. It's a wonder he hasn't been sued."

"Well, I know he used to let Drew eat at the bar."

"Yes, Drew and only Drew." Brid said sourly. "And don't you know that a few fights have almost started over that I can tell you." What Brid didn't tell her was that Des's standard answer was, "He's my son."

"This reminds me of a confessional," Franny said, looking around her.

"I will have to take your word for it," Brid chuckled. "It's been a long time since I've seen the inside of one of those. In Ireland, the snug was available to the local priest if he wanted to have a pint in privacy. The women out drinking without a man to protect them also used it." She pointed to the panel in the wall. "If you open the panel, you will see that we are directly behind the bar. The drinker, be it the good Father or some woman who wanted to slip away and have a drink in peace, had only to knock and the bartender would slide the panel open and hand over the drink. The patrons in the bar would be none the wiser."

Ronan returned and quickly laid the table with a heavy Irish linen cloth and the necessary silver and glassware. Ill at ease, he hesitated for a moment watching Brid warily as he spoke.

"I don't suppose you'll be wanting to order a drink then? Will ya?" It was common knowledge in the bar that Brid no longer drank.

"I'll have coffee, black, and not from the pot Da keeps at the bar."

"Ah, it'll put hair on your chest," Ronan said, grinning, relaxed once more.

"Just make sure it comes out of the pot in the kitchen. What would you like to drink, Franny?"

"I'll have a Perrier with lime, thanks."

Franny ordered the small filet mignon, baked potato, and a garden salad. Brid opted for the new salmon dish, asking if it was as good as her father bragged it was.

"Must be," Ronan said, scribbling their orders on his pad. "We can't keep it in the kitchen. Jim's talking about making it a Craic Classic," he said, referring to the list of items Craic was famous for. He closed his order book and pulled the door shut behind him.

"I can't believe that Drew never showed this room to me," Franny said, looking around her. "I thought I had seen everything there was to see. He was so proud of Craic. You would have thought it was his. Maybe he didn't know this was here." Someone in the bar began to play the piano. The music drifted into the small room where they sat. Brid remembered the last time she had been in here with Drew.

Des was playing the piano outside in the bar. Brid had just hung the portrait of Countess Markievicz when she turned to find Drew in the doorway. In his hand was a tumbler of scotch, his fingers caressing the heavy Waterford crystal in the Colleen pattern she had agreed to keep on hand for his personal use. His expression, as he took in the finished room, was triumphant.

"*Come on, Mick, admit it. It's fabulous.*"

"*If it makes any money, then it will be fabulous, MacCullough.*"

"*This will be the hottest dinner reservation in New England by the end of the month. I'll bet my soul on it.*"

"*And who the hell would want it, blackened by a life ill led, such as it is?*" *Not bothering to answer her, Drew wandered around the room, checking to make sure that each of the tables was level. He walked over to the wall and flipped the switch, igniting the gas fireplace. He studied the glowing logs, a frown creasing his handsome face.*

"*I wish we could burn wood or, even better, peat.*"

"*You're mad, stark raving bonkers. Peat stinks. Who do you think wants to pay this kind of money for dinner and smell a peat fire? If they do, they go to Ireland, not Lynton, New Hampshire. Where, come to think of it, if they are paying that kind of money, they will not be subjected to the smell of peat!*" *Not replying to her, he crossed to the back of the room and opened the door into the tiny room behind the bar.*

"*Mick, come over here for a minute.*"

She glanced over her shoulder, looking at the portrait trying to decide if she liked where she hung it, as she joined him at the entrance to the secret Snug. Without warning, he slipped his arms around her waist and swung her around into the small space, depositing her sprawling on top of the table. As she struggled to get up, he pulled the door shut behind him. She could tell that he was figuring something out. She knew that look. Leaning forward, he straddled her, and placed his legs on either side of her own. He gripped her arms with his hands as she twisted to extract herself. His eyes looked into hers. She was struck by the achingly familiar scent that to her would always mean Drew. A combination of his aftershave, still Polo, she observed in some detached part of her brain, cigarettes, and the smoky bite of fine scotch.

"Let me go, you bastard, or I swear to you, I will kick you right in the balls."

"Of course." He dropped his hands from her arms, reached behind him, opened the door, and backed out. Brid scrambled from the table, shooting out of the tiny room like she had been scalded.

"Hey, I only needed to make sure it could be done. Don't flatter yourself, I didn't mean with you."

She was halfway out of the room. Turning, she replied, "You're a pig!" The sound of his laughter followed her out the door.

Laughter coming from the other room jerked her back to the present.

"You know, you could have a drink if you want one." Brid said, quickly to cover her woolgathering. "I don't mind if people drink when they're with me."

Franny laughed. "I'll pass. I know you won't believe this after the other night, but I'm not much of a drinker." She grimaced. "I don't care if I ever have a drink. I'm an eater. Drew said I was addicted to food. When he died, I lost weight, but since then, all I've done is eat."

"How clever of him to have figured all that out for you," Brid said. Franny appeared to miss the sarcasm in her voice. Brid wondered if it was possible that she really didn't have a clue as to what a bastard Drew could be.

"He hated fat women. He would die all over again, if he could see me now," Franny said. "But you, of all people, must know that. He thought you had the greatest body in the world."

Brid snorted. "Except for the small matter of my breasts," she flashed Franny a grin across the table, "no pun intended."

Franny gave her a bewildered look. "I don't understand?"

"Drew hated my breasts. He said it was like making love to a boy, a malnourished one at that. He wanted me to have plastic surgery, to get breast implants." She enjoyed the memory. "I told him to get a pair himself if he was so keen on them."

"But...he told me you were perfect." Franny dropped her voice. "It was right here, at Craic, sitting out there at the bar one night that he told me, 'You'll never be in the same league as Brid.'"

"He told you that?" Brid said. "You should have slapped him." She gave Franny a sympathetic look and asked, "Did he not ever tell you about Leslie Millingham?"

"It was Elaine who told me about Leslie. She pointed her out to me one year at the Holly Ball. She said what a shame it was that Leslie and Drew never made a pair. But I don't think Leslie ever mattered to Drew, it was you," she insisted stubbornly.

"That sounds exactly like Elaine. She is such a witch." Brid reached into her purse and pulled out the pack of Marlboros. She took out a single cigarette, broke it into three pieces, and began to shred it. Franny watched her, fascinated. "I'm trying to quit," Brid said, grinning.

"You really hate his mother don't you?"

"Yes, as a matter of fact," she looked up from the tobacco she was pushing into a neat pile. "I do."

"But...why? I know that she can be very snooty, but really don't you think she's kind of pathetic? I mean," Franny lowered her voice to a conspiratorial level, "I think that she might have a drinking problem."

"She's a drunk," Brid said, incredulously. "I suppose for that I should show her some compassion." She grimaced as her fingers played with the shredded tobacco. "But I can't. Not her. She treated my mother like dirt and for that I'll never forgive the sodden old hag."

Franny seemed surprised. "Elaine? Really? Her mind is so full of her social calendar and what she is going to wear for dinner at the club that I can't imagine her deliberately being cruel to someone. She would have to think about them first, wouldn't she?"

Brid laughed. "Good for you. At least she hasn't completely fooled you. Maybe she's mellowed or drowned a few more brain cells since my time. Let's say that, when I married Drew, she would have done anything to stop it. When that didn't happen, the bitch tried everything she could to end it. She never planned for her precious son to bring home some Irish peasant raised over the local bar." Brid sighed. "Sometimes I think one of the reasons he married me was to stick it to Elaine. You realize that she drove him mad."

"I know he adored you. He told me often enough," Franny said stubbornly.

"Drew MacCullough adored no one except himself." Before Franny could protest, she changed the subject. "What did you want to talk to me about?"

Franny reached into her purse and pulled out a folder and thrust it at Brid.

Brid hesitated before she opened it, dumping a stack of 5 by 7 photographs out on the table, silently flipping through them. She saw that each was a study of the same toddler, a boy. In some of the pictures, he was alone and in others he was either in a group of children or with a tall laughing girl in her early twenties dressed in overalls. The pictures were well done. The photographer had an excellent eye. Each shot was beautifully framed and the resulting images were delightful.

"Where did you get these? They're good pictures. Whose child is this?" Brid asked, frowning at the pictures spread out on the table.

"I took them. Sometimes I do photography. Drew bought me a great camera and I took a course last year at the Art Institute in Manchester. That's Lorie's son," Franny said, pulling the studio portrait of Drew as a child from her purse. The picture had been ripped in half and then painstakingly taped together. She picked up the stack of pictures on the table and flipped through them until she found the one she was looking for. She placed the two pictures side by side facing Brid. "They could be the same child," she said in a voice filled with pain.

"No," Brid answered sharply, shaking her head. "It's only two little boys with dark hair who are the about the same age. That's all."

"How can you say that? Look at them." Franny stared intently at the two pictures, convinced the likeness was obvious.

"Holy Mother of God! Are you crazy?" Brid asked as a new thought occurred to her. "Are you now stalking this child?" She wanted a cigarette desperately. "Do you want to be locked up?"

"It was a brilliant idea. Even Drew would have been impressed. The day that we had lunch together at the Chayne outing, Lorie told me how wonderful The Little Black Lamb daycare center was. She was so happy to have Alex enrolled there. I went over there and told them I was checking out daycare for my college roommate who was moving east from California the end of the month. I said I wanted to see what they had available for children between eighteen months and two years. I asked them if I could take some pictures of the center to send to her. So she could get a feel for the place." Franny laughed. "They were only too happy to accommodate me. They could not have been nicer."

"How did you even know which one was the right child?"

"Easy. He's the only Alex." She looked down at the pictures again. "But I would have known it was him, he looks like—"

"He does not!" Before Franny could protest, Ronan arrived with their dinners. Brid, relieved to end what was turning into a futile argument, focused her attention on the salmon dish.

"Can I get you anything else?" Ronan asked after serving each of them.

"Nothing. This is lovely." Brid smiled up at the young man.

"All right then, I'm off."

They ate in silence, each occupied with her own thoughts, the only sound in the small space the muted conversation seeping in from the larger rooms surrounding them.

Having eaten only half her meal, Brid laid down her silverware and gazed across the table at Franny who was demurely slicing her filet.

"At least Drew must have been delighted with your table manners," Brid said, an amused smile playing around her mouth.

"My table manners? What do you mean?" Franny asked in surprise, looking up from her steak.

"Drew said I had the table manners of an Irish peasant." She sighed. "I suppose the shrinks would say he had a love/hate thing about the Irish." She shook her head. "Listen to me, Franny. Drew's dead. I know that you loved him, perhaps you'll always love him, but he's not coming back. He's dead," she repeated slowly for emphasis. "And you are not."

"I have to know if this is his child," Franny insisted. "I have to."

"For the love of God, why?" Gritting her teeth, Brid pushed the thought of a cigarette away.

"Because, at least then it would make sense to me. If he was drunk and got Lorie pregnant, I would understand it. Don't you see?" Franny's eyes filled as she stared across the table. "I always thought it would be you. I used to look for signs that he had been with you. I wondered what perfume you wore. I was too afraid to ask him. God knows he told me enough about you without my asking for more." Brid could hear the bitterness behind her words. "You're beautiful, talented, slender – a sharp girl," she finished using Drew's highest praise for any woman.

"Oh yes, I know all about his sharp girls," Brid said, softly. "They were figments of his imagination. Women he conjured up in his head, not real women who sometimes got blemishes on their chins and runs in their panty-hose or occasionally slurped their damn soup." She watched, fascinated, as Franny's expression turned ugly with anger and jealousy.

"What could he have seen in her? She was nothing like the kind of woman he admired. She had a TATOO! He was always complaining to me about the way she dressed." She took a deep breath to keep her tears from falling. "I tried so hard to be what he wanted me to be, to become what he wanted me to be and he cheated on me with her?"

Brid picked up the two pictures once again and studied them intently. "I can't pretend to see what I don't. There's a superficial resemblance, the hair color; perhaps the shape of the eye, but it's only superficial. Young children look so much like one another. You see it because you want to see it, not because it's so." She placed the pictures down on the table and shook her head.

"You truly don't believe that this is Drew's child?" Franny asked. For the first time since she had brought out the pictures, she seemed hopeful.

"No, I don't."

"How can you be so sure?"

"I told you, young children look alike. The likeness you see is only superficial." She hesitated, reluctant to continue.

Franny immediately picked up on this. "What? There's something else, something you haven't told me. What is it?"

Brid was thoughtful for a moment, realizing that if she continued, she would only add to Franny's pain. Grudgingly, she said, "All right, I don't believe that the child is Drew's because," she stopped again and sighed. "He never would have given him up."

CHAPTER 18

"Want to go shooting with me after work tonight?" Surprised to hear Neil's voice when she answered the phone on a dreary morning late in February, Brid's first thought was of Franny. What now?

"Shooting? Are you mad? Or have you been nipping? At what," she looked down at her watch, "ten thirty in the morning?"

"Come on," Neil argued. "You used to beg me to take you shooting when we were younger."

She laughed. What he said was true. She had begged him to take her with him to the gun club when she and Drew were married. "Ah, yes, so I did. But that was when I had someone I wanted to shoot."

Neil continued to press her to join him. "I'll pick you up right after work and we can shoot for an hour. When we're finished shooting, I'll take you out to dinner. It'll be fun."

She started to say no, but then she thought, Why not? What did she have to look forward to this evening anyway? An hour spent on Craic's books or more frustration at her easel struggling with the portrait she was painting. "Fine, Malone, you can get off your knees, you've convinced me. What should I wear?"

Neil's laughter spilled out of the phone. "Brid, only you would ask that. Jeans and a sweatshirt will do nicely. The most important thing is that you cover enough of your body to hide the fact that you don't have a tattoo."

"Are you telling me that you do?" She asked, shocked. She didn't understand tattoos, unable to imagine anything she would want engraved on her body that God hadn't already put there. She shivered in revulsion whenever her eyes happened to fall on the snake crawling down Lilah's leg.

"I'm not telling," he teased her.

She could hear the amusement in his voice and realized he, of all people, would never have a tattoo. "Well, fine, then. Pick me up at home at six. I'll need to change first."

"It's a date, then. I look forward to it. See you later."

For a moment longer, she stood holding the phone, the dial tone buzzing in her ear. He was right. She had made a date with him. What had she done? Hanging up, she stared at the traffic splashing through the rain on Main Street.

Her last real date, other than those related to the gallery and they didn't count, had been six years ago. She had broken one of her rules and started dating a guy she met at her meeting. It was not a good idea, which AA was quick to remind you. People did it all the time, of course, mostly with bad results.

Mark was an architect. He shared her passion for the American Impressionists, preferring them, as she did, over the French. He had been sober only six months and his sponsor was against it from the start.

She had not had a drink in almost eight years. The gallery was turning a profit, not a large one, but a profit and she was able to lift her head and take a breath. Craic, as Drew predicted, was doing a booming business. Her role, beyond that of providing Des with an occasional shoulder to cry on and keeping the books, was finished. She no longer had any reason to talk to or see Drew. She supposed, looking back, she was lonely. She had enjoyed arguing with him on a weekly basis over which lamp fixture to use and what wine to stock.

Mark, with his quirky smile, and his soulful eyes, was charming. It was the charming ones that did her in. They had fun for a few months. Things changed when Mark started to drink again. It began with a glass of wine before dinner, only one, he assured her, which initially he seemed able to control. One became two and two became three and an after dinner liqueur. He tried to convince her that abstinence wasn't necessary, that they could drink again in moderation. There was literature now to back that theory up but she didn't believe it.

Oh, she wanted to believe it, to have another Guinness before she died, only the thought of going back to where she had been stopped her. The risk was too great. She might not find her way back a second time. So she ended the relationship and the belated realization of how close she had come to disaster had frightened her badly. She ran across Mark at meetings. They were cordial, as former lovers can be, but she never let herself be pulled in again.

Since then, there had been no one. To her surprise, it had been easy to let that side of her life go. It was another of God's little jokes that she had ended up living like a nun; the last thing she ever thought that she would become. And now, Neil Malone had convinced her to go on a date with him.

He picked her up promptly at six. Wearing her running shoes, worn jeans, a Mass Art sweatshirt, and an old ski parka, she was out the door and sliding into the car before he could get his own door fully opened. He smiled approvingly at her outfit. "I was afraid you might wear that beaver-lined cape."

"Oh, don't be ridiculous. I'm not daft." Trying not to be too obvious, Brid checked out what he was wearing: a barn jacket, faded jeans, a chamois cloth open-neck shirt that had seen better days, and old tennis shoes. She relaxed, for some reason the worn clothes made him seem different to her, less sure of himself, younger. She rarely saw him in casual clothes anymore. During the six years she and Drew were married, he had been in and out of their home like family, which as far as Drew was concerned, he was. They had fun, although the Neil that she remembered was always the serious one, the adult in a group of overgrown children. He had been dating Maureen Meehan then. Brid wondered what had become of her. When she and Drew divorced, Neil's loyalties and company went with him. He was friendly to her when their paths crossed, which was often enough. Lynton was a small city and their circles overlapped. And now, here she was riding around with him in a car with a gun, wherever it was. Glancing into the rear seat, she asked, "Where's your gun?"

"I keep it in the trunk. I have a permit to carry it, of course, but a gun on display would make a cop really nervous if he pulled me over."

"You're full of it tonight, Malone. You've never had a speeding ticket in your life." Brid grinned.

"Me, I'm a frustrated Indy driver," he answered, even though the speedometer made a liar out of him.

"I'm surprised that you still shoot after all these years," she said, openly curious.

"I do it as a way of relieving stress and I suppose because it makes me feel close to my father. He's the one who taught me to shoot." He was silent for a moment. "It was really the only thing we ever did together besides eating breakfast and going to church. I still use his revolver, a Smith & Wesson thirty-eight Police Special. It's outdated. The cops use Glock nine millimeter semi-automatics now. I still like the Special and have never bothered to replace it."

"It's hard to think of your dad in connection with things that are violent; even though I know he was a cop. I remember him as being such a gentle soul."

"Well, in many ways he was, which is why he never made detective. He was railroaded by that mentality the Irish had when he was growing up: 'Be a cop or a fireman.' He was afraid of fire so he became a cop." He added, "He was a hell of shot, though. He taught me everything I know about guns." Taking advantage of the red light, he glanced at her. "He taught Drew to shoot, too."

"Drew? I didn't think Drew even liked guns."

"He didn't, I talked him into it. Dad taught us both to shoot out in that field at the end of Willow Street. Elaine MacCullough had a fit when she found out about it. Drew's father didn't agree with her. He said, 'Do that boy good to know how to handle a gun.'" Neil chuckled. "Drew might not have liked guns, but he was a better shot than I was. But then, everything he ever did, he did well."

Brid said nothing. What could she say? He was right.

Neil swung the Mercedes into the gun club parking lot. Turning off the car, he asked, "Are you ready?"

"I suppose I'm as ready as I'll ever be." Her eyes scanned the parking lot dotted with pickup trucks and SUVs. The battered red Bronco in front of them sported a torn 'Charlton Heston is my President' bumper sticker. "Am I going to be the only female in this place?"

"I doubt it. About thirty percent of their members are women." His eyes rested on Brid in the quick appraising look of a man looking at a woman and liking what he saw. "I have to say most of them seem to have considerably more meat on them than you do."

"I'll have to eat more, then, if I decide I like this," she said, pushing the heavy door open.

Neil retrieved a black gym bag from the trunk of the car and they crossed the parking lot toward the concrete block building. Inside, Brid's nose wrinkled in distaste at the smell of cordite. The only furniture was a long glass case filled with pistols and ammunition. Open boxes holding headsets, protective plastic glasses, and stacks of targets ranging from small round bulls-eyes to life-size outlines of people were piled along the walls and on the counter.

"Hey, Neil, how are ya tonight?" A tall, heavy-set man with a head of thick gray hair, old acne scars, and bulbous nose greeted Neil.

"Evening, Eddy. How are you doing? Not working too hard I hope?"

The man laughed. "Not me, never."

"Eddy, I would like you to meet a friend of mine, Brid Sheerin. Brid, this is Eddy Mancuso. What he doesn't know about guns isn't worth knowing."

"Hello," Brid said, smiling.

"Nice to meet you, Brid." Eddy Mancuso smiled, but his eyes examined her carefully, probably speculating where she fit in Neil Malone's life.

"Eddy, we need a headset, protective glasses, and a setup in booth four." He told Brid, "You pick out the target."

"Can we shoot at those big men with your gun?" She asked, pointing to the pile of targets stacked on the counter, oblivious as to why every man within earshot grinned at her question.

"Those are women. We don't shoot men here." A young man with a devil tattooed on his bicep laughed.

"Shut up, Randy," Eddy said, smiling at Brid. "These targets are gender non-specific." He placed the glasses and the headset on the counter. He tore several life-size targets from a pad and waved them at Randy. "Make yourself useful and set up number four. You need any ammo, Neil?"

"No, thanks. I'm set there. Put this on my account."

Eddy peered through the plexiglass window into the range. A red light glowed at booth four.

"Your booth is ready," he said, gesturing toward the hallway on the left. Neil thanked him and picking up the equipment, headed down the hall toward the sound of gunfire. Brid strode behind him. He walked past the first three doors and opened the one marked with the number four. Politely, he stepped aside to let her enter the long narrow room first. The room reminded Brid of a lane in a bowling alley. The paper target Brid had selected hung from a metal frame against the far wall. Neil opened the gym bag and removed the gun. "First, the most important rule: Never point a gun, loaded or unloaded, at anyone." He passed her the gun. "Here, you hold it. Don't worry, it's not loaded." She was surprised by the weight, but was able to hold it in one hand. "Bring it up to about your shoulder and hold it with both hands about eighteen inches in front of you." Following his directions, she found that keeping the gun steady was harder.

Neil took the gun back from her and removed six cartridges from the box of ammunition and inserted them into the chamber. Removing a headset and a pair of protective glasses from the gym bag, he told Brid, "Put on your equipment and stand behind me." Brid did as she was told. He slipped the headset and glasses on and raised the gun in his right hand. Widening his stance slightly, steadying the gun with his left hand, he drilled six neat holes across the chest of the paper man. Holding the gun down at his side, he said, "I haven't been up here for a couple of weeks, so that's not bad." Flipping the cartridge chamber open, he ejected the empty cartridges into a box and replaced them.

"Okay, Madam. Your turn."

Gingerly, she took the gun from his hand and held it up the way he had, wrapping both hands around the handle. She sighted the target, pulled the trigger back, and fired. The recoil took her by surprise, but not as much as the fact that the bullet she had so carefully aimed at the paper man's nose pierced the paper above the left shoulder.

"Loosen up, you're stiff as a board and bend your knees. You need to aim at the body and hold the gun steady." Neil stepped closely behind her, his large hand covering hers on the grip of the gun. She was conscious of his nearness: the solidness of his body behind her, his cologne – Old Spice, the same scent her father wore – the minty sweetness of his breath, the beating of his heart. With his help, she pulled the trigger again and stared in wonder at the hole that blossomed in the center of the target's chest.

The hour went by quickly, as they each took a turn, one after the other, with the gun. Brid's shots got better. As she stepped up to take her last six rounds, she asked, "Do you ever pretend that it's a person up there, someone that you know?"

"Never." He answered without hesitating.

Brid thought about that as she took aim. In her mind, she saw Franny obsessing over the baby pictures the night they had dinner. She slipped the image of Lorie Derouin over that of the paper man. She raised the gun and fired. Behind her, Neil crowed.

"Hey, Annie Oakley, you're a natural!" Brid stared at the hole in the center of the paper man's heart, keeping her thoughts to herself.

"That was fun," Brid said as they drove back toward Lynton. "I'd like to do it again, if you're willing."

"How about coming with me Wednesday?" He asked, quickly.

"Well, I," she floundered and thought, the hell with it. "Okay. Wednesday it is."

"My Wednesdays are free now. So it would be great to go shooting with you."

She was struck by the sadness in his voice before she remembered. He and Drew had played tennis at the Lynton Country Club every Wednesday night that Drew was in town, for the last twenty-three years.

"Let's call Bertucci's and get a pizza and take it back to my place. We're both pretty grubby to be going out. My treat," she added, emphatically.

"And deny me the chance to buy dinner for a beautiful woman?"

"Don't be such a chauvinist. Women take men out to dinner in this century, in case you haven't heard."

They called from the car and ordered a large sausage and mushroom pizza with anchovies on two slices only, for her. "Why don't we stop and get some beer for you on the way home?" she offered.

"No, soda's fine for me. I don't need any beer."

"Neil, really, I have no problem if you drink in front of me," Brid persisted, certain he was being gallant.

He answered her gently. "I am sure you don't. I know that you believe that all Irishmen can't live without their pint, but trust me on this one, I can."

"Okay then. I just don't want you to feel—"

"I don't." He smiled, placing his hand on top of hers. "I don't."

Brid unlocked the door into the flat and Neil followed, carrying the pizza.

"Don't look too closely; the place is a bit of a mess. Whenever I am working on a painting, my housework suffers."

While she went to get the plates and the soda, Neil set the pizza on the oak coffee table and wandered over to the easel standing in front of the windows. His eyes widened in surprise. The artist pad was filled with sketches of Drew. "I didn't know you were painting Drew," he called to her.

Brid came in from the kitchen balancing plates, paper napkins, forks, and two cans of Coke. "I wouldn't say that I am painting Drew, not based on what you see there. I don't think I have captured anything, not in those anyway. And don't ask me why I'm doing it because I can't tell you. I feel called to it."

"But the likeness is there."

"The likeness is there, but not the soul. Of course, that could be the problem, trying to find his soul."

Neil slid the two pieces of pizza with the anchovies on them onto a plate and placed it on the table in front of her, going back to help himself to two more. Settling down on the sofa across from where she squatted, lighting the fire, he said, "You don't have to try so hard to convince me that you hated him, because I know it's not true."

Brid watched, as the dry logs surrounded by rolled newspaper knots, caught and flared filling the room with bright light. She sighed. "I did hate him, truly I did, often, over the years, but you're right, I don't hate him now. It seems strange to say that I miss him because I rarely saw him, but I do. I miss knowing that he's here in the same world that I am." She sighed. "I know it sounds mad."

"Not really, not to me," Malone replied, intent on studying the flames in front of him.

"How could you understand? You thought he was perfect, you and—"

"You really believe that?" He interrupted her, more angry than she ever remembered seeing him. "That I thought he was perfect? You think I didn't know what a bastard he could be? Or that he could be controlling and cruel to the women he loved? That I, as you say, of all people didn't understand that he was a drunk? When I let myself dwell on this last cock-up, which to his credit has to be his finest, I become furious. When I think of that poor confused girl up there in Hiram's Forge, I want to slug him."

Agitated, he got up and walked back over to the easel to stare down at the page filled with thumbnail sketches of Drew. "He was an arrogant, self-aggrandizing shit and my oldest and truest friend. I would have trusted him with my life." He came back again to sit on the sofa. "Do you know how we met?"

"Playing baseball, wasn't it?"

"Yes. Drew, Harry, and I, were all on the same Little League team. But we were friends before that. When I was nine years old, I wanted to play baseball. I was an athletic kid and I could run, but I hadn't really played baseball. I was so afraid that I would disgrace myself at the tryouts. My father was working a three to midnight detail and he couldn't practice with me. So my mother said, 'Go down to Lacey field, there are always boys playing there. They'll help you learn how to play.'" He stopped for a moment lost in thought.

"I went and it was that crew of little snots from the North End, Rick Ballard, Billy Kingsley, Scott Tremont, and the rest. Harry and Drew were playing with them." He sighed. "After forty years this still hurts. I asked if I could play and Tremont said, 'Hey, Malone, this game is for North-Enders, only. Go back where you came from.' Drew stepped in and said, 'Sure.

You can play."' Neil smiled. "And those guys listened to him maybe because his old man was president of the bank or maybe because even then, young as he was, he could dazzle people. I don't know. Anyway, he made them let me play. And by Jesus," Neil smiled at the memory, "I played."

"Did you know about this thing with Lorie Derouin?" Brid asked.

"The first time I met Lorie Derouin was that night at McKenna's." He said, not looking at her. There was a stack of old pictures in a basket on the center of the table. She had been looking through them in her attempt to capture Drew's face. Neil picked one up. It was a group shot taken one summer when they had all rented a place on Martha's Vineyard. They were all there: Drew and Brid, Neil and Maureen, Harry and the girl he had come closest to marrying, Anne Sheldon. They had asked someone fishing off the dock to take it for them. "We had a fun that time on the Vineyard," Neil said, looking down at the faded color snapshot.

"Yes." Brid took the picture from his hand to look at it. "We did."

"Did Drew ever tell you that he saved my life?" She shook her head. "You see? Now that's something he wouldn't tell you. But remember how we had to listen to how he was a marketing genius until we could recite it with him. Hell, I don't know, maybe he was. But he did save my life."

"You tell me about it." She waited to hear the story.

"We were in the eighth grade and we were hanging around down by the river one afternoon, someone, probably Drew, had a pack of cigarettes. The same cast of characters who wouldn't let me play ball decided it would be a great idea to swim across." Ruefully, he smiled at her. "Well, I wasn't much of a swimmer. Anyway, they all jumped in down there by Hobbs Landing and started across. I was a big kid, cursed by the same bulk that would land me a spot on the football team the next year. I didn't want to do it, but they started to ride me, calling me a chicken and a sissy. I felt I had no choice. I had to do it, too. By then, they were all on the opposite bank. I jumped in and started across." He stopped talking and stared into the fire before going on. "I was in the middle of the river when I got a cramp. I panicked, certain I was going to drown. The next thing I know, Drew's in the water next to me, butting me like a dolphin, actually swimming underneath me to get my head above the water. Somehow, he got me close enough to the bank for Harry to help him. They pulled me out."

Brid said nothing, picturing a young Drew leaping fearlessly into the water to rescue his friend. Her eyes drifted to the easel. If she could put that part of him into the damn portrait, she might have something. Neil sat lost in thought for a while and then, slapping his hands on his knees, stood up. "It's crossed my mind, that if we had met as adults, I might not even have liked him. The truth is we didn't have much in common as men. What we had was history together and you and I know being Irish, that is often everything." He walked over to her, jacket in hand, and said, "I really enjoyed tonight, Brid." Brid started to say that she had too, when he kissed her, filling her mouth with his tongue. She felt a surge of desire, like an electric shock ripple through her groin, and she was kissing him back, her fingers entwined in his thick hair to bring him closer to her. Her hungry mouth eagerly met his.

"This is a mistake," she murmured, reluctantly breaking away to stand slightly breathless in front of him. "We have to stop."

"Why?" He asked, pulling her to him once again, his lips against the pulse in her throat. "Don't tell me that we have to stop." Without letting her go, he took a step back from her and asked, "Do you have any idea how long I've wanted to do this?"

"Your mother would turn in her grave, if she knew you were here with me," she said, unable to keep the bitterness out of her voice. She was well aware of what Peg Malone had thought of her both before and after she had married and divorced Drew MacCullough.

"Yes, she would, but Ma's opinion of you never mattered to me and that's the truth." He hesitated, his eyes searching her face trying to see into her heart. "They both are in their graves, Brid."

She sighed and having made up her mind, took his hand and led him toward her bedroom.

Trailing behind her, Neil felt the enormity of what he was proposing overtake the desire that only a moment before had been pushing urgently against the zipper of his jeans. What the hell did he think he was about to do? Inwardly, he cringed at the memory of passing the full-length mirror on his bathroom door as he stepped each morning from the shower. When Brid turned to him, the reality of the king-size bed behind her overwhelmed him. In his mind, he saw Drew as he had last seen him alive, trim in his tennis whites, returning a serve with effortless grace.

Involuntarily, he took a step backwards. "Brid, I don't think—"

She laughed a low musical sound that slowly built upon itself until it filled the room with peals of mirth, a sound he had loved for as long as he had known her. "Ah, no, Neil Malone don't you even begin to think about sliding back out the way you've come. I am afraid you are in for it." As she spoke, she unbuttoned her shirt and let it fall to the floor. Reaching around and unsnapping her bra, she shrugged it off her shoulders and watching him, she hooked her fingers over the tops of her jeans, pulling them down and stepping out of them as they pooled around her ankles on the floor.

Neil's breath hissed between his teeth at the sight of her standing unselfconsciously in front of him, her slender body showcased by the winter moonlight pouring through the window. He had seen her nearly naked a dozen times before, cavorting on the beach in the barest of bikinis. But this was different, instinctively he understood that this, this was for him and for him alone.

"My God, you are so beautiful," he said as his eyes took in the small, high breasts with their deep rose-colored nipples, the curve of her hips and the slight protrusion of her belly over the lush thatch of dark curls between her legs.

Brid smiled, but didn't argue with him. The truth was that at that moment standing there in the soft light from the window, her body, unmarked by childbirth and honed by daily yoga, was beautiful. "How is it now that one of us is as naked as the day they came into this world and the other is not?" Before he could answer her, she tugged the shirt from his pants and slipped her hands under it, each one finding a nipple that she began tease and caress until it hardened to marble under her fingers. Groaning, Neil's mouth once again found hers even as he fumbled urgently to undo his belt and zipper.

Impatiently kicking himself free of his pants and shoes, he moved the two of them backwards toward the bed. He bent and lifted Brid onto the mattress as she wrapped her long legs around his hips.

He slid his tongue down her arched throat and tasted the cleft between her breasts. He suckled first her left and then her right nipple urged on by the low moans that came from deep in her throat. Raising his head from her breast, his eyes met hers and once again the doubts came rushing back. Brid whispered in a voice hoarse with desire, "Now, Neil," as she guided him between her legs. The years fell away and he was young again, his only thought was to meet the demanding rhythm of the beautiful woman beneath him. He felt her crest and fragment beneath him, the sound of her cry of pleasure in his ears as his slid beneath the waves of his own climax.

The numbers on the bedside clock read 4:30 when Brid woke with a start, aware that something was different. The memory of the night before came flooding back to her, as she tentatively reached her hand behind her, seeking the man she had taken to bed. A small movement in the corner of the room drew her eyes to where Neil was quietly dressing.

"Are you leaving, then?" She asked, smiling at him, uncharacteristically shy. Shoes in hand, he came back to sit next to her on the edge of the bed.

Bending down, he kissed her, his thumb caressing the side of her cheek. "Yes, I need to shower and change before mass." Seeing her stricken expression he added, "Don't look so sad, I was going to leave you a note."

"Do you regret it, then? Are you sorry that we slept together?"

He smiled at her. "I am only sorry that I woke you and that I have to wait until I can climb back into bed with you again."

Kissing her again, he stood up and headed for the door. He didn't quite manage to duck the pillow that she threw at him.

CHAPTER 19

Franny sat primly in a chair outside Johanna Caras's office under the curious eyes of her administrative assistant. Aware of the women's surreptitious looks, Franny thought guiltily, I should remember her name. She was sure that Drew had introduced the two of them either at the annual Christmas party or Chayne's summer outing at Miller State Park. The woman had come to his wake, too, as had most of the people that he had worked with here at Chayne. But, unable to remember her name, Franny smiled and said nothing when their eyes met.

Johanna had seemed surprised, and Franny sensed, less than thrilled when Franny called and asked to meet with her. "I have some questions about Drew's last month at work, I think you can help me with," she had told Drew's boss. Johanna agreed to see her on the condition that they do it at the end of the day. Franny had been happy to agree, knowing as she did, that Lorie left at 4:30 to pick up her son from the daycare center. Franny viewed not running into Lorie while she was at Chayne as an unexpected gift.

Johanna Caras stepped from her office at exactly 5:15 and gave Franny a reserved smile, one that stopped before it got to her eyes. "Good afternoon, Mrs. MacCullough, I'll be right with you."

Johanna walked over to the blonde girl's desk. "I think that's everything for today Kara, you can leave now. We can finish the presentation for the Hoeflen account tomorrow. I'm going to make some changes this evening." She turned back to Franny and said, "Come into my office." Franny got up from her chair and followed Johanna into a spacious corner office with two large windows set at right angles overlooking the man-made pond. An office like this, Drew had explained to her, was one of the perks awarded to people fortunate enough to become vice presidents — people like Johanna Caras.

"Please, have a seat," Johanna said, indicating one of the two chairs facing her desk. The desk itself was teak and almost bare. If its surface was any indication, Johanna tolerated no clutter. Thinking of Drew's desk, crowded with family pictures – herself, Cynthia's kids, Sofia, the two dogs – Franny was struck by the fact that there was not a single personal item on Johanna's desk.

"How can I help you, Mrs. MacCullough?"

"Please call me Franny."

Johanna smiled again, this time looking slightly more human. "Okay. How can I help you, Franny?"

"Well, I'm still not sure why Drew spent the night before he died at the Sheraton… instead of coming home, I mean, and I wondered if there had been some problem that day here at work. I know now that he was in the office that afternoon. I thought that he was coming home the following morning on the red-eye. Obviously, his plans changed but I don't know why." She hated asking the question, but she had to find the answer.

Something that might have been pity flickered, momentarily, in the other woman's hazel eyes and she appeared to hesitate before she spoke. "I am not sure there's anything to be gained by going over the past. You, and for that matter, those of us here, have to go on without him."

"But was he unhappy in his job? Did something happen?" Franny's voice rose slightly on this last, making her desperation evident.

Johanna looked at her incredulously, "Surely, you must realize that he hated his job, or to be fair, I suppose, that he hated working for me? Unfortunately, Drew and I did not form the team that I thought we would when I came onboard last year."

"Well, yes, I suppose I knew you two did not exactly hit it off," Franny answered softly, remembering Drew referring to Johanna as "The Wicked Witch."

"That would be one way of putting it." Johanna's eyes narrowed as her glance assessed Franny, "You don't work do you?"

"Well, no, not really, not in a place like Chayne, not anymore. I have a little business. I sell dolls to collectors. I did work here once, but…" her voiced trailed off under Johanna's condescending stare.

"Oh, yes. That's right. Dolls. I think I did know that." She smiled thinly. "Drew must have mentioned it." She got up from her chair and moved restlessly over to the window, staring out into the darkness to where the pond would be if you could see it in the dark. She turned and told Franny. "Your husband was a dinosaur, did you realize that? He'd worked here for what? Twenty years?"

"It was twenty-five years in May. He joined the company six months after it was founded."

"Twenty-five years. And he never worked any place else, right?"

"No, not really," Franny answered, meekly.

"Drew could have had this job. In many ways, he was the obvious candidate but he just didn't understand that the world changes in twenty-five years." Johanna shook her head. "He thought he could use the same model." She hesitated before continuing. "The same style he'd always used, but he was wrong. It didn't work anymore. He had been told that several times. But, of course, being Drew MacCullough, he didn't listen. Somehow, he just didn't get it. We did have a disagreement the day before he died over the appropriate way to act when you're out with a customer. Drinking yourself into a stupor, which is what he did in Seattle, is no longer acceptable." She stopped and looked once more at Franny, sighed, and continued. "Let's say we exchanged words that were less than pleasant over it."

"But he didn't quit, did he?" Franny blurted this out, seeing in her mind the letter she found in Drew's briefcase.

"Quit?" Johanna asked incredulously. "No, he didn't quit. In fact, he wished me a Merry Christmas on his way out the door."

"How are you really doing?" Johanna asked changing the subject, appearing human for the first time since Franny's arrival in her office.

"I have my bad days and my not so bad days." Franny smiled wanly.

"I've never been through it myself, but they say it does get easier as time passes." Her eyes drifted to her watch, a trim Rolex glinting with diamonds. "I truly hope that life begins to get better for you. Sometimes things happen that don't make any sense to us and we have to accept them. I wish you well." She extended her hand to Franny.

Franny took her hand and thanked her again for making the time to see her. Trying not to think about what Johanna said about Drew's getting drunk in front of the customer in Seattle, she made her way toward the stairs. She felt drawn to the opposite wall and the cluster of offices there. She wondered if Drew's office was still empty or if someone else was already busy living a life there: eating a quick sandwich, calling his wife, writing long range plans, talking to customers, playing games on the computer on the sly, like he had all the time in the world. She was tempted to go past Lorie's cubicle to look once more at the picture of the little boy in the Winnie the Pooh frame, but forced herself to continue walking toward the exit. She couldn't afford to get caught snooping around there. She had to hurry in order not to be late for the yoga class where she had promised to meet Brid.

Driving back to the center of Lynton, Franny parked the car and walked up Coal Street, thinking, I must be crazy agreeing that I would go to yoga.

She had been reading the obituary page, circling the names of the people who were younger than Drew, when Brid called to invite her. There were two. Three or more made her feel better. Some days, there were none and on those days she was desolate, wondering, why Drew?

"How are you doing this morning?" Brid's lilting voice came over the line.

"I'm reading the obituaries and trying to work up some enthusiasm for the bowl of oatmeal and blueberries in front of me, if that tells you anything." She stared mournfully at her breakfast. She had decided to get serious about her diet. Food, at least when she was eating it, was a comfort, but she needed to lose the weight she had gained since Drew died. She didn't have to like what she was eating.

"The Irish Comics? Da says the main reason to read the obituaries is to make sure that your name isn't in there and that your enemies are. I have an idea. Come with me to my yoga class tonight and afterwards, we'll get take-out salads at The Big Wooden Bowl and bring them back to my place. I need to talk to you."

"Yoga? Are you kidding me?" Franny laughed.

"Don't be difficult. It's a class that's open to all levels. It will be good for you."

"Drew always said I was terrible at—"

"Mother of our Precious Lord! It's not yet nine o'clock in the morning and I have to listen to words of wisdom from Drew MacCullough! Just come. It's not the Boston Marathon. Meet me at Namaste on Coal Street at six thirty. It's directly past the Dunkin Donuts on the left."

"I'm not wearing a leotard." Franny said, wavering.

"Wear sweats, wear shorts, wear your damn snowsuit if you want, just meet me there."

Namaste appeared in front of her, where Brid had said it would be. Carrying her gym bag containing sweat pants and a long tee shirt, Franny joined the chattering group of women as they entered the lobby. A slender blonde who looked like she had stepped off the cover of Yoga Journal greeted them at the door. There was no sign of Brid. The girl looked up at Franny, a question on her face.

"Hi," Franny said, nervously looking around. "I'm Franny MacCullough. I've never done this before but—"

"Oh, you're Brid's friend. My name is Aly. Welcome to Namaste." The girl had a beautiful smile. "The dressing rooms are through that door," she said, indicating a doorway to the right. "Once you've changed, come on into the studio and grab a mat."

"What do I owe you?" Franny asked.

"A drop-in class is fifteen dollars, but we can settle up after class."

A few minutes later, Franny self-consciously stepped into the softly lit studio. She joined a group of twelve women of various ages and sizes dressed in workout clothes ranging from baggy sweats like hers to biking shorts and sports bras. She was relieved to see that two of them were heavier than she was.

"Over here, Franny, come sit by me." Dressed in black yoga pants and a rose-colored top with spaghetti straps, Brid sat on her mat in the lotus position near the door.

"Don't sit by Brid," said the woman in front of Franny who turned around to smile at her. "She's so perfect that it's painful to watch her! Sit by me. It will make you feel better. I'm Vicky, by the way."

"Don't scare her. I had a hard enough time getting her to come," Brid laughed.

"No squabbling, ladies. Remember we are seeking serenity." Aly scolded them from her mat in the front of the room. "Okay. Everyone find a comfortable seated position."

As the class progressed, Franny relaxed. Brid was right; no one was watching her or cared if she couldn't complete a pose. Realizing this, she began to enjoy herself. To her surprise, she found that she was able to do many of the poses without too much difficulty. By the end of the class, she understood what Vicky meant about Brid being perfect as she watched her slip effortlessly into the Wheel, her long arms and legs holding her slender torso in a rounded arch high above the floor.

"How did you like yoga?" Aly asked Franny, when she inquired shyly if she might become a regular student.

"I liked it very much. It wasn't as hard as I thought it was going to be." She flushed, adding. "And the fact that I am not exactly thin didn't seem to matter that much.

"It's really about what your individual body can do in this moment. You did fine."

Franny followed Brid's Jeep to The Big Wooden Bowl where they ordered large salads to go taking them back to Brid's condo.

"You are losing weight, aren't you? Good for you," Brid said, eyeing her speculatively as she laid out the silverware.

"I've lost around five pounds, but as you can see, I have at least twenty more pounds to lose." Franny said, carefully pouring only half the dressing over her salad. For a moment, she was envious of Brid's slight frame accentuated by her tight yoga pants and fitted jacket. "I bet you've no idea what it is like to want something and not be able to have it."

Brid looked at her incredulously and began to laugh until her peals of laughter brought tears to her eyes. "Mother of God, you're funny! I'm a recovering alcoholic. Hardly a day passes that I don't want a drink. My first choice would be a Guinness, or even better, a Black and Tan. In a pinch though, I would settle for an American beer."

Franny sat staring at her salad, at a loss for words. Tentatively, she asked, "How long has it been since you had a drink?"

"Thirteen years, ten months, and six days." Brid answered her without hesitating, having stopped laughing.

"Does it ever get better?"

Brid leaned back on her heels and thought about it. "Some days are easier than others. It's always there, like a low grade toothache. Other days something: a song, a smell, a person, a situation can suddenly make it as hard as it was the first day I quit, the way hitting the nerve in the tooth can make the pain suddenly unbearable."

"Why did you stop drinking?"

"I suppose that saying 'I got tired of it.' sounds very simple doesn't it? But I did, I got tired of smelling like stale booze, feeling queasy and anxious, and having no control over my life."

"Had you been drinking too much for a while?" Franny asked, shyly, not quite meeting Brid's eyes.

Brid shook her head in wonder. This woman had lived with an alcoholic and she didn't have the slightest understanding of the problem. "I was drinking regularly from the time I was fifteen years old. It was what we did in my house when I was growing up, the way other families played board games like Scrabble. We drank. My parents were both true to their gender, as it tends to take the Irish. My father is a blathering, red-faced, pugnacious, and at times weepy, drunken Mick. My mother was secretive. She took her Bushmills in her tea, and hid her bottles in the clothes hamper, or the linen closet. At first, she became more carefree, happy, really, but as she got drunker, she got quieter, her mouth got tighter. Unfortunately for me, I'm a brawler like Da."

"But I don't think I've ever seen your father drunk in all the times I've been in Craic."

"Would you recognize it, if you saw it? He has his rules, you see, like all highly functioning alcoholics, one of those being that he never takes a drop of whiskey before midnight. Of course, a *pionta*, a pint that is, doesn't count."

"Did you go to AA?" Franny asked. She couldn't picture Brid doing that from what she knew of the program, which admittedly wasn't much.

"To be sure. I went to ninety meetings in ninety days when I first stopped drinking. Now I only go weekly, if it's one of those hard times. I make a point to show up at least once a month though. It still helps." She hesitated before adding, "I tried to get Drew to go to AA when he was arrested for DUI."

"You knew about that?" Franny asked, embarrassed all over again for Drew.

"It was in the paper, Franny." Brid answered.

"What did he say? I mean, of course he never told me that he talked to you about it."

"He said that I was crazy, if I thought he was going to sit in a circle holding hands with a bunch of strangers, sending up prayers to his Higher Power."

"Well, it's not like he was a drunk. He had a problem sometimes with alcohol, but after he was arrested, he stopped drinking completely."

Brid restrained herself, and began gathering up the plastic salad containers. "Would you like some tea? I've both Irish Breakfast and herbal."

"Herbal tea would be nice, thanks." Franny replied, sinking backing into the deep, squashy cushions of the sofa.

Brid brought the teapot and two mugs along with a Beleek honey pot filled with raw honey and set them on the coffee table. Pouring the steaming tea into each mug, she handed one to Franny. Then she opened the French doors and lit a cigarette. She stood in the doorway smoking to calm herself. Finishing her cigarette, she joined Franny where she sat on the sofa.

"We need to talk. I like you and I've enjoyed getting to know you. As bizarre as it will seem to people, I want us to be friends." She sighed. "But, there are things you need to know, things about my relationship with Drew."

Franny turned pale and the mug in her hand began to shake.

"I knew it. He was sleeping with you. I knew it." The cry came straight from her heart, the hot tea splashing unfelt on her thigh as she confronted Brid.

"Never. Not since the day he walked out the door."

"What then? What things about your relationship with Drew?"

Brid took a deep breath, let it out, and began. "It's about

Craic. Ten years ago when it became clear that the bar was going under, I came up with the plan to renovate the place. I asked Drew to convince Da to go along with it because," bitterness laced her words, "while Da would never listen to me, I'm not a man. You see, he always listened to Drew. In the end, Drew did much more than that." She took a sip of her tea, adding more honey. "Craic, as you see it today, was very much Drew's conception. He gave me the money that I needed for the renovations."

"I remember when the bar was renovated," Franny said. Drew was excited about it. He said Lynton really needed a classy place for people to go to eat..." Her voice died as the knowledge of the depths of her husband's deception washed over her. "But, how? How could he have done that without my knowing it?" Even as she asked the question, she realized how easy it would have been for him. She had known nothing about their finances beyond cashing the generous monthly check he gave her to run the house.

"It turned out that he never closed our joint checking account. He put the money in there. I paid the bills from that account. After Drew died, Neil brought me a life insurance policy for two hundred and fifty thousand dollars. I was the beneficiary. Drew left a letter telling me to pay off the mortgage on the bar." Franny sat completely still, her tea growing cold in her hand. "He said the money was not for me, but for Da, to make Da feel secure during his last years. He didn't want you to know that he had left me the money because he said he would never want to hurt you." She waited for Franny to react in some way, to say something. When she remained silent, in desperation, Brid went on. "I put the money in a CD. You can have it. Or I will put it in writing that when I inherit the place I will turn it over to you. I'll get Neil to put some big seal or something on it. Mother of God, I don't want the damn bar. I've been trying to get away from the place my whole life."

"Can I see the letter?" Franny's voice was small, the voice of little girl asking for a favor.

Remembering what Drew had written: *you will always be a ghrá mo chroí,* Brid told the first lie. "I don't have it. I was so angry when I understood what he had done, the position that he put me in, that I burned it."

"I don't care about the money. Why do I need more money? Drew loved your father. He told me so." She took a sip of her now cold tea and made a face. "What hurts is that he hid it from me. I'm beginning to think that I never knew him at all." Putting down her mug, she walked over to the easel and glanced at it. She looked across the room at Brid. "I didn't know that you were painting a portrait of Drew."

"Don't ask me why because I can't tell you. I felt called to do it. Sometimes it happens like that and I start to paint."

"He looks alive," Franny said, touching the canvas gently.

"It's only a beginning. The mouth is wrong, but I'm working on it. Come and sit down, there's something more I need to tell you."

"More? How can there be more?" Close to tears, she came back and sat stiffly on the sofa.

"Last October Drew came here to see me. It was very late and he was very drunk."

"I told you, Drew stopped drinking, he—"

"Was very drunk that night," Brid finished for her. "I asked him where you were and he said you were at some spa."

"Yes," Franny answered dully. "I went to Canyon Ranch in Lenox for a long weekend in October. Did he try to make love to you then?"

Brid's eyes drifted toward the kitchen where Drew had

stood kissing her throat, his fingers caressing her breasts and she told the second lie. "No, he told me that he needed to talk. I got the feeling that he was in some kind of trouble." Franny appeared to have stopped breathing, so intently was she listening to what Brid was saying.

"Did he tell you what was bothering him?"

"No. We ended up having a terrible fight and he left in a huff." Brid walked over to the oak sideboard and opened a drawer. Reaching inside, she retrieved Drew's cigarette lighter and handed it to Franny. "He left this behind and I never found a way to return it to him. You should have it."

Franny took the lighter turning it over in her hand. "I wondered where this was. I looked for it in his bag when Neil brought it back from the hotel. When I couldn't find it, I figured he had lost it. It wasn't the first one I gave him."

"I know. I gave him a couple myself."

The two woman stared at one another and finally Franny said, "This is crazy isn't it, you and me?" When Brid didn't answer, she continued talking, "I still don't know why he was at the Sheraton. It's driving me out of my mind. I went to see his boss, Johanna Caras today and asked her if he had quit his job."

"Quit?" Brid was stunned. "He believed he was indispensable in that damn job."

"I found a signed letter of resignation in his briefcase dated the day he died."

"Mother of God." Brid stared at her.

"Neil had a fit when I showed it to him. He was afraid that if Drew had actually submitted his resignation I wouldn't receive his life insurance. Johanna looked at me like I was crazy, so Drew must not have done anything with the letter. She told me the last thing he said to her was 'Merry Christmas.'" Avoiding Brid's eyes, she continued. "Johanna also told me that Drew got drunk in front of the customer he was seeing in Seattle." She sighed, "So…I guess…he was drinking again."

"Writing that letter sounds like something Drew would do in a fit of temper. Sometimes he acted like the spoiled little rich boy he once was. Thank God the fool didn't actually quit. As far as the drinking, what does it matter now? He's dead. Alcoholism is a curse. It's a terrible, soul-killing disease but you won't find people holding a 'Run for the Drunks' or a 'Ride for the Sots.'" Brid sighed. "Drew wouldn't be the first person who couldn't get out from under it. Speaking of Neil Malone, you are not going to believe this. I still don't believe it myself. I went out with him the other night. We went target shooting together."

"Out? On a date? You and Neil?"

Flustered, Brid laughed to cover her embarrassment. "I don't quite believe it myself."

Franny beamed. "But that's wonderful, Brid. I am so happy for you."

Brid thought, no wonder Drew fell in love with you. Cynical to a fault himself, he could not have helped being drawn to someone capable of such spontaneous happiness. "Franny, it was one date. I'm not marrying the man."

"Maybe you should consider it. Drew told me that Neil's had a thing for you for years. And he's such a nice man."

"Neil Malone and I could not be more wrong for one another. He's serious, steadfast, and true, to say nothing of being a daily communicant. And I would be a professed atheist if I weren't so damn superstitious," Brid answered, attempting to convince herself, as well as Franny.

"I think you're wrong about you and Neil. Are you going out again?"

"Yes, next Wednesday."

"That's wonderful," Franny said, laughing and clapping her hands. Still smiling, she stood up. "I have to go. The dogs haven't eaten and Ollie's been getting in trouble when he feels that I'm neglecting him. He jumped through the screen door on the porch the other day. Thanks for inviting me to the yoga class. I really enjoyed it. And thank you for telling me about you and Drew." She opened the door, started to leave, and stopped. "I almost forgot what I wanted to tell you." She looked triumphant. "Do you remember when you told me pay attention to the words that Neil used when he told me something?"

Brid nodded.

"Last night I was thinking about what you said. I couldn't sleep so I went down to the kitchen and made myself a cup of chamomile tea. I was sitting there at the table and I thought about what Neil said to me when I asked him if Drew told him about Lorie. He said, 'I swear to you on my mother's grave. He never mentioned Lorie Derouin's name to me.'" Lowering her voice, Franny took a step back into the flat. "I know that you are going to think that I am crazy, but this is true. I felt Drew sitting there, with that look he got sometimes, the one that said, 'Pay attention, Franny. This is important.' He would never have used Lorie's name. He would have said something like, 'Jesus, Neil, I'm involved with someone in my office. What the hell am I going to do?'" Suddenly, she threw her arms around Brid, giving her a hug, leaving her standing in the door behind her.

CHAPTER 20

Sofia grimaced and gripped the door handle of Brendan's old truck, feeling like she was on an amusement ride. Sitting beside her, Brendan grinned, which infuriated her. "When are you going to get the shocks fixed on this thing?" Normally, she refused to ride in the truck and they used her black Saab convertible. She drove, very sure of herself and a little too fast. Brendan was content to ride shotgun, his Red Sox hat pushed back on his head, only occasionally suggesting that she might want to slow down. A suggestion she ignored even though this had resulted in her receiving two warnings and a ticket in the last year. Not a great record for an officer of the court.

"It's a truck, Sofia; it's supposed to ride like this. Doesn't bother me," he shrugged.

"It bothers me! I can't even read my BlackBerry." To prove her point, she brought the BlackBerry she held in her hand closer to her face. "Let's do our long run tomorrow. It's going to be a nice day, not too cold and we could head out toward Hollis."

"Sure, on one condition." He looked over at her. "We go out to dinner tonight. We could try that new Italian place, Dolce. The food is supposed to be pretty good."

Good and fattening, she thought. "As long as I can get a salad—"

"I said eat, not graze," he interrupted, his usually mild tone, firm.

"You obsess about my eating, do you realize that? Why do you care what I eat?"

Brendan took his eyes off the road and looked directly at her, his usual affable mood gone. "I care about you starving yourself, and I care about picking you up off the road."

"Like you've ever had to," she snapped. Continuing in a lighter tone, she agreed. "Okay, I'll eat. You can even choose my dinner. Are you happy, now?" She flashed her most winning smile at him, trying to make peace.

"Absolutely ecstatic," Brendan answered, his good mood restored.

"And for your information, I don't starve myself," she said, needing to have the last word. "I know there's a pack of gum in here. I just bought it." She rummaged through her bag.

"Try the glove compartment."

She gave the dented door a dubious look and popped it open. Inside, was an unopened six-pack of Trident sugar free gum. "Brendan, you are the best." She blew him a kiss to prove that she meant it.

"I was a Boy Scout – always prepared. So, how do you think Franny is doing?" He asked. "Are you being nice to her?" She blinked, surprised by his question. She and Franny were not really talking. Twice they had been together at their mother's for dinner. Both times had been awkward; Sofia had been bossy, peppering Franny with questions, and Franny had been withdrawn, refusing to talk about anything but the weather and Marie's pictures from Florida.

Sofia was surprised when the phone rang earlier in the week

and it was Franny asking if Brendan would mind repairing a screen door that Oliver had shredded. "I'll be glad to pay him. It's impossible to find anyone to do such a small job. I could ask Harry, he's been good about calling to see if I need anything. The truth is: I don't think he would be any better at fixing it than I am."

"Don't be silly. Brendan will be glad to do it for you. He's always asking me how you are. And it will take him no time at all. I think he's off this weekend. Unless you hear from me otherwise, plan on us coming over Saturday morning around ten."

That's why they were in the truck filled with Brendan's tools this morning instead of her Saab. She looked at Brendan. "What do you mean am I being nice to Franny? I am nice to Franny." Promise me you'll be nicer to Franny, Drew had said.

"No, you're not always nice to her and neither was Drew." Brendan answered, his tone level, his eyes on the road.

She stiffened. "What are you saying? That Drew wasn't nice to Franny? My God, he practically wiped her nose for her."

"Your brother-in-law could be a real prick." He delivered this astonishing opinion like he was telling her that it was going to rain.

For a second, she was speechless. Finding her voice, she cried, "What!"

"Look, Babe, I know you thought he walked on water, but you weren't married to him. While he was alive, I pretty much ignored him. But now he's dead, and I decided it was time you realized it." He held up a hand to keep her silent. "I was only with them a few times, but every time I was, he was telling her that she didn't know how to do something, or that she wasn't smart enough to do something. You were right in there agreeing with him."

"Are you saying that Drew thought Franny was stupid?"

Her eyes widened as another even more disturbing thought occurred to her. "Or that I think she's stupid?"

He gave another maddening shrug. "I'm telling you what it looked like to me and what I bet it felt like to her." Brendan appeared to think about it for a minute and continued. "I don't know, maybe he needed her to be stupid."

"My sister went to Wellesley. She majored in English Literature. She reads things like the new translation of *Beowulf* for fun!" She said through clenched teeth.

"Okay, then why do you talk to her like she's an idiot?"

"I do not!"

"Have it your way, but try listening to yourself sometime. It sure as hell sounds like you do from where I sit."

They continued toward Hiram's Forge in an uneasy silence. The radio was broken and Brendan, happy enough to be alone with his own thoughts, saw no reason to fix it Of course she didn't think Franny was stupid. Hadn't she listened to her father insist that Franny was "the scholar" her whole life? But what had Franny done with her life? Not much since she married Drew and not a damn thing in the four years since the baby died. For the first two years after that, she had barely gotten out of bed. When she had, it was only to go to the bookstore or to see that shrink, Wohlander, who had done nothing except zone her out on anti-depressants. At least she was working again at her doll business, ridiculous as that was.

"How many guys do you think would have put up with what Drew did for the last four years? My sister was pretty lucky to be married to him."

"I'm sure she agrees with you about that."

Sofia shot him a look, but his expression gave nothing away. "This may come as a shock to you, but Drew, prick that you think he was, stopped by my office the week before he died and asked me to be nice to Franny, too."

The truck rumbled up the MacCullough driveway, setting off a chorus of barking from inside the house, interspersed with Oliver's unique style of doggy singing. "You would think she had a pack of wolves in there from the sound of those two," Brendan said. He liked the dogs and played with them whenever he saw them. Shutting off the engine, he told Sofia, "Here's your chance."

Dressed in a pair of baggy jeans and a red fleece, Franny stepped through the battered screen door followed by the dogs. Lucy carried a stuffed alligator in her mouth. Brendan crouched down to greet her. "Great gator, you have there, Lucy," he said, picking up the toy that she dropped at his feet.

"Brendan, I don't know how to thank you for doing this. I really appreciate it." Franny smiled at him.

"No problem, it will only take me a few minutes, although I'll admit Oliver did a good job wrecking this." Brendan inspected the tattered remains of the screen that still clung to the doorframe. "Ollie, did you do this? Huh? Did you?" he asked the dog sitting patiently at his side.

"He's such a brat." She crouched down in front of the dog. "Aren't you Ollie?" She kissed his nose. "I think they call it, acting out. He was mad because I was outside and he was in. I think that they miss Drew." Her smile slipped. "Maybe I should take them to a shrink?"

"I hope you're not serious?" There was a definite edge to Sofia's tone. Brendan shot her a look, his unspoken message clear: Be nice.

"I'm kidding. Do they even have dog shrinks?" Franny laughed. "I suppose they might out at the vet school at Tufts, but one of us in therapy is enough." Her eyes went to her sister, dressed in black running pants and fleece, a UVA baseball cap pulled low, hiding her eyes. "How are you Sofia?"

"Busy. Things pick up this time of year. How are you doing?" Sofia asked. There was something different about Franny this morning, something Sofia couldn't put into words.

"I'm okay. Come on in. I'll get you something to drink."

The two women went into the kitchen while Brendan unloaded a roll of screening from his truck under the watchful eyes of the dogs. Franny filled a glass with crushed ice and handed it to Sofia along with a can of Diet Coke without bothering to ask what she wanted. The big airy kitchen, neat and organized when Drew was alive, seemed different, too. The large granite island in the center was filled with what he would have disapprovingly called clutter: books, catalogues, several DVDs, and a manila folder. There was an arrangement of yellow tulips in their last stages of life in a cobalt blue vase on the round oak table. In front of the wood stove, Thomas lay sprawled on the rocking chair, basking in the warmth of the fire.

"Have you lost weight?" Sofia asked, beginning to get a better sense of what was different about Franny.

"Nothing spectacular. Maybe five or six pounds. I'm trying."

"I can tell. You definitely look better." Sofia took a closer look at her sister, who was measuring coffee into the coffee maker. "Since when do you wear hoop earrings? Drew hated them on you." And he had, insisting that they made her already round face look even rounder.

"Well, Drew's not here," Franny said, touching the earrings with obvious pleasure. "Aren't they great? I got them at Brid's gallery."

Sofia gaped at her. "Brid Sheerin's place in Lynton?"

"Yes. Have you ever been in there? It's fantastic. She's got some wonderful things, very unusual. Everything is imported from Ireland."

Sofia took her drink over to the oak table and sat down. For a moment she said nothing, trying to figure out who this person was who looked like her sister, but behaved like someone she had never met before. "I don't get it. I remember when you thought Brid Sheerin was your greatest enemy in life. When," she paused for emphasis, "you were convinced your husband either had or was about to climb into bed with her. And now, suddenly you're buying things in that tacky gift shop of hers?"

"It's far from a tacky gift shop," Franny said bringing her coffee over to the table and sitting down. "I was wrong about Brid. While I was worrying about her, he was busy somewhere else."

"Franny don't start—"

"No, you listen." She interrupted. "Please." Sofia closed her mouth in a stubborn line, a mulish expression on her face. "I know that you love me, even though I drive you crazy. And I'm more grateful for that than you will ever know. But you don't understand what these last three months have been like for me." She looked into her sister's eyes and took a deep breath, "I'm not tough like you." She sipped her coffee. "Dr. Wohlander asked me last week to draw a picture that represented my relationship with Drew. I drew a circle. I told him that Drew was the line and I was the inside of the circle and if you took the line away, there was nothing left. That's how I feel about myself without Drew, like I'm nothing."

Sofia sputtered to life. "Why do you have to be a drama queen? How can you say you're nothing? Tell me what did the great Dr. Wohlander have to say about your circle?"

Franny grinned. He said, 'Very interesting, Franny. Now let's explore why you feel this way.'"

"That quack is like a character in a Woody Allen movie. Even the name, Dr. Wohlander! I hope to God he's not medicating you into oblivion again," she said, referring to the months after Franny had lost the baby.

"Do I look like he is?" There was anger in Franny's voice, something else that was new. "I told him when I started seeing him again that this time I wasn't taking medication." She got up and refilled her coffee. "I want to feel what's happening to me, not sleep through it." There was no point in defending her decision to go back and see Dr. Wohlander. Sofia despised the man, even though she had never met him, partly because she could never imagine relinquishing that much control to anyone. Franny understood this, but believed that Wohlander had helped her come to terms with her baby's death. "He really can't help what his name is, Sofia."

"With a name that stupid, he should change it!"

Franny laughed, not a polite social laugh, but a real laugh, spontaneous and amused. "I'll be sure and tell him you said so the next time I see him." Slowly, she stirred her coffee. Looking up, she met Sofia's eyes. "I was wrong about Brid Sheerin. She's not anything like I thought she was. Like Drew made her out to be. She's been very kind to me. I like her."

"She's a bitch and Drew hated her!"

Franny sighed. "Are you so sure he hated her? I'm not."

"What do you mean you aren't sure? How many times did he say he did?"

The Gospel According to Drew MacCullough, Franny thought, hearing Brid's voice the night they had discussed dogs. "I know what he said. I just don't think he hated her, but then I was never privy to what Drew thought." She sighed. "I know that now." Putting down her empty coffee cup, she went to the window and watched Brendan finish replacing the screen in the porch door, the two dogs sitting on either side of the sawhorses watching him. "Let's not fight about Brid. I'm not asking you to like her. Anyway, Brendan's almost finished."

"I told you it wouldn't take him very long. He's good at that stuff."

"Brendan's a nice guy. He's crazy about you. I can see it in the way that he looks at you."

"Drew—"

Exasperated, Franny cut her off. "Didn't know everything! I know he thought that he did, but he was wrong. He didn't think that Brendan was good enough for you." Facing her sister again, she cautioned her, "Don't let Drew's opinion make your decision for you." Franny glanced out the window again, looking at Brendan, crouched now in front of Oliver, pointing at the newly repaired screen door, talking to the dog. "You might let something really wonderful slip through your fingers, if you do."

Franny went to the granite island and picked up the manila folder that was lying there. "I want you to look at these before Brendan comes in." She removed two pictures: the black and white study of Lorie's son and the baby picture of Drew. She placed them side-by-side in front of her sister on the oak table.

"My God, did you tear this picture in half?" Sofia asked, as she examined the carefully repaired photograph.

"Yes, I did. Sometimes, I think I hate Drew."

"What? How can you even think that, let alone say it?"

"You would be surprised how easy it is. But never mind that. Tell me if you think these two children look alike."

Sofia stared at the two pictures. "Whose kid is this?"

"That's Lorie's son, Alex." Franny waited.

"Why are you showing me these pictures?"

"Look at them carefully." Sofia examined the pictures again.

"Maybe I do see it. It's the eyes, isn't it?"

"The eyes and the curve of the jaw," Franny answered, certain of it now, tracing it with her finger on the newer photo.

"How could it have happened?" Sofia wondered, studying the pictures again.

"I don't know. I've been making myself crazy trying to figure it out."

Sofia picked up the picture of the Derouin boy and examined it more closely and, in a voice that was barely audible, asked softly, "Why?"

Unable to answer, Franny busied herself pouring another cup of coffee.

"It makes no sense," Sofia said, once more sounding like a lawyer. "Why hasn't Lorie said something, or," she scowled, "asked you for money?"

"I don't know. Maybe she's afraid of what her husband would do. Maybe she's not sure who the father is, or keeping her family together means more to her than money. Drew's not coming back."

"I still don't believe it. He would never have cheated on you!"

"Look at the pictures." Franny said, in a voice hardened with anger and pain.

"Does Neil know?" Sofia asked, looking again at the two pictures side by side on the table in front of her.

Remembering her discussion with Neil the night they had dinner, Franny said, "Of course he does. Drew told him everything."

"Did he tell you that he knew about Drew and Lorie?"

"And betray Drew? He never would. He would die first."

"You're right, he would," Sofia agreed. "What are you going to do?"

"I don't know." Franny finished sipping her coffee.

Brendan came in the door, the dogs on his heels. "All set. And this character," he looked sternly at Oliver, "and I had a talk. There'll be no more clawing through the screen. Right, Oliver?" The dog circled him, his stub of a tail wagging in agreement. Franny poured Brendan a cup of coffee and sliced him a piece of almond coffee cake, he glanced at the stack of catalogues on the island. "Are you going back to school, Franny?"

"Yes. I think so."

"You are? Where?" Sofia pounced.

"I don't know, yet. I want to look into an MBA concentrating on small business management. It needs to be somewhere close enough to commute. They say you shouldn't move in the first year." She sighed. "Where would I go anyway? The animals have had enough upheaval as it is."

"I think that's great," Brendan said, smiling encouragingly at her.

Sofia said, "I do, too. I was afraid that you would end up like that Miss Havisham character in Dickens. You know, the one covered in cobwebs."

Franny laughed. "Miss Havisham was a jilted bride, not a widow."

"What does it matter? She was stuck there in some decaying house surrounded by rats for years and years. Right?" Sofia stood up, indicating that she was ready to go. "Let me know what you decide to do about the picture thing. Are you ready, Brendan?"

"Yup. Great cake, Franny." Brendan picked up his jacket from the seat of the rocking chair where he had dropped it, getting ready to leave.

"I can't thank you enough. Are you sure you won't let me pay you?"

"Franny, I told you he's glad to do it." Sofia interrupted, impatiently.

Brendan smiled at Franny. "And I am. Glad to do it. In fact, here's my card. Call me if you need something else or if Oliver forgets his promise."

Franny picked up a bottle of red wine sitting on the kitchen counter. "At least let me give you this," she said, handing him the bottle. "I thought you would like the name."

Brendan took the bottle and read, "Big Red Truck, huh? Thank you. Your sister and I will take care of this for you."

Franny waved as the truck backed around the front of the house and slowly pulled out of the driveway. She could see Sofia talking and gesturing excitedly with her hands as they drove away. Franny wrapped the coffee cake and placed it in the freezer. It was less of a temptation there, and she hated to throw it out even though it would have been safer.

She poured herself the last of the coffee. Removing the pictures from the manila folder, she stared at the two little boys who looked back at her. She had studied them so many times that to her they had become the same child.

CHAPTER 21

Franny edged the silver Lexus close to the curb in front of the Sheerin Gallery and waited with the engine running. Through the windows, she could see Brid talking animatedly to the girl with the snake tattoo. They were laughing about something. Brid glanced at her wristwatch, said something to the girl and turned, striding confidently through the door. When she saw Franny, she waved and hurried toward the car. She opened the door and started to get in. Seeing how Franny was dressed, she began to laugh. Franny's hands, gripping the steering wheel, relaxed, and she smiled at Brid's obvious mirth.

"If you're going into battle, the most important thing to do—"

"Is dress like you intend to win," Franny finished, a catch in her voice, one of Drew's favorite exhortations usually sternly delivered to his own reflection in the mirror.

"The bastard lectures from his grave. Where do you suppose he learned that nonsense? At that fancy prep school he went to?" Brid asked. She nodded her approval of Franny's black suit, pearls, and matching earrings. "You look very nice."

The jeans and cashmere sweater Brid normally wore were

gone. For today's lunch, she was dressed in a tailored black wool suit, the skirt hemmed to show her long, shapely legs to advantage. Around her neck she wore a single strand of pearls that left no doubt that they were real. Diamond studs twinkled in her ears in place of the heavy gold loops she usually favored. She wore a large amethyst ring encircled by diamonds. Franny had never seen it before. She wondered if it had been a gift from Drew. Looking at her, Franny thought of the old cliché "dressed to kill." Only the wildly curling black hair was familiar.

"And you," Franny said, as she swung the car into the heavy midmorning traffic on Main Street, "look gorgeous." Not for the first time, she wondered how Drew had been able to give up Brid who seemed to be everything he had desired – everything he had futilely tried to make her become.

"Funny we both wore black, the Widows MacCullough." Franny said, taking her eyes off the road for a moment to glance at Brid.

"I don't think by definition a man can have more than one widow. And that," Brid smiled at Franny, "is you." Looking down at herself, she shrugged. "This is the only suit I own. Besides, Lorie may outdo both of us and wear the outfit she wore to the wake."

Franny headed toward the 99 Restaurant where she had agreed to meet Lorie for lunch.

"I talked to Sofia this morning," Franny said.

"I'm sure that was lovely. And what does she think of this meeting?"

"At first she was totally against it. She thinks Lorie's nutty." Franny sighed. "She and Neil."

"I have no doubt the woman is nuts. The question is: Is she a liar, too?"

"Sofia wanted to come with me."

"I'll bet she did. Another thing for her to manage," Brid answered, tartly.

"You don't like her very much do you?" Franny stole a quick glance at Brid as she waited for her answer, even though she was sure what it would be.

"I don't know her. She's arrogant, and she has a great deal to learn about life. I think she could have showed a little more compassion for you when Drew died." Brid hesitated for a moment before she added, "And so does Neil."

"Really?" Franny was surprised. She had never seen Neil perturbed about anything except the letter she found in Drew's briefcase. "He said that?"

"With Neil, everything is couched in that lawyer blather, but I know he was upset by some of the things Sofia said to you right after Drew died. Your sister is a control freak. You see them everywhere in AA, people that need to be in charge." Brid shrugged. "I tend to be one myself. It's one of the reasons I do yoga. It teaches you to let go of things."

"Sofia isn't an alcoholic—" Franny protested.

"No. She's an exercise freak who loses it if she doesn't get her run in every day." Brid softened her voice. "Addiction's addiction. It just wears different faces. Trust me. Your sister has, as they say, 'issues.'"

"Sofia loves me, and she's only trying to help." Sensing Brid's resistance, Franny continued. "She does! She was crazy about Drew and she can't bear to think that he would ever do anything less than honorable." She sighed. "You have to understand that Drew was a hero to Sofia. We were only married six months when my father died. Sofia was eighteen and she was devastated. We all were. Drew filled a huge hole for both my mother and for Sofia, as well as for me. I don't know what we would have done without him. I think he got into heaven based on how good he was to my mother that summer."

Brid did not dispute what Franny said nor question the certainty that Drew MacCullough was actually in heaven. She reached for her purse. Remembering where she was, she reluctantly pushed the thought of a cigarette out of her mind. She shifted restlessly in her seat, staring out the window at the passing March landscape, the dismal browns splashed here and there with a suggestion of the vibrant colors to come. She wondered, not for the first time that morning, why she had agreed to go to this lunch. A biker flew past them, the roar of his Harley reminding her of the day that Drew had taken her mother for a ride on his bike.

"Ah, come on, Rosie, let's go for a ride. You'll love it. Come on."

Her mother stood at the back door of the bar dressed in the cheap polyester uniform she wore to wait tables, her neatly turned ankles overpowered by the carefully polished white oxford nurses' shoes she wore to ease her aching feet. Her hands nervously twisted her apron as she looked at her son-in-law straddling his Honda. His blue eyes laughing, Drew continued to cajole her to get on the motorcycle behind him.

"It's mad you are, Drew MacCullough, to think I would ever get on that great beast of a machine. Isn't it bad enough that you take the life of my only daughter in your hands when she's on there with you?"

"Ah, Rosie, how can you be saying that about this beautiful bike?" Drew mimicked her Irish lilt. "Get on and come for a ride. With the wind blowing in your face, it's back to Ireland you'll think you are."

"It's foolishness, that's all, and no doubt a sin, as well."

"True, the lads will see your legs, but surely with legs as lovely as those it would only be a venial sin, wouldn't it now?"

"Stop making fun of me, you horrible man." She flapped her gingham apron at him in mock anger.

"Then come for a ride with me and I promise I won't say another word."

Rosemary looked longingly at the Honda. "All right, then, I'll go. Let me just take off my apron."

Brid watched as Drew gently fitted the extra helmet over her mother's head, overriding Rosemary's protest that he would ruin her hairdo. Gingerly, Rosemary hoisted herself behind him, modestly pulling down her skirt. With a wink at Brid, Drew took off slowly, her mother grinning like a teenager as she clung tightly to his waist.

She was brought back to the present by Franny's voice. "I told her you were coming with me." Franny smiled grimly, remembering Sofia's voice changing from astonishment to outrage.

"She must have thrown a fit." Brid answered.

"Let's say she wasn't happy about it," she said, hearing Sofia's tirade in her head. *What is it with that bitch? Have you all lost your minds? First, Neil and now, you. When did Brid Sheerin suddenly become everyone's best friend?*

They were early. It was twelve fifteen when Franny parked the Lexus in the parking lot of the 99 Restaurant. They had agreed to meet at twelve thirty. The lot was half empty. The restaurant was not one of the popular lunch spots in Lynton. It was frequented by travelers staying at the attached Comfort Inn and by people looking for an out of the way place where they could have lunch without being noticed. There was no sign of Lorie's bright red Toyota Rav 4 with the "Believe in angels and other magical beings" sticker on its rear bumper.

Franny had been stunned when she had answered the phone two days ago and heard Lorie's voice on the other end.

"I need to talk to you," Lorie said flatly, her tone indicating that she was not willing to take no for an answer.

Why not? Franny thought. Knowing things couldn't be worse than being caught between the truth and what I once believed to be true. They agreed to meet for lunch, settling on the 99 as a neutral place where they would be unlikely to run into someone either of them knew. It was only later when the enormity of what she planned to do hit her, that Franny pleaded with Brid to go with her. Brid had balked at first. Sensing the younger woman's panic, she relented. She warned Franny that Lorie wouldn't like it and might walk out the restaurant when she saw her.

As Franny had anticipated when she suggested it, the restaurant was only half full. "Someone else will be joining us shortly," Franny told the hostess, as she slid across the bench into the booth.

"Can I get you something to drink?" The waitress asked as she slapped two menus in front of them.

"I will have coffee, black, please," Brid answered, her eyes searching the restaurant, already seeking an escape route.

"Just water, thank you," Franny told the waitress attempting to smile.

Lorie came through the door wearing a long purple skirt and matching sweater with a multi-colored scarf looped casually around her neck. Catching sight of Franny, she smiled tentatively. She took a step toward the table and froze, her eyes widening when they fell on Brid.

She slipped into the booth next to Franny, ignoring Brid. Lorie appeared almost gaunt, having clearly lost weight since Franny had last seen her. The weight loss only accentuated her high cheek bones and large green eyes. Typical, Franny thought, I get fat and Lorie gets even more attractive.

"What is she doing here? It was supposed to be you and me."

"I asked her to come. I thought it would be better if someone else was here, someone who really knew Drew." Franny answered, closing her menu and placing it on the table.

"Neither one of you really knew Drew, not like I did." Lorie sniffed. "But I suppose it doesn't matter now, does it?"

The waitress returned and took their orders: veggie burger with coffee for Lorie, tuna salad and ice tea for Franny, and a large salad with more coffee for Brid.

"Why did you want to see me?" Franny asked, attempting to hide how anxious she was to hear Lorie's answer.

"I wanted to tell you that I was sorry." Her voice faltered and she took a sip of water. "I realized after we talked that night that you didn't have a clue and that I never should have told you about Drew and me. It was a mistake and I wish I hadn't done it." She reached for Franny's hand. "It was cruel."

"What are you sorry for? That you slept with my husband or that you told me you did?" The heat crept into Franny's voice unbidden, the way the embers in a log fire suddenly catch and flare without warning.

Sitting beside her in the narrow booth, Lorie dropped Franny's hand. Warily, she continued, "He was your husband, not mine, and I regret causing you any more pain."

"The sixth commandment, isn't it?" Brid spoke for the first time. "In that you were both married at the time," she added dryly, "to other people."

"I'm not talking to you. I'm talking to Franny." Lorie squared her shoulders and indignantly hissed. "I know what you did."

"Really?" Brid's tone indicated she could care less what Lorie knew.

"Yes. Drew told me. He hated you." Lorie glared across the table at Brid. "He called you a cold-hearted, unnatural bitch."

"So he did. To my face, many times." Reaching down, Brid pulled her cigarettes and lighter from her purse. She paused, the lighter in her hand. "I am going to have a cigarette. You must understand that, because I'm sure Drew smoked when you were together. He always loved smoking a cigarette after he had sex." Beneath Brid's casual tone, there was an unspoken warning: Don't mess with me. The other two women both heard it. Brid slid out of the booth and strode toward the exit.

The waitress brought their lunch, asking them if they needed anything else. They both said no and began to half-heartedly eat the food in front of them. Twirling a French fry in the catsup, Lorie looked up and said, "I can't believe that you invited her! Why are you having anything to do with her? You must know how much Drew hated her!"

"What does it matter how he felt? He's dead. She's the only one who believed me." Franny stopped for a minute and laughed bitterly. "Or I should say believed you, when you told me that you and Drew were lovers! I needed someone else to hear what you had to tell me today." Franny sighed. "What do you want from me? Why did you ask to meet me?"

"I need you to tell me that you forgive me. My angels are giving me the message that I need to obtain your forgiveness. The cards are clear that I should seek forgiveness from someone I have harmed."

Franny was stunned. Whatever she had been expecting, it was not this. Instead of answering her, Franny asked a question of her own. "The thing that I don't understand is," she stopped, her voice choked with emotion. "Why did you wait until he was dead to tell me?" Blinking fiercely, she looked away in an effort not to cry, her eyes focusing on a large Easter Bunny advertising the upcoming Easter Brunch. Could it really be Easter already?

"Because she wanted you to know and she wouldn't have dared tell you when he was alive." Brid answered, returning in time to hear Franny's question. "That's the truth isn't it?" She asked her tone filled with contempt. Lorie refused to acknowledge her question.

Brid unenthusiastically poked her fork at her salad. Calling the waitress over she asked, "Do you have any fresh ground pepper?"

The waitress looked at her, surprised. Picking up the pepper shaker from the table, she examined it carefully. "Do you think this is stale? I could get you one from another table."

Franny didn't dare meet Brid's eyes, afraid if she did she would burst into hysterical laughter. Brid stared at the girl. She seemed about to say something, but changed her mind and replied calmly, "Never mind, I'm sure it's fine."

"Everyone who knew Drew," Franny said softly, not looking at Brid, "keeps telling me that you're making this up."

"I'm not! Drew and I loved one another. We never meant to fall in love, but it happened. Is that so hard for you to understand?"

"I thought we were happy." Franny's voice dropped until it was barely audible. "Things were getting better." She swiped at her own tears. "He promised me that he would always love me. Why would he have an affair?"

At this last, Brid lost her temper. "Enough!" Out of patience, she glared at the two stunned women sitting across from her. Around them, all conversation stopped. Brid lowered her voice, "He was drunk. Don't you see? So drunk, I'll wager he wouldn't have known if he slept with that Easter Bunny over there." Half rising, her hands on the table, she challenged Lorie. "He was, wasn't he? Tell her!"

Shrinking back against the rear of the booth, Lorie was silent. Disgusted, Brid turned back to Franny. "He was no doubt in a blackout. He would have had no memory of any of it when he woke up the next morning. Although I'm sure that this one," she nodded her head at Lorie, "was quick to tell him what happened. God knows he was a charming man, but is it really possible that neither of you realized that Drew MacCullough was also an alcoholic?"

Franny cried, "I didn't even know he was drinking again until Johanna told me."

"An alcoholic? Sure he liked to drink, but he was not an alcoholic!" Lorie said, indignantly.

"I haven't seen him have a drink in years," Franny said. "He stopped completely after he was arrested." Franny recoiled from Lorie's incredulous expression and the pity in Brid's eyes. "He promised me," she insisted.

"I told you. You didn't know the first thing about him," Lorie smiled triumphantly. "He drank all the time when he traveled." Lorie was flushed with importance – the girl at the pajama party who knew the dirt. "I found out that he and Johanna had a huge fight about his drinking the day before he died." She lowered her voice and continued, "He got really drunk with the customer he took out to dinner in Seattle and the guy called and complained to Johanna before Drew even got back from the West Coast. Johanna threatened to put him on corrective action."

For the first time since Drew's death, something finally made sense to Franny.

"So that's why he—"

Under the table, Brid kicked her sharply and Franny

stopped. Lorie looked at her, waiting for her to continue. "He didn't call me when he came home early from Seattle," she finished lamely. Franny saw that Lorie was growing restless. If she was going to find out what she wanted to know, the time had come to ask the question that had brought her there. "Is Alex Drew's child?"

"What? Of course not! He's Steve's son. Don't you dare suggest that he's not! Drew was right. You are crazy."

"Why did you tell me that he looked like his father the day that I picked up Drew's things from his office?"

Lorie stood up; her voice shook as she told them, "Because he does look like his father – my husband, Steve."

"No. He doesn't. He looks like Drew." Franny reached into her purse and removed the carefully taped baby picture and placed it on the table in front of her.

Lorie looked at the picture in dismay and then back at Franny.

"Alex is Steve's child. Why are you doing this?" Lorie's eyes darted toward the exit.

"Because I think that he's Drew's son. I think that's why he continued to see you."

"You can't believe that he loved me, can you?"

"No." Franny eyes went to Brid. "If he loved any of us, it was Brid."

"Brid? He hated Brid. If you understood him at all, you would know that." Lorie reached for the check that the waitress left on the corner of the table. She fumbled with her wallet and dropped ten dollars on the table. "I hope you find some peace, Franny. If you would let me read the cards for you, I could help you with that. I really could. Call me, if you change your mind."

"Drew thought that Alex was his son, didn't he?" Brid

looked at Lorie, waiting for her answer.

"I don't know what Drew thought. If he did, he was wrong. What does it matter now? He's dead." Lorie was clearly rattled. "I have to get back. I am on lunch break and I am already late."

"Wait." Franny put her hand on Lorie's arm. "Did you spend the night before he died with Drew?" She sat very still, her hands gripping the edge of the booth, braced for the answer.

"No. I told you the truth. Drew called me the night before he died and said that he had something urgent to discuss with me outside the office. He asked me to meet him for coffee the next morning at the Sheraton. When I got there and went up to his room, he was still in his pajamas. He looked awful. He said he had been having terrible indigestion all night." She started to cry. "He asked me to call the office and let them know that we were meeting offsite and that he would be in later and I did. But the pain kept getting worse. I told him he was having a heart attack. He said if I was going to get hysterical, I should leave." Lorie wiped away the tears. "If you don't believe me, ask my husband. I spent the night with him." Without another word, she turned and walked out

"Are you all right?" Brid asked, looking at Franny's ashen face.

"No." Franny whispered, shaking her head. "I'm not."

Brid picked up the check, studying it for a moment and reached into her wallet. Brid added fourteen dollars to the money on the table.

"Are you ready?" Franny nodded.

They were surprised to find Lorie waiting for them in the parking lot. Her car was parked next to Franny's, the engine running. She rolled down the window. "There's one more thing you should probably know." She looked at Franny. "He died calling your name." Wordlessly, the two women watched as she drove away.

CHAPTER 22

"**G**et in the car," Brid ordered, taking charge.

Franny made no effort to stop Brid from removing the keys that dangled from her limp fingers. Her eyes followed Lorie's Toyota as it weaved through the parking lot and headed toward the highway. She focused on the angel bumper sticker until she could no longer read it. None too gently, Brid nudged her toward the passenger side of the Lexus, impatiently reaching past her to open the door.

"Get in, Franny," she repeated more insistently.

Franny got in slowly, reaching for her seat belt as she slumped down in the seat. She felt cold and found herself shivering despite the warm sun streaming through the windshield. Brid fumbled with the seat controls to accommodate her long legs. Satisfied with her seat position, she turned the key in the ignition and started the car.

"Do you think that she was telling the truth?" Franny asked.

"God knows. Neil's right. That woman's living in a fantasy."

"But do you think that Drew did that?" Franny persisted. "Called out for me when he was dying?"

Brid put the car into drive and as they began to move pushed down firmly on the pedals to gauge the play in the brakes. The car stopped abruptly, pitching both women forward into their seat belts. "Not much like my Jeep is it?" She asked Franny, who was staring out the window.

"Do you think he did?" Franny persisted, refusing to be distracted.

Brid sighed. "How would we know if she's telling the truth?"

Unhappy with the answer, Franny didn't reply. Her eyes begged Brid to say what she so desperately needed to hear. Brid continued. "Of course, he would. For God's sake, you were his wife!"

The tears that Franny had contained all through lunch came then. Sliding down her cheeks, she made no effort to stop them. "Why not you? Why wouldn't he have called for you? He never got over you. I think he was still in love with you."

Merging onto the highway in the unfamiliar car, Brid concentrated on driving. Only after she was safely heading south did she respond. "You're wrong. He wasn't still in love with me. The more I think about it, I wonder if he ever was." Franny began to protest, but Brid cut her off. "Drew was in love with the idea that he could take an unsophisticated girl who grew up over a bar on the edge of a slum and turn her into this – what the hell did he used to call them? – oh, yes, 'a sharp girl', and shove her straight down his mother's throat." She let her mind dwell briefly on her former mother-in-law. "I'm not sure he even knew who I was, only the woman he thought he could turn me into. If he called for anyone, it would have been you, but," taking her eyes from the road for a moment she looked over at Franny and added in a gentler tone, "don't you see, you'll never know for sure. The only truth that you have now is that he's dead and you are not." She repeated herself in a voice both fierce and soft at the same time. "You're not."

They rode in silence oblivious to the world outside the car, each occupied with her own thoughts. Franny was in the room at the Sheraton, an invisible spectator to Drew's dying, willing him to call her name. Brid was going over the conversation at lunch again in her head.

"Why did you and Drew break up?" Franny's voice startled Brid.

"It happened a long time ago. Why does it matter now?" Brid answered

"I always wondered if you were so perfect, so right for him, why your marriage didn't work out."

"Did you not ever ask him?"

Franny thought about those times, when weeping with frustration after Drew had made some seemingly casual comment about his first wife, delivered with the unerring accuracy of a stiletto, she had shrieked at him, "If Brid was so damn perfect, why did you let her go?"

"He said it just didn't work out between the two of you." With a start, she saw that after all these years of viewing Brid as her nemesis, of hating her, what she felt now was a desire to protect her. What Drew had actually said was, "She's a selfish bitch who cares only about herself."

Brid snorted. "I suppose that's the truth. It damn well didn't." With a sigh, she seemed to make up her mind. Her voice went flat and colorless, the musical quality that Franny found enchanting, gone. "We got a divorce because I had an abortion."

Franny stared at her in stunned disbelief, not sure that she had heard correctly, her own pain forgotten. "But he never said. He never even hinted at it." Thinking about what Brid had just told her, against her will, she began to remember.

They were walking through Boston Public Gardens and stopped to watch the children climbing on the statue of the mother duck and her ducklings. Drew smiled at her and said, "You and I are going to have two children. One beautiful little girl who will look like you and a son who hopefully will not be as disreputable as me."

"Why didn't you and Brid have children?" She asked him, both repelled by and drawn to information concerning his first marriage and his ex-wife. His smile vanished and was replaced by a look that she was not sure she had ever seen before, part anger, part wistfulness.

"She never wanted them. Wasn't about to compromise her precious talent by wasting her time having kids."

"But you wanted them, didn't you?" Franny asked, although she was certain she knew the answer.

"Yes. I wanted them. What man doesn't?" He took her hand. "There's an old saying: A man isn't a man until he's written a book, planted a tree, and had a son." He grinned. "Or something like that. I can do those other things myself, but I need you to have my son."

"Now I have shocked the good little Catholic girl in you haven't I?" Brid's bitter laugh brought her back to the scenery flying past her as they sped down the highway.

"How could you do that?" Franny asked, her voice barely above a whisper, afraid of being overheard despite the fact they were sealed inside the warm cocoon of the car. The idea of abortion was so totally removed from her own world that she was incapable of concealing her horror. For her it was an issue outside the bounds of politeness, aborting one's child was beyond her mind's ability to grasp. "It's murder, Brid."

Brid had attended twelve years of parochial school, the first eight at Our Lady Queen of the Angels in Lynton. After that, despite her protests, she had gone on to high school at the exclusive Marian Academy. It had been her mother's wish that she go there. It was Rosemary, not Des, who had paid the tuition, working an early morning shift in the kitchen at St. Luke's before starting her long day at the bar.

By the end of her freshman year, Brid had parted ways with the dogma of the Church irked as much by its droning hierarchy of righteous old men as by anything else. She had kept this to herself as long as her mother was alive, reluctant to add more pain to Rosemary's life.

She rejected the neatly fitting trilogy of heaven, hell, and purgatory. It was not the fires of hell that she feared, but moments like this one. How was she going to explain what she had done to this grief-stricken woman who had given birth to a stillborn son and would never have the chance to carry another?

Brid took the first Lynton exit off the highway and pulled the car into the parking lot of the Lynton Mall, coming to a stop in the far corner facing away from the line of stores. Switching off the engine, she began to talk. "It all happened a long time ago and it's really none of your business. But I can't help feeling that some of Drew's obsession with having a child began with what happened between us. He was used to getting what he wanted, to getting his way. And for that I feel that I owe you the story." She reached for her purse and opened the door. "But first I need a cigarette."

"Just roll down the window." Franny answered.

Closing the door, Brid shrugged and removed a pack of Marlboros and her lighter from her purse. She lit a cigarette. "I met him at Craic. He came in with Neil on a Saturday evening in August. He was wearing an Izod shirt of the palest shade of pink. Trust Drew to have the balls to wear a pink shirt. It was the perfect foil for his dark hair and those eyes." She smiled. "I suppose it was the artist in me that was drawn to him first. The colors, you see? Slumming, I guess he was. Craic was nothing but an Irish dive in those days. Not one of the usual watering holes for the likes of Himself. He did most of his tippling in Boston or at the country club."

She stopped to take a puff on her cigarette. "I was living in Boston, going to school part time, and working in a gallery there. I would come home to wait tables on Saturday night so that my mother could rest. God knows Da wasn't about to pay a waitress, when he had her there. And she would never have asked." She stopped talking, gathering her thoughts, and continued. "Drew played the piano that night." There were scenes from her past, both painful and pleasant, that she made a conscious effort to shy away from thinking about. The night Drew walked into Craic was one of them. She flipped the cigarette out the car window. She smiled ruefully at Franny. "Well…I don't have to tell you what he was like." It was the closest they had come to discussing the fact that at one time they each had been passionately in love with him, captivated by his charm.

"Didn't you ever talk about having kids?" Franny asked.

"I suppose it must sound strange to you, but, no, we didn't." Brid sighed. "We were both young, although he seemed so much older than me, so sophisticated and very cosmopolitan." She shrugged, forgiving herself. "I was only twenty. Later, when having a child became an issue, he said in that maddening way he had, 'but you're a Mick. I assumed you would want kids. They all have litters of them.' But we never sat down and talked about it, never said we were going to have two or three or ten, for that matter."

"But why? I mean, why didn't you want them? How could you not want them?"

Brid lit another cigarette and sat smoking for several minutes as Franny waited impatiently for her to continue. "My mother was pregnant nine times. She had five miscarriages, a stillbirth, and two sons who died before either was two days old. In the end, I was all she had. Each of those dead babies took something from her – her spirit, her strength, and her will to live. I think it was exhaustion as much as the cancer that killed her. 'It's God's will,' they said every time a pregnancy ended in disaster. She kept on because to do anything else would have been a mortal sin. Do you know what her greatest regret was? What she wept about when she was dying?"

Shaking her head, Franny was struck by the depth of bitterness in Brid's voice.

"That she had disappointed my father. She felt she had let him down because she had not given him his precious son." The second cigarette followed the first out the window. "And Da, he never let her forget that because of her he was a man with no male heir to carry on his name."

Her voice broke and she looked out the window for a moment before going on. Her anger underscored her words. "I swore that I would never let any man turn me into my mother. She sacrificed everything for Da, her looks, her health, her love of learning and the arts – everything for a man who I never once heard thank her or tell her that he loved her." She shook her head to emphasize her point. "I wanted to paint, to go to Florence, to live life passionately – to live," she said fiercely. "Not drag myself through life at the heels of some man. And Drew, with his fancy cars, tickets to the ballet and trips to Europe promised me that he would give me all that."

"How did it happen?" Franny hesitated. "I mean, how did

you get pregnant?"

Brid laughed, amused despite the bleakness of the conversation. "In the usual way." Franny blushed then and Brid continued.

"I was on the pill. It seemed so easy. And, of course, the pill and the bottle don't mix. And there were lots of bottles. We both drank a lot, at home and when we went out. I would forget to take my pills or think that I had taken them. It's amazing that it didn't happen sooner than it did. One day I found myself pregnant." She shuddered at the memory. "We had been married five years by then and I had my BFA. Drew had started to make noises about having a child. We argued about it. I was working in a gallery on Newbury Street and painting whenever I had a free minute." She shook her head as she groped for another cigarette. "Painting badly I might add, which is why I suppose the drinking had really begun to get out of hand. It was slowly dawning on me that I was never going to be a serious painter—"

"But you paint beautifully," Franny interrupted. "That picture in the Snug is wonderful."

Brid shook her head dismissively. "That picture is one step up from paint by numbers."

"So what happened when Drew found out?"

"He was traveling a great deal, then. He was visiting customers for as long as two weeks at a time, which was fine with me. It was all unraveling by then. It gave me more time to paint without him distracting me, without him demanding that I act like a wife." She smiled at Franny. "Surely, you must realize that he didn't appreciate coming second to anything – although he loved to brag about his wife, the painter. And by then, I had begun to suspect that my paintings were no good. My reaction to that was to paint more and more frantically. And to drink more and more frantically, too. Shortly after I discovered that I was pregnant, Drew left for Texas for two weeks. The day after he left, I had an abortion. When he came home, I told him." She lowered the window of the car and flipped the cigarette butt onto the pavement. "He had a right to know. What he didn't have the right to do was force me to have the child." She fell silent remembering his towering rage. "It wasn't the abortion itself that bothered him. What you would see as the murder aspect of the whole thing. He didn't, as he told me, suffer from my 'papist' ideas that life began at conception. What enraged him was that I destroyed his child. He never forgave me for that."

"I can't believe that he didn't tell me. He told me so many things about you. Intimate things that I never wanted to know and should never have heard."

"He never told you because he understood that if you knew what I had done, you would realize that I was never a threat to you. And he needed me as a threat to you. He constantly compared me to Leslie Millingham, reminding me that she was a debutante and that she had gone to Smith. His favorite thrust was that, unlike me, she was a lady. It comes as no surprise to me that he compared you to me. I am certain that he compared Lorie to you."

"Does anyone else know? About the abortion?"

"Almost no one knew about it. I think in some way Drew felt that it reflected badly on him and that stilled his tongue. He couldn't believe that I wasn't overjoyed to be having his child." Brid reached for another cigarette, staring at it with loathing, with an impatient shake of her head, she lit it. "I'm the one who had the abortion, not him." She sighed. "And as God knows, I'm the one who has to live with it." She took a puff, falling silent as she watched as the smoke wafted toward Franny. "But still he made it his damn tragedy!" Angrily, she tipped the ash from the cigarette out the window. "Of course, he told Da."

"He told your father?" Franny shivered, as in her mind she pictured and then shied away from her own father's reaction to such news about one of his daughters.

"Ah, they were a pair, those two. I don't put much stock in all that blather the psychiatrists sputter, but that thing about marrying your father must be true. God knows in more ways than I can count, I sure as hell married mine."

"But what did your father say to you?" Franny asked, trying to picture the Des's reaction.

"Say to me? Directly? Are you mad?" Brid snorted.

"But—"

"You don't understand the Irish. It's not our way to communicate directly. The more serious the subject, the more smoke and blather we throw over it." Brid's mind played out the scene in the bar the night Drew died. "He lets me know every now and again that he knows. I don't care about Da. He's in no position to judge me. Believe me, he's no saint. Sure, I love him, he's my father. I do my best to look out for him, but I love him because of my mother, because to not love him, would hurt her so." Once again, she was silent, lost in her thoughts, her hands painfully gripping one another to keep from reaching for yet another cigarette.

"Your mother was already dead, then?"

"Dead two years. Dead at fifty, an age that has begun to look and feel very young to me, I might add. Had she not been dead, I would have had the baby."

"But—"

"Make no mistake, my reasons for not wanting it would not have changed, but I could never have done that to her. It would have truly broken her heart." She paused reflectively. "I'm not sure that Drew ever understood that." Brid shrugged and suddenly ripped the remaining cigarettes from the pack and, holding them out the window of the car, viciously began to shred them. "Damn cigarettes. I despise them!" Once the destruction was complete, she stared morosely at the small pile of tobacco littering the pavement. "God, I hope I don't poison the birds."

Franny was overwhelmed with a sense of sympathy for Brid who seemed drained by their conversation. For the first time since Franny had gotten to know her, Brid had lost the control she prided herself on keeping. "Why don't I drive?" Franny said. The two women switched seats, passing each other wordlessly in front of the car.

"Do you think Neil knows why you and Drew got a divorce? Knows about the abortion, I mean?" Franny asked the question tentatively, not wanting to dig deeper into Brid's pain.

"Of course he does. I don't believe that there is anything about Drew MacCullough that Neil doesn't know, but you'll never hear a word about it from him." Franny nodded, having come to believe this to be true.

Heading back toward the center of Lynton, they were silent, each emotionally spent and attempting to come to terms with the afternoon and its revelations.

"I am amazed that Drew told Lorie though, that does surprise me," Brid said, breaking the silence.

Franny asked, "Told Lorie? What are you talking about?"

"I thought you missed that," Brid said. "Lorie said to me, 'He told me what you did.' I'm betting she was referring to the abortion. I wonder why Drew would have told her. It doesn't make sense to me."

"Unless they were discussing abortion because she was having his baby!"

"You've got to leave it alone. She told you that little boy was not Drew's child. Why can you not accept that?"

"Because, I don't think it's true!" Franny was adamant.

Brid's voice was gentle. "Then you must make it true in your mind. And you must make yourself believe that it's true in your heart."

"But why, why do I have to?" Franny pleaded with her.

"Because you have no other choice. Even if the child is Drew's – and I don't believe that he is – he will never be your child. You have no claim to him. Do you not see that? He's Lorie's, not yours. All you can do is bring misery and pain to that little boy and to yourself if you persist in this." Brid's voice became more insistent. "You must let it go." Franny said nothing, refusing to concede that Brid was right. Pulling into a parking space in front of the gallery, she said to Brid, "Thank you for going with me this morning. I couldn't have gotten through it without you."

"You underestimate yourself. But, if my being with you helped, then I am glad I went."

"I'm sorry about the other thing." Franny said, shying away from the word abortion. "I hope dragging it all up was not too painful for you."

"As I told you, it happened a long time ago. I would do it all over again. I only regret that I had to do it in the first place. I was careless, for that I'll never forgive myself." Pivoting on the seat, Brid extracted herself from the car.

"Brid," Franny stopped her as she began to close the car door, "do you really think that Drew called out for me before he died?"

"Yes. I believe that he did."

EPILOGUE

Neil stood at the bay window in his office. Lost in thought, he watched the downy snowflakes as they fell soundlessly into the slate blue waters of the Merrimack River. It was not a real snow storm, just a tease to remind everyone this was New Hampshire and it was December. Reviewing tomorrow's appointments, he considered canceling the day and going skiing. If he could talk Brid into playing hooky from the gallery and coming with him, he might take the day off.

He laughed softly at himself. He was too old to throw off the habits of a lifetime and he knew it. As far as he was concerned, this nonsense about having a mid-life crisis was overrated. The snow, tempting as it was, would be there on Saturday. Behind him, the phone rang. Picking it up, he told Erica, "On my way."

Franny sat in the same chair she had been sitting in the first time she had come to his office not quite a year ago, the day he had read Drew's will to her. She was engrossed in the book she was reading and she didn't see him standing in the door watching her. She had insisted they do this today. "I want to do something important, something big, to mark the first anniversary of his death." This was certainly big, not that he approved.

"All set, Franny?" He asked, walking across to where she sat, his hand extended. She took it, but then impulsively stood on her toes and kissed his cheek.

"Thanks for seeing me today. I really appreciate it."

"No problem," Neil said, returning her smile. "Everything's ready for you to sign."

She followed him back to his office, where he politely stepped aside for her to precede him through the door. Settling herself into the black Windsor chair in front of his desk, she said, "He's dead a year, today. In some ways it feels like I saw him this morning and in others, it's like he's been gone forever. Almost as if the time we spent together never happened." Her smile disappeared. In its place, there was a look of desolation so stark that he felt himself draw back from her. As quickly as the expression had come, it was gone, replaced once again by her subdued smile. He didn't point out to her that he knew it was a year as well as she did. It was the first thing he thought of when he opened his eyes.

"I had a mass said for him at Our Lady's this morning," he said, letting her know that he had remembered.

"Did you? I wish I'd known that. I would have gone." Franny giggled. "Drew would have laughed at you."

"I know he would! He used to say to me, 'You damn Micks, constantly working the angles, even when you're dead.' The truth is I did it more to comfort myself. He's no doubt long since charmed his way by Saint Peter." As an afterthought, he added, "Des was there." He had been surprised to see him shuffle past on his way to communion. It was near two a.m. by the time Des, usually deep into the Bushmills, finished closing the bar and was in bed for the night. It was a rare thing to see him before nine in the morning. Attendance at the early morning mass was a true sacrifice.

"Mr. Sheerin loved Drew. Brid said he couldn't have loved him more, if he had been his own son." Neil nodded his agreement.

He sat down. Reluctant as he was to proceed there was nothing to be gained by delaying and he knew it. A manila legal folder lay in the center of his desk. He toyed with it, his beefy freckled fingers, neatly manicured, slid it around on the slippery mahogany surface, but he didn't open it. Across from him, Franny watched him and sighed.

"You still don't approve of what I'm doing, do you?"

"Franny, I'm your attorney. My role is that of an advisor. It's not up to me to approve or disapprove. It's your life. And even more to the point, it's your money."

"I really want to do this, Neil." She looked at him intently. For a moment, her resemblance to Sofia was striking. Funny, he had never noticed it before. The same widely spaced eyes and high cheekbones, that same damn intensity. Studying her, he realized that while she was not as slender as her sister, she had lost weight; the fullness that had effectively blurred her facial features was gone. She was a lovely woman.

Examining her more closely, he saw that she was changed in other ways as well. She seemed more comfortable in her own skin. The tension that he had always felt, the diffidence like she was afraid of committing some grievous social sin, was gone. Even the way she dressed was different. It had always seemed to him as if someone else put the clothes on her, like she was dressed to please someone other than herself. Drew, he supposed. Today, for the first time since he met her, she looked like she enjoyed the clothes she was wearing.

She was dressed in slim black pants and a softly draped sweater, a color somewhere between ivory and bone. She wore a Hermes scarf in a riot of blues, casually draped around her neck. Her bright gold hoop earrings flashed even on this gray day. He noted that she still wore her wedding ring on her finger.

"Why are you so against this, Neil? I can afford to do it and you know it." Franny asked.

"I am against it because I don't believe that Drew would have wanted you to do it." Neil chose his words with care. "He intended this money for you. He took care to make sure that any other obligation that he had was taken care of. He was an honorable man."

Franny smiled. "You mean the money he left Brid, don't you?"

"She told you about that, did she?" he asked casually.

Franny laughed. "Yes, she told me months ago. She seemed bothered by it. I think she feels she doesn't deserve it."

"It was Drew's way of taking care of her father. He was very fond of Des Sheerin." His eyes met hers. "Actually, it was Rosemary he loved. I think she gave him something during the brief time that they were related that he had never gotten from his own mother."

"You know what he was like: the elderly, animals, and damsels in distress." Neil detected neither irony nor bitterness in her tone. "He had a soft spot for them all." Franny's eyes grew moist. "Not that he ever wanted anyone to know it."

He made no move to open the file on his desk.

"Franny," he began, "you're a young woman. The odds greatly favor you marrying again." He hesitated, choosing his words with infinite care he continued. "While I realize that you can't have a child of your own, you may decide that you want to adopt or marry a man with children. This money—"

"Was Drew's, not some child's who may or may not figure in my future life. As you said, it's my money. I need to do this for myself. Once it's done, I think that I can let the past go and move on." Franny's voice was firm despite his obvious disapproval.

At last, Neil lost his temper. "Jesus, Mary, and Joseph. You're wrong, I tell you. If he had wanted to provide in some way for this child, he would have done so himself. And he damn well did not."

"You don't believe that this child is his, do you?" For the first time, she sounded uncertain, once again the old Franny looking for reassurance.

"No, I most assuredly don't. I never have."

"Did Drew talk to you about Alex?" Franny asked, hoping that Neil was about to finally tell her what he knew.

"Let's get started, shall we?" Neil said, avoiding her question.

Without another word, he opened the folder and removed a multi-page document, flagged in several places with the yellow stickers that indicated that a signature was required. "I've set up a revocable trust as you asked. It stipulates that the sum of one hundred thousand dollars will be held in trust and invested accordingly for Alexander Stephen Derouin until he reaches his thirtieth birthday, at which time the money will become his outright. It may be drawn against for educational expenses before such time at the discretion of the trustees consisting of a representative from this firm and you." He turned the document towards Franny. "If Alexander should die before he attains his thirtieth birthday, the money reverts to you."

Franny smiled. "Thank you. It's exactly what I wanted." He returned her smile somewhat sourly, but made no comment.

Pressing a button, he picked up the phone. "Erica, I need you and Pam to come in here and witness a document." Moments later, the door opened and Neil's pretty young secretary came in followed by an older woman.

"I think you've met Erica." Indicating the second woman he said, "This is Pam Delbino. Pam works for Mike O'Shea. This is

Franny MacCullough, Sofia Chiesa's sister." The women murmured their hellos the way people awkwardly do in such contrived situations.

"The way this works," he said, speaking to Franny, "is that you will sign in the places that are indicated and Pam and Erica will sign after you, attesting that they have seen you sign the document of your own free will."

Franny reached for the pen he extended towards her and signed her full name, Francesca Chiesa MacCullough, in the places that were marked. Neil neatly gathered the papers as she signed them and passed them to Erica who, after signing her name, handed them to Pam.

"Thank you, ladies. As always, you do a great job." The women laughed. Neil tapped the pages on the desk before slipping the signed document back into the manila folder. Franny added her thanks as the two women filed out the door.

Neil smiled at her, a gracious loser. "It's done, then. The only thing remaining to do is fund the trust." Relaxed now, he was obviously relieved to be finished with what he had considered to be an unpleasant, if unavoidable, task.

"Brid tells me that you're back in school?" he asked.

"Yes, I have the last of my first semester's exams tomorrow – marketing strategies – pretty interesting." Her voice revealed her excitement. "I can't wait to move forward with opening my shop downtown." She grinned. "I'm going to need an attorney—"

"I'm your man. Let's plan on meeting early next year. I'm really happy for you, Franny."

"Thanks, Neil. I am so excited. But first, I'm going to Ireland with Brid on my break when she goes scouting for the gallery."

"Yes, she told me. I imagine you two will have fun."

"I don't know how I would have gotten through this last

year without Brid's friendship."

"You and Brid." He shook his head, thinking of Drew's reaction to that improbable pairing. "Drew would have gotten a kick out of that – the lioness and the lamb."

"No more than of you and Brid." She retorted with a sly smile.

Neil returned her smile. "A gentleman never discusses his relationship with a lady." He said primly, looking at her over the top of his reading glasses.

"And no one could ever accuse you of not being a gentleman."

She gathered her coat and her purse and turned to leave only to stop, her purse dropping from her hand to the floor with a thud. She gazed wordlessly at the small watercolor hung on the wall opposite the desk.

"Brid told me that she had finished it. I knew it would be wonderful. She's very good, despite what she says." Franny continued to gaze at the portrait. Her voice dropped to near a whisper. "I never thought it would be so true to life." Behind her, Neil studied the picture of his oldest friend. The tilt of his head, the broad smile that was sweet while at the same time just shy of lascivious, the remarkable aquamarine eyes, and the arrogant jut of the chin.

"Yes. I think it's her best work. I'll always treasure it."

Franny turned, reaching out to him, "Neil—"

"God, I miss him." Neil's voice was thick with unshed tears. "I have to remind myself that he's really gone, that the phone is not going to ring and I'll pick it up and hear him say, 'Jesus, Neil, you didn't really believe that I died, did you?'" Neil squared his shoulders. "It's 'Himself,' as the Irish say, no two ways about it." He shook his head, bemused, "And to think she would give it to me."

"You should be the one to have it." Again, Franny stared across the room at the portrait, straight into her husband's eyes. She crossed the small space between them, to hug Neil, her forehead brushing his wet cheek. He held her without a word, his eyes still on Drew's portrait. Gently, she disengaged herself, picked up her purse, and walked to the door. "I believe," she said, "of all of us, you loved him the best." Still staring at the picture, he made no reply.

It was dark when Franny left Neil's office, even though it was not quite four o'clock. It was, she realized, almost the shortest day of the year. She debated using her car. She decided to walk. The night was cold but clear so different from last year, when it had been foggy with a raw, freezing rain, suggesting that perhaps Lorie's angels had wept at Drew's passing.

The gas lamps on either side of Craic's wide double door twinkled invitingly as she walked past them. The place was quiet. A middle-aged man, who could have been a banker or a lawyer, sat nursing a beer on one of the green velvet love seats, engrossed in the Irish Times, left there for the customers. Three women all in their early thirties had their heads together over a trio of martinis near the end of the bar, an occasional burst of laughter coming from the circle of their shinning heads. Des's cronies, Mahoney and Shanahan were nowhere to be seen tonight. The stools where they usually sat were empty. In the dining room, Ronan, who over the year had assumed the position of maitre d' was checking the table settings and placement of the reserve cards. Behind the bar, the bartender another lanky red-head who she knew was in all likelihood a relation of Brid, was carefully chopping small green limes in preparation for making the twists he would need for the evening's drinks. He looked up at Franny and smiled, a slow toothy grin that took its time moving across his face.

"And what could I be gettin yah?"

"Oh, I'm not here for a drink. I came to see Mr. Sheerin. He's not here?"

"It's Des you're wanting, is it? He can usually be found in the Snug this time of the day." He winked at her. "It's going over the books, he says he is, but I'll wager good money you'll find him with his feet up by the fire."

Franny made her way down the short hallway that led to the Snug. As the bartender predicted, she found Des sprawled fast asleep in one of the wing chairs that stood on either side of the fireplace. She stood for a moment in the doorway and watched him. Marveling as to how the elderly could look like the breath had left them when they slept. She cleared her throat hesitantly. Des's eyes fluttered for a moment before they opened.

"Excuse me, Mr. Sheerin. I wondered if I could talk to you for a minute." Still slightly disoriented, he struggled to get to his feet, even as she begged him not to. "Oh no, please don't bother to get up."

But it was up that he got, gallantly directing her to the chair on the other side of the fire. "Ah, Mrs. MacCullough, of course, of course, you can have a word with me, as many as you wish." He nodded toward the wing chair that stood companion to the one that he had been sleeping in. "Have a seat with me here near the fire." Franny sat in the chair beside the gas-burning fireplace. "Of course, it's not the real thing, after all. There's nothing like a wood-burning fireplace. Or, even better yet, peat." He sighed. "But this keeps our friends at the fire station happy."

"The gas logs work as well as the real thing without all the mess. Drew made such a big deal out of fires. He loved them and he made the most wonderful fires."

"He would, wouldn't he?"

Franny nodded and the silence lengthened between them.

"I've been thinking of him all day," the old man said, as he looked sideways at her. "Of course, it's much worse for you. This day, marking a full year, as it does, puts even more distance between the two of you."

She sighed, amazed to find that he seemed to understand why she had dreaded this anniversary. "It does. Beginning tomorrow, I can no longer think, a year ago today he was here and we did this or that."

"I know you'll not believe me, but I'll say it, if only to comfort myself, it will be getting better. Time is the great healer of hearts that have been broken. When you live as long as I have and have lost more than you still hold, you'll understand what it is that I'm telling you. Now, what was it that you wanted to talk to me about?"

"I have something for you. I should have given it to you before this, but for some reason I couldn't." Reaching into her purse, she removed a small white box. Wordlessly, she handed it to him. Des took it from her and opened it. They both stared at the Celtic cross nestled there. The old gold's brightness, muted by the years and the sweat of the men who had worn it, glowed in the soft light of the fire. In her mind, Franny could hear herself confronting Drew about the cross.

"Why, tell me why, do you still wear that cross? You're not even Irish!" She was consumed by jealousy, tormented by images of Drew and Brid. "You still love her, don't you? That's why you wear it isn't it?"

Sighing, Drew answered. "No. I wear it because I still love the old man, he's the one who gave it to me."

Des cleared his throat, bringing her back to the warmth of the Snug. She had come dangerously close to throwing the cross out when Neil had handed it to her after the funeral. Reluctantly, she had taken it from him, seriously considering tossing it into the trash. Something, or perhaps someone, had stayed her hand and she had buried it in the bottom of her jewelry box where it had remained this long, sad year. Seeing the reverence in Des's expression as he stared into the box in his hand, she wondered now if had been Drew himself who stopped her from throwing it away.

"I never thought I'd see it again. I figured it had gone into the ground with him." He smiled at her, his rheumy blue eyes bright with unshed tears. "It was my da's and his da's before that. My mother gave it to me when he died. I was his eldest son, you see, the first male of my generation." He sighed again. "It was to have been for my son." Looking up from the cross in his hand, his eyes met Franny's. "Don't you see we have that in common, you and I, we, each of us, have no son?"

"But you're lucky, Mr. Sheerin. You have Brid."

"Ah. Brid. Brid is a good girl to be sure. But she's no son." He fell silent. "I'll tell you this, Mrs. MacCullough, a man needs a son." He looked away from her, his eyes focused on the glowing logs. "Your husband, now, he was a son to me. I came to love him like my own flesh. He was that good to me." His eyes narrowed. "It was Brid's fault that the marriage ended. Not a thing did he do wrong, I swear to you that. If I had been him, I'd have given her the back of my hand." He sighed. "It might have helped." He shook his head. "But not him. He never did. Not once did he ever raise a hand to her."

Franny found herself drawn to Brid's defense. "But, Mr. Sheerin, it's never only one person—"

"It was the children, you see. He wanted a son. What man

does not?" His voice hardened and his eyes grew cold. "And her, the bloody selfish bitch, would have none of it. Mortal sin that it was." The color began to recede from his flushed face. "I'll leave her to God to forgive, as I can not." He took the cross from the box and held it in front of him by the chain. "I'll be sending this home to my nephew, Michael. He's the next in line, the first male of the generation born after mine." Looking over at Franny, he smiled. "I'm grateful to be getting it back. Will you do an old man one more favor this night?"

"Of course, if I can." Franny slipped her coat back on in preparation for leaving.

"When you think of Drew, try to let the mistakes he made go. In his own way, he tried his best, God love him, to take care of us all. He was only a man and flawed as God knows we all are, but he was good man and a fine man, too. That's the way you should be remembering him. Will you do that now for me?"

Not trusting herself to speak, she nodded. Satisfied, he waved her on her way. She left him gazing down at the cross in his hand. She slipped silently through the awakening bar and into the cold clear night.

She had her exam to study for tonight. Tomorrow she planned to decorate the tree. Neil and Brid were coming, as were Sofia and Brendan, who had offered to bring dinner. Both women, still wary around one another, had promised to be on their best behavior. Brid had insisted on one condition or she wasn't coming: five strings of only colored lights. Happily, Franny had agreed, grateful for an excuse not to have to untangle the bag of white lights she had dumped in the back of the closet last Christmas. The five boxes of colored mini lights were sitting in a Wal-Mart bag in the back of the Lexus, waiting to be strung on the tree.

The earlier flurry of snow had stopped and the night sky

was alive with stars. She had the sensation that Drew was not far away. It had happened before. Instead of being upset by it, she found it comforting. It was to him that she said aloud, "Brid is right. It's time for a change. You'll have to hang your thousand lights in heaven." Picturing his reaction to that heresy, she smiled to herself and began to walk back towards Neil Malone's office where she had left her car.